The Earth
Beneath us

TARREN GUY

Books by Tarren Guy

Veritas Rerum Novels
Power of Will

ISBN: 978-0-6489721-1-2

Dedication

For Amanda
1 Year my wife
Forever my heart
Always my soul
I will love you into eternity
Happy Anniversary

<u>Chapters</u>

Prologue – Written in the stars

Many believe that life was created by some omnipotent being tenderly crafting each soul, mapping out each journey with perfect precision, creating purpose and meaning to everyone's existence.

Others, that a massive explosion of energy and elements set the course of creation into motion. That everything that's happened has been through circumstance and chance, negating any notion of a grand design. The truth of the matter lies somewhere in the middle.

The universe is crafted of raw energy: clashing, combining, repelling, and changing. Always, this energy sought more in life. It longed to grow and see all the universe had to offer. Most forms of energy did this by taking on a physical body and experiencing life gifted by the planets. And like an omnipotent being the energy crafted a life for itself in the form of a book. It created the world and experiences it wished to achieve, good and bad, for itself and in that way could learn and grow.

Most energy would undertake such a personal journey on their own. To experience just what was needed to fulfil the deep longing inside for that which was new. Some may succeed in satisfying this longing with one life before moving on to try something else like becoming a newborn sun. Others would need countless lives in many forms to satiate their desire. Always, it was a decision made by an ever growing, ever sentient form of energy.

Sometimes, two forms of energy would come across each other or be drawn to one another. A bond would be created that would be almost inseparable by external forces. These are the types of energies that form galaxies spiralling together until the ends of time. In the physical, this type of attraction would be deemed as twin souls, soul mates. And would live a life designed to experience the fierce love and attraction they share for one another.

Far above a blue green Earth, orbited by a single moon, two such energies were found. Their essence in the form of the humanoids that lived on the planet below, an arm outstretched in the direction of a glowing, golden book before each. As they thought, words filled the silken pages preparing the lives that would be experienced. For any who

1

watched as they wrote would see a life of love and warmth almost identical to one another as it was a life designed to be shared.

After 10 years of careful design and creation, each book finally closed. The energies looked at one another, smiles radiating from each face. The female drew her book close to her chest, protective over the life she made.

"I'll be the first to go," the male energy said. His telepathic voice was rich like starlight as it fed straight into the mind of the female. It always sent tingles through her when she heard it.

"I'll come within the year. I left some parts blank so that I may surprise you. I don't want you to see as I write them," the female was whimsical like a multi-coloured nebula dancing to the tune of a nearby sun.

Without another word the male nodded and after a last embrace, floated down to the Earth below. His book engulfing him in pure, gold light as he prepared for the life ahead.

A giddy sensation like she hadn't felt before made the female essence come alive in anticipation. Sparks rippled off the cosmic dust around her and she opened her book once more to fill in the last minor details to make their lives complete.

Too engrossed was she in her creation that she hadn't realised there was indeed someone looking over her shoulder. An energy that had also crafted a book but unlike the story in the golden books of the mated pair, this story was of heartbreak and longing. It followed the lives of those it had read but always kept itself at a distance, seeing the couple but never coinciding with them. As this new energy crafted its book, it left gaps where the female energy had in her golden book, not knowing just what would be written there but trusting that life would follow anyway.

Impatient, this dark form rushed the female creating a pulse of energy opposite to her own repulsing her back. The being snatched the golden book from the female leaving its own tattered creation. Before the female had a chance to recover the invading energy fell to earth taking on the story not her own. It was a trick this being had used many times. In this way it would steal the life energies of the male through their close bond within the physical world and should the female choose to enter in the story it created, the being could feed on the tragedy and longing experienced by her. The trap had been set perfectly and ensnared two strong energies.

The female energy raced forward and opened the book crafted by the invading force. Immediately, her heart dropped, her life essence dimming as she read the words on the rotting pages. She would never bond with her male counterpart in this life and to take the time to rewrite another book she would miss her chance to experience a life with him at all. Maybe even lose their bond altogether.

Reluctantly she picked up the cold, dark tome and floated towards the earth. In the last moments before her transcending into a body she saw the gaps in the written word, recognising the moments. With a quick flick of the wrist new golden words filled one empty space early in the story. She couldn't be certain the affect these words would have or even if they would succeed in coming across at all but it was all she had. A dim, barely visible, light encircled her body as her descent quickened.

Chapter 1 – Home is a four letter fantasy

...Accompanying my father will be my first great love. He will be someone I see only from afar and when given the chance my words will not reach him. For all my days there will be a longing for this man I could never fulfil. Thus, I continue to live out my days on my father's farm. With no other company than my old dog, I would start to wonder which life was worse... My father had a child to another woman who came to live with us. He liked to play pranks on me and make me feel uncomfortable... All I would know is sadne l j ao p e mlt .;a jh.

~ The altered book of Blair.

Broken and bare. To anyone glancing in from outside, they would swear the apartment was abandoned. Originally a blue violet, the walls had faded to patchy shades of grey with neglect and time. Threads and scraps of material were hanging from the windows keeping out only minimal amounts of light. They did however make a mediocre barrier to any prying eyes from adjacent buildings. A single, lumpy mattress with a sheet for a blanket and small cushion for a pillow was pushed into the corner behind the open entryway. It was thought that any invaders would move deeper into the apartment giving a chance for anyone inside to slip out unharmed. And this was employed on two occasions.

Most of the light filling the living space came from the Kitchen window. The kitchen was a small alcove at the far corner of the apartment made tighter by the two seater table at its centre.

A splash of colour had been hung up around the kitchen and table today. Balloons had been drawn on paper in different colours and stuck to cupboards and walls. Strips of coloured paper were attached around the rim of the table and a small cupcake with a single unlit candle was sitting on the table. Seated before the cupcake was a young teen. Picturing a flame upon the candle the teen blew it out.

"Happy Birthday, Blair," she whispered. A single tear crashed down onto the table. Wiping her eyes, Blair started to pick at the cupcake. She knew it would be one of the only things she got to eat today and wasn't about to finish it all at once.

A knock at the door broke the celebration. Blair hadn't been expecting anyone and cautiously approached the door. Each step gentle so as not to make the floorboards creak alerting whoever was outside that she was home. Peering through the peephole, Blair could make out the uniform of a courier local to the city.

"Whatever it is just leave it at the door," Blair called out.

"Sorry, miss, the parcel needs to be signed for," came the reply. "If I'm turned away now you'll need to collect the parcel from our depot across the city."

Biting her lower lip, Blair contemplated letting him go. With no response given the courier started to turn away but Blair flicked the handle of the door, swinging it open. The security chain had snapped a long time ago and the simple door lock was intermittent at best. Snatching up the pen, Blair had signed for and taken the small parcel shutting the door again before the courier had a chance to say, '*Have a nice day.*'

She waited until the retreating footsteps had rounded the far corner of the hallway before studying the box. Apart from Blair's name and the postal sticker, there were no indications as to who could have sent this. Slumping to her mattress, Blair released the packing tape and tentatively opened a flap.

Inside was a small black flip phone accompanying a folded letter. Immediately, Blair recognized the fancy cursive of her father's handwriting spelling out her name. It wasn't the first thing he'd sent since her mother's death a year prior. Normally it would be a letter inviting her out to the farm she grew up on before the divorce 6 years ago. An invitation she could never accept having no money to travel the five hours it took. Sometimes, there would be money enough for a nice meal, but Blair made that stretch as long as she could, being extra careful.

Since her mother's death, Blair had to fend for herself. There were no relatives in the city she could stay with and as she happened to be between schools, there were no close friends either. Making friends had been difficult. Feeling the weight of her mother's death, Blair had been reserved with the other students. It didn't take long before she was labelled a freak, and no one would go near her. Not even the other outcasts of the school. This was now Blair's life.

Each package her father sent only enhanced the feelings of loneliness. He spoke in dreams and fantasy. Each letter offered a life far removed from this one. It spoke of things Blair could only imagine, unable to keep three meals on her table each day through the two jobs she worked around school. Where was he to give her these things, to pick her up and say everything would be okay as he whisked her off to a new life? They were only words on paper with no true worth. He was nowhere to be found.

Blair opened the next instalment of her dad's fantasy novel. It wasn't a long letter keeping to the length of previous letters but as her eyes scanned the words the well of sadness at the tip of her throat deepened:

My Dearest Blair,

> *My thoughts are with you for your 17th Birthday wishing you great joy with your friends and much excitement for whatever you have planned. I know you kids these days have such fan dangled phones with your blueteeth and your googlebooks but I thought you may have wanted a trinket of your mums. The phone inside was Karen's. I found it while sorting through some work things and thought you would appreciate it. Sorry I couldn't find the power lead.*

Love Dad

A small watermark at the bottom of the page sporting her dad's initials, B.T., finalized the letter. These stood for Bryan Thompson. That was it. There were no offers of flight and fantasy. Nothing Blair could hold to at night when all there was were tears. Had he now finally given up completely with teasing her?

Depressed, Blair moved back to the kitchen and started pulling down the hand drawn decorations before sliding them into a folder titled 'Birthday Decorations'. Pausing, Blair tried to swallow back the lump building in her throat. Tears came unbidden, tumbling down to dampen the pages of balloons and streamers. The walls became constrictive,

6

closing in to make breathing difficult. Blair dropped the pages she held and ran out of the apartment. Out into the dirty streets her feet carried her not quite knowing where they ran. No one in this part of town cared for the miseries of one girl. Everyone had their own hardships to deal with.

slowing to catch her breath, Blair looked around. The buildings were tall here, their closeness holding back much of the sun's rays. Everywhere she looked was graffiti and rubbish. Blair knew this was a rung below even her part of town. Glancing across the small street Blair made eye contact with two teens about her age. Instantly, she regretted this as they considered her, tilting their heads one way and then the next, looking Blair up and down. Tattoos of words, guns and women ran up their arms into loose fitting shirts and jeans. Blair felt silly catching herself blushing to see their underwear far above the tops of their pants. The one on the left sported a crimson bandana over long dark hair while the other wore nothing on his bald head. A jagged scar running over the top from ear to ear.

"What have we 'ere, Bill? A little bird 'as found 'er way into our nest," the man with the scar, Johnny said. He had pulled a small flick knife from a deep pocket and moved to the left. Bill was already moving to the right as they started to cross the street in an attempt to trap her in.

Panic started to rise in Blair and skirting a skip bin, she fled down the dark alleyway next to her. The footsteps behind rising in tempo to show they were now in pursuit. Blair didn't dare look back but focused on escaping. A man stood up ahead of her.

"Help," Blair screamed out to the man. Turning the man assessed the trouble coming his way. He was unshaven and Blair couldn't know whether he would end up being a greater threat, but she knew the two teens behind her were trouble and he was all she had.

"Little 'elp, Greg," Blair heard her pursuers call and her heart sank as the man before her extended his arms to block her path.

Blair came to a complete stop unsure now how to free herself from these men. Able to take their time, the men slowly closed in. They jeered and teased, reaching out at times to pinch Blair but she slapped them away. Spinning in circles Blair tried to watch all of them at once but couldn't keep up.

"I'll scream," Blair said. Her voice coming out in squeaks.

Johnny laughed loudly as Bill let out a heart chilling scream. Anyone who heard that would swear someone had just been murdered or worse. "As you can see, little bird, there is no one who will care," Johnny said.

Greg rushed in sweeping, the struggling Blair up in his arms. He pulled her up off the ground and as her feet came back down again, she rammed both heels into Greg's feet. He let her go giving Blair a chance to slip around him.

"Fucking Bitch," Greg swore as his arm snaked out to catch her once more. "For that, I will not make this quick."

Johnny jumped as a hand came to rest on his shoulder. Glancing across he pulled back quickly.

"It may be in your best interest to let the girl go," the face that appeared inches from Johnny's said. The Man was in his late thirties with hard, tanned skin. Anyone could tell he was a man of the land, choosing to spend his days working under the harsh sun. The hand that was slowly gripping Johnny's shoulder tighter only emphasized a life of labour.

"Piss off, old man. This doesn't concern you," Johnny said trying to pull his shoulder away. The man only motioned to Johnny's other side and Johnny turned to come face to face with the barrel of a shotgun. Another young man stood calmly cocking the hammer with a chilling click. "Fuck." Johnny jumped back, the man letting go of his shoulder.

As Bill cottoned on to what was happening, he too jumped back. Though he didn't have a young man pointing a gun at his face, it was the sharp teeth and snarling growl from the blue heeler that had him retreating.

"Greg," Johnny said tapping the other man on the back. He had turned away unaware of the newcomers and was now fiddling one handed with his belt. "Greg," Johnny said again, more urgency in his voice.

Irritated, Greg turned and froze. He still had a grip on Blair's arm but knew he was outmatched.

"Hand her to us and leave," the older man said.

Throwing Blair to tumble over the trash cans at the side of the alley, Greg took off. Bill and Johnny not far behind.

8

"Go ready the truck, Tanner, I'll see to Blair," the older man said. Moving over to where Blair still lay, resting against an upturned trash can, the man checked her visually. There was a small cut on her left knee, already congealing, and a scrape on her arm. He placed a reassuring hand on her shoulder. "Are you alright?"

Eyes flaring, Blair struck the hand from her and tried to crawl away.

"Blair," the man said. He raised his voice saying the name twice more before he got through.

Blair studied the face before her. "Dad?" She finally said. Tears came once more and Blair jumped into his arms. "Oh Daddy, I was so scared."

"I'd been waiting outside your apartment for you to come out. I didn't want to interrupt any plans you may have had," Bryan told her. "When I saw you running from the building with tears in your eyes I followed you. I'm glad I did now."

"Why were you here? I already got your parcel," Blair said.

"I send you letters all the time and you never reply. I wanted to see you. To know that you were okay. I wanted to spend a lunch or dinner with you for your birthday. Maybe you might like to come out to the farm for the end of the holidays?"

"I... I couldn't,' was all Blair said.

Bryan's lips became stern and he nodded. "Come on. I'll take you home." Bryan bundled Blair up in his arms and ushered her to the large pickup truck. He helped her into the back to sit behind the young man who helped her. Tanner didn't look back. A whistle and the blue heeler leapt into the trayback.

It was a short trip back to the apartment block. Blair had little time to comprehend everything that had happened but the sight of her home now sent shivers down her spine. Her dad was here in the flesh. The fantasy of his letters now had a chance to be real.

Bryan looked back as he parked outside the main entrance. "Maybe you might have some free time tomorrow to do breakfast?" He said. "Tanner's finished with everything he was doing and doesn't mind staying one more night in the city."

Blair just shook her head and a sense of disappointment came over Bryan.

"At least I got to see you," Bryan said.

"No," Blair replied. "I don't want to go back to that apartment."

"What are you saying?" Bryan asked. A rush of hope swelling in his chest.

Blair was quiet. She needed to build the courage to ask for help. It wasn't something she'd done before. "Take... Please take me with you."

Bryan's smile could not be any brighter. "Tanner, run up and get Blair's things. She need not set one more foot in that apartment."

Before Blair could object, Tanner was out of the car. Before Blair could work out her door was set to Child lock, Tanner had disappeared into the building. She realized that when she had left in such a hurry the door was wide open. He would have to have some knowledge of her apartment number also with how confident he entered the building but to have a stranger find she had nothing... Blair's face started to turn red in embarrassment.

It wasn't long before Tanner appeared once more. Blair knew he'd found the room as he was holding her mother's flip phone.

"Just a moment, Blair. He may be having trouble finding the room," Bryan said before exiting the pickup. Blair watched as Tanner leaned in to speak in hush tones. He showed Bryan the phone and Blair noted the look of heartbreak come over him. She thought he might burst into tears on the spot.

She looked back to Tanner. Any other day, Blair may have thought him cute. Today, under these circumstances, Blair was mortified to meet him.

Bryan returned to his seat. "Shall we be off then?" He asked without turning back. The vehicle rumbled to life and they pulled out onto the road.

Blair felt a small nudge on her leg and realised Tanner was passing back the phone.

"Thank you," Blair said. Taking the phone, a small spark struck her hand as she grazed Tanner's.

With a yawn, Blair stretched her arms above her tussled mess of brown hair. It'd been years since she slept so well and glancing out the window, Blair could see the sun was high in the sky. The farm was already in full swing and from her vantage point in the attic room on the third floor, her childhood room, Blair could see most of the land.

The eastern side of the farm grew sunflowers that followed the sun like a religious cult in worship of its light. They stretched far beyond the angle that Blair could see around her window and off into the distance.

Driving in late last night, Blair could see the Southern side of the house was full of sunflowers also. It was all she could see with the crop far and above the top of the pickup truck. This was the main source of her dad's income and it was almost time to be selling. Blair could see her dad at the edge of his crop showing it off to a potential customer.

The Northern stretch, as seen from Blair's bedside window, held the small chicken shed and large pig pen. This provided the eggs and a supply of bacon for the morning's breakfast. Also on special occasions a roast of pork would be shared amongst Bryan and his farmhands. They would cook a whole pig on a spit over a pit of red hot coals. There would be music and dancing and Bryan would open his vast supply of liquor, stored behind lock and key in a shed next to the house, for all to savour.

The North-western reaches of the farm became hilly and a vast forest encircled the Western front. It provided a wind break in the harsh fall season when winds could be blowing a gale for weeks on end along the grassy plains nearby. Hidden within the trees was a large lake that the farm utilised through an underground pipe network to water crops and kept the farm functioning through long drought seasons. This, though, seldom occurred.

Blair loved this farm. Her fondest memories were here, memories with no precursors to the trouble and sadness her life would bring. This farm stood as a reminder that she was happy once and she hoped with all her heart that it would once again work its magic to set her life back on a happy path. The chicken shed was where Blair got up to her biggest mischief. She would chase those plump hens around for hours on end while her dad worked in his crops. It was weeks before Bryan could work out why the hens weren't laying. Too stressed out by his offspring, they were always on guard.

Bryan's answer had been a large Wolfhound by the name of Shadow. And did he earn his name. Shadow had been trained to become Blair's shadow. If Blair started causing havoc in the chicken coop Shadow would catch her by the seat of her pants and drag her back. He would follow her around the yard from a distance keeping a watchful eye on the girl. The young, sharp eyed, Blair started to notice and would stop chasing the chickens, giving only pretence enough so that Shadow would catch her and drag her away. This became her new game.

It was a sad day, saying goodbye as Blair left with her mum. Shadow couldn't hope to fathom the reason for her departure at the breakdown of their family. Blair did the calculations in her head. Shadow would have been 12 now. Two years beyond the lifespan of a 10 year dog.

The sound of an approaching car stole Blair back from her reminiscence. Racing to the southern window, Blair could make out the yellow markings and sign plate resting on the roof of a taxi bumbling down the uneven road. It was a curious thing to see as, normally, a taxi was a one way trip for anyone inside. Her first thoughts were of Tanner, the farmhand who helped her the night before. Warmth started to fill her cheeks turning even her ears red. She would die before having him stay on the farm. He knew far more than she wanted anyone to know about herself. As fast as it had come though, Blair dismissed it. Anyone that worked the farm either shared a lift in and out or brought their own vehicles. This was someone coming to stay. Images of women ran through Blair's mind and she shook them away. 'No not that,' she thought to herself knowing full well it was the most likely answer. She wasn't ready to share the house with another woman. It felt like a betrayal to her mum's memory.

Slowly, the car pulled up in the driveway and a small figure could be seen in the window. As the door to the cab opened Blair's heart dropped. This was a far worse predicament than she could have anticipated and she had premonitions of her road to happiness falling apart. From the cab jumped the 7 year old love child of her dad and his mistress. The child that announced the end of Blair's parent's relationship, Jacob.

From under the eave of the veranda, Blair's dad strolled

out to greet his son with a tender hug before grabbing the luggage. This stabbed at Blair's heart harder than their parents' divorce. Jacob waited until Bryan paid the taxi driver before rushing in to ask a question Blair couldn't hear. Bryan's gesture pointing to Blair's window made the question quite obvious and as Blair ducked back out of sight she saw Jacob rush into the house.

"No," Blair said aloud as she heard the feet upon the staircase. Each step thumping in her chest with impending doom.

Hesitation outside her door gave Blair hope that he would turn around and leave not wanting to intrude on a closed room but this wasn't the case. The door swung wide and with a wide smile, Jacob rushed in.

"Sister," he shouted joyfully. "I've waited so long to meet you."

Before Blair could react to the sudden charge, Jacob had pounced wrapping his arms around her.

"Sister," she almost spat. She tried to struggle out of his grip but he held true. "I am NOT your sister. You are the reason my parents divorced. You are the reason for the loneliness and emptiness in my life. I hate you!"

Jacob released his grip and Blair flung him back. The smile hadn't faded from Jacob's face but there was pain evident in his eyes. Picking himself up and dusting himself off, Jacob made to talk again but Blair cut him off.

"Just get out. Don't you ever come into my room again!" She waited a few moments but Jacob didn't move. "Well?"

"I'll leave. I just want you to know that I didn't choose to split your parents apart. I didn't choose to make your life miserable. I am sorry for my role in your despair. I have dreamed of having siblings to play with, find joy and create memories with. I want to prove to you that I can be a good brother. One day, you may even call me so." With that Jacob left the room closing the door behind him.

"That day will never come," Blair whispered as she slumped back at the Northern window. Tears began to roll down her face like old friends as her emotions started to collapse in on themselves. She was almost swept away under waves of sadness when she noticed a hairy, grey figure amble into the chicken pen and enter a small house at its side. "Shadow?"

Her worries forgotten, Blair catapulted from the window sill and raced out of her room. On the staircase, she almost collided with Jacob. The latter dodging across as she came sweeping by. Racing out the back door, fly screen barely saved from being ripped off its hinges, Blair slowed as she entered the chicken pen. A dog house, easily years old had a small tuft of hair sticking out. Reaching in, Blair gently caressed the dog's head. It was old but as it gently lifted its head Blair saw those familiar stormy eyes looking back at her.

"Oh, Shadow," Blair said. "I've missed you terribly."

Shadow put his head back down to resume his napping. This act of unfamiliarity hurt Blair but she knew that over the six years, his memory would have built a wall of stone around her image. A chicken came clucking by and with nothing else to take her frustration out on she yelled at it, chasing it away.

A small yelp escaped Blair's mouth as she felt something latch onto the back of her pants and start to pull. Turning back, she saw that Shadow was tugging her back to protect the chickens.

"You do remember me, old boy," Blair said, a soft smile touching her lips. She spun back around and hugged Shadow's face into her own. "I'm back now and the chickens are safe. Rest."

Shadow stayed in this position a moment longer before retreating to his bed.

"I haven't seen him do that before. Even when Jacob used to chase the chickens," said a voice behind Blair.

She knew without turning who was standing there but this didn't prepare her to make the turn. Slowly, Blair spun around to look at Tanner standing at the edge of the chicken coop tossing feed into the pen. A shock like electricity stormed through her entire body rooting her to the spot. Her eyes became wide, darting left and right to avoid looking straight at him.

"Mustn't trust you with the chooks," Tanner gave a rich laugh as he continued to throw the food.

Blair knew he was expecting an answer but at each moment she tried to talk her mouth became that of a goldfish, opening and closing incoherently. All her mind could focus on was the glints of sunlight reflecting from the sweat of his skin covered only by, from what she could tell, his overalls. Looking away Blair tried to fight past the images creeping into her mind.

"He's my dog," she was able to squeak. When no reply came, Blair looked up to find Tanner had already moved far out of hearing range. She traced the well-defined muscles over his back... Her eyes darted away.

Watching from his vantage point on the deck, Jacob smiled mischievously.

Chapter 2 – We don't like her

Grumbling to herself, Blair trudged down the stairs. She made a point not to venture out of the house after yesterday's run in with Tanner. Tomorrow marked the start of a new school term. The prospect of meeting new people and finding her place in an already established world irked Blair. She knew it couldn't be worse than her last school skimming around the outskirts of people's awareness. The only positive being while she was at school Jacob wouldn't be trying to create a bond.

Jacob had changed since their first interaction. He started playing pranks and acting as though Blair being in the house was such a burden. She could see it was all a farce and was getting fed up with it. She just wanted some peace and quiet.

"One more day," she told herself. "One more day and then she could settle into the backdrop of her new school. Life could settle down once more."

As Blair reached the bottom of the staircase, she could hear her dad and Jacob arguing over something most likely insignificant. If she had of listened to the topic of conversation, maybe she would have held off entering the kitchen. As it was Jacob latched onto her the moment she walked through the door.

"Blair can take me," Jacob said. "We've been getting along well."

Blair's heart sank at the thought of taking this cretin anywhere. There was little love for the boy that should be her half-brother. Just being in the same room caused her emotions to bubble over. Her Dad just had to say no... that was until he answered.

"Blair may not be up for the task," Bryan said. "I'd like you home in one piece."

"Excuse me!" Blair exploded. Both Bryan and Jacob turned to look at Blair, eyes wide in shock. To hear just what her father thought of her hurt. "I've done just fine looking after myself these last few years. I'm still in one piece. Jacob will be like nothing."

It was Jacob who recovered first turning to look back at Bryan. A large grin had coursed its way across his face. And seeing his Dad he knew he had won.

16

Bryan's shoulders sagged. "Fine," he said. "But I want you home by 10."

"Last year I got to stay..." Jacob started.

"10!" Bryan cut in. There was no nonsense in his voice and Jacob nodded. With his part in the conversation over Bryan made to leave the room. Pausing by Blair, he placed a hand upon her shoulder and leaned in close. "Take no offense to my idle comment. A simple no doesn't sway the boy. I needed to remove you from the equation. But I trust you and know you'll take care of him. See me later for some money." Bryan then walked from the room.

Blair realised her mistake and regretted getting so upset over a comment. She just had no real trust in the man yet. "What have I gotten myself into?" Blair asked. She hadn't turned to look at her father's spawn.

"Our town's Harvest Fair. There's little excitement in this small town of ours and this is one of those nights you don't want to miss. Happens each year just before school heads back. The lights, the rides, the..." Jacob said.

"Alright," Blair cut in. Her lips were pursed realising just how much effort she was going to have to put in. The fair was a fond memory of hers from many years passed. Now, it was going to be spoiled by Jacob. She was tempted to leave him to his own devices for the night but if she was going to start to trust her father, he would also need to be able to put his faith in her. Blair turned to scowl at the young boy. "Just be ready to leave when I say so. I won't spend more time at this thing than I must."

"Of course," Jacob said with a smile.

Large chunks of time were slipping through Blair's fingers as she wasted the day away in her room. The long, slow day she had wished for was not going to be granted. Just another thing to be denied to her and with that in mind Blair just knew the night would come screeching to a halt as she counted the minutes. At least tomorrow she could escape into the background of the school. The student's lives were already established so her presence was of little consequence.

"Well mum, I guess you can see the situation I've gotten myself into," Blair said. She was holding onto the power depleted phone of her mothers. Such a small thing yet it

17

was something her mother's words had fallen on. Something her mother held close to her and Blair in turn felt close to her mother again by simply holding it. "I know he isn't a terrible kid, but he is the physical manifestation of Dad's infidelity. I can't form a bond with him."

"And *him*... have you seen how he affects me? How do I speak without getting so flustered? It's like he brings me to life and takes away my breath all in a single moment. I don't know how to push through this. Did you ever feel anything like that?"

A knock at the door caused Blair to pocket the phone and look up. She could see the partial form of her father standing just behind as the door softly swung open. After a moment's hesitation, Bryan shimmied into the room making note that Blair had been waiting to hear of the reason for his visit. Blair saw how awkward Bryan was trying a number of times to find a suitable position to talk before sitting at the end of the bed. Even then a long, silent moment crept in.

"How can I help?" Blair finally asked.

Bryan shook his head. "Sorry," Bryan started. "You just had the look of your mother about you. It stunned me for a moment. I mentioned money for tonight..."

"Don't worry about it," Blair told him. "The least I need to do the better. And not having much money allows for that excuse."

"I'd feel less worried knowing that if something unexpected were to occur you would have some backup funds on hand.Even just for a cab." Bryan held out a few notes bouncing them to try and entice Blair to take it. "And, either way, the more you do the faster the night'll go."

Blair's lips pursed as she considered the money. One more bounce and she finally took it. "But only as a precaution. I won't be using it if I don't have to."

"It's all I ask," Bryan replied. He studied his daughter's eyes. "You doin' okay? I know it's hard settling back into a life on the farm, especially when a lot has changed."

Blair considered the old man. A small crack appeared in her defences in the form of a soft smile. She could see he was trying. "Yeah Dad, I'm getting there. It's still better than the lonely city... and Shadow is still around to hunt me off the chooks." Blair tried to grin but it was strained and awkward.

Bryan seemed sad as he nodded before heading towards the door. He paused as he crossed the threshold. "In a half hour when you're ready, go see Tanner about getting a lift for yourself and Jacob. He knows to expect you." With that Bryan left Blair to her peace. A peace now in complete turmoil.

Tanner! Blair's face took on a deep crimson hue. Could this night get any worse? Moving to the edge of the window and Blair peaked out. Coming down the driveway in an old pickup was Tanner. He pulled up out front and stepped from the vehicle. Blair's breath caught in her throat. Jeans and a white shirt, sleeves rolled up to just above the elbow. The farm life had toned his body and tanned his skin. Blair hadn't realised but she was staring, her mouth hanging open slightly. Her fingers curling through the curtain draped down the side.

From the outside, Tanner must have seen the movement of the curtain or seen the small outline of Blair as his attention was drawn her way. Leaning back against the pickup he waved causing Blair to jump back with a yelp. She tripped on the edge of the bed to fall into a heap on the floor.

"Come on, Blair," the voice above her said. "Tanner's already here."

Blair tilted her head to find Jacob had snuck into her room. "Get out you little mongrel!" Blair said swinging an arm into nothing.

Jacob had been too quick in his retreat. "You're not going to be wearing that, are you?" Jacob asked referring to the baggy pants and oversized shirt Blair slept in the night before.

"Just go!" Blair shouted. She heard Jacob's laughter all the way down the stairs. Grabbing the blanket dangling over the edge of her bed Blair smothered her head and growled out her frustrations. A few moments later, due to obligation more than want, Blair sat up and looked in the long mirror by her dresser. Her dark shoulder length hair was all tangled and she could see dried drool across her chin seemingly missed this morning. Jacob was right; the pyjamas though comfortable were not fair attire. But what to wear?

Moving to her dresser she pulled open a few drawers to scour through the small amount of clothes she had accumulated while on the farm. It was a quick look and nothing seemed to suit. Lips pursed, thinking what she could do, her attention fell upon a large chest near the dresser. It wasn't hers and she didn't want to snoop but a small scrap of fabric could be seen caught under the curved mahogany lid.

Curiosity got the better of her and, after a moment fidgeting with the lock, Blair flung open the lid. She was amazed with what she found. A treasure trove of dresses, pants, shawls and all other variety of clothing she might want.

Atop the clothing was a small piece of paper that read simply, your mother left these behind. Blair smiled, realising her Dad had wanted her to open the chest. She smiled more to have another gift from her mother. Almost instantly, Blair dove in pulling out different outfits, holding them up to herself, looking in the mirror. She was in a dream to be able to look this good, to have such a selection of clothes.

A horn sounded outside pulling her back into the waking world. She remembered her obligations tonight and was a little annoyed at Tanner for being so rude. She moved to the window to glare down at the man but instead found him wrestling Jacob from the pickup. Should have known.

A small giggle escaped her lips as the younger boy got the better of the older sending him sprawling backwards to land on a bale of hay.

Catching herself, Blair moved back to the clothes. They were all far too fancy for her to wear. She could never live up to her mother's clothing. In the end, she went for something simple. Dark pants and a soft pink off the shoulder shirt that exposed Blair's little belly button. There was even a small black clutch that Blair transferred her Dad's money into before heading out the door.

As she made her way down the stairs, Blair was able to get most of the tangles from her hair to look somewhat decent. A last check in the hallway mirror and she shrugged her shoulders. "I've left the house looking worse," she told herself.

Walking to the car she found a sulking Jacob and a stern Tanner standing over him. Blair's eyes toured over Tanner, the way he held hands on hips, the strong, no-nonsense stance and the stern look etched into that... perfect face. The eyes turned on her and she immediately looked away. Warm drafts escaping her top to flow over her face.

Jacob was straight to his feet and racing over to her. "I'm not sitting next to Tanner," he said pointing back at the farm hand.

"I don't expect he would want you next to him either."

Jacob smiled knowing he caught her in his scheme. "So you agree? That I shouldn't bug Tanner while he is driving?"

"Definitely," Blair responded innocently. "It's bad enough you bug me around the farm. We don't need you causing an accident because you were annoying our driver. No, you need to be seated far from Tanner."

Tanner was just shaking his head. "Well then, if we're all ready to go?" Tanner held the door and motioned for Blair to hop in.

With a shy smile Blair moved to the vehicle and looked in. Immediately, her faced changed. She seemed confused and worried all at once as if she didn't know how to proceed.

Tanner leaned in close, behind Blair. "He never says what he truly means." Tanner's voice caused Blair to jump, her skin rising in goosebumps. "I'll give you as much room as I can but I'll be too busy driving to corrupt your honour... if that is your worry."

Blair's face hardened and she climbed into the single cab trying to display an uncaring attitude. She glared at Jacob as he got in next to her but this had no effect on the boy who sat with a large grin. As Tanner jumped into the driver's seat Blair set her face forward. She couldn't look his way lest her face burn crimson. If it wasn't already.

The engine rumbled to life sending a shudder through the vehicle. It felt as though Blair sat upon a vibrating plate that coursed through her body. Not an unpleasant feeling but her afternoon could have done without it. Tanner's hand reached down towards Blair's leg causing a large jerk from her before realising he had only been reaching for the gear stick.

She was conscious now of the heat surrounding the man next to her. It was warm and inviting and Blair did all she could to resist the urge to have it wash over her. Every bump and pothole causing issues as she would bounce into Tanner. His arms solid to touch. Arms that could reach out for her. Arms she wouldn't jerk away from this time...

No, no, no... Blair told herself, shaking her head and "Sorry," she said to Tanner as if he had any idea on what she was talking about. He just nodded a reply.

Turning from the driveway onto the road 20 minutes from the fair Blair was pushed up against Tanner. She realised Jacob was rolling into her with the swing of the vehicle.

"Jacob! Stop acting like a little brat and sit still," Tanner said. His voice was strong and authoritative. A voice that echoed through Blair's mind like a warm summer breeze.

"It's your driving," Jacob replied. "You're all over the road."

Jacob sat back up allowing Blair the ability to move again. She hesitated only a moment before sitting upright.

"You're okay?" Tanner asked while shooting Jacob a dirty look.

"Yes, thank you," Blair replied, her voice barely above a whisper.

Another left bend and Jacob rolled again. Blair winced as her shoulders turned in front of her squished between the boy and the man.

"Jacob!" Tanner seemed more annoyed now. "Keep it up and I'll make you walk the rest of the way."

Jacob just laughed and coming up to another corner Blair could see his intentions plain as day. Turning her back slightly to Tanner she was able to find a more comfortable position to be squashed in. What happened next though was unexpected. An arm reached around her to keep her stable. Tanner's arm. A small yelp escaped Blair's lips and sure as anything, her face flared red.

"Sorry. Just until the child settles a bit." Tanner said softly in her ear. The warmth from his breath caused goosebumps to run over the right side of her body and she shivered a little.

"Okay," Blair blushed harder as her voice came out in a

squeak.

Her mind swimming, Blair could barely think straight. This was a position she tried so hard not to imagine with her dad's farm hand yet here he was holding her close. His arm sat snug across her chest and down a little so that his hand cupped the curve of her waist. Without the ability to fight her thoughts she settled in to savour the moment as another corner came along.

Not through lack of trying, Jacob was held at bay. Blair realised Tanner was also protecting her. His strength plenty enough to keep the boy from squashing her. The rough, gentle hand settled back at her side.

Looking to Jacob, Blair found the boy was already looking back up at her. A mischievous grin etched across his face. As he noticed her attention, Jacob shot a quick wink then turned to face out the window. This worried Blair for what he would do next but found he didn't try anything more as they passed a number of corners.

An unsure realisation nestled inside Blair's mind trying to make even a small amount of sense out of Jacob's actions. A realisation that the boy had manipulated both Tanner and herself to place Blair into the man's arms. This was the only thing that made sense and Blair couldn't understand why Jacob would do that other than to be an annoying brat. Whatever the case, Blair was here now. She may as well take advantage.

Shifting her shoulder just slightly to find a more comfortable position Blair froze as Tanner raised his arm a little. No, Blair's mind screamed, her body not ready to give up the warmth flowing over her, through her. Unsure of how to proceed, whether to sit up or stay still, Tanner answered it for her. He had just been waiting for her to settle before repositioning his arm around her. This time his arm curled in just above her hip. The hand resting on the exposed skin of her belly.

Electricity immediately shot though Blair and she let out a soft, heated sigh. She had never felt so alive in her life and didn't wish for this to end. She noticed Tanner's heartbeat gain in tempo also. And though Jacob didn't try anything more, Tanner remained holding Blair until the entrance of the Fair.

Tanner's arm unfurled itself from around Blair to grab

the wheel once more. A cold emptiness rushed in to replace the heart racing warmth and with regret Blair sat upright. It took only a moment to find a park in the fairgrounds, having driven to the back of the parked cars and taking the next empty space in line.

Jacob was the first to leave the vehicle, bouncing around the side of the car, his excitement running high. As Blair slide across to step from the truck the freshly familiar warmth anchored into her shoulder. A crimson blush grew across her face as she found Tanner's hand holding gently. Her mind immediately giving images of the man pulling her back for a stolen kiss. Without realising, Blair had moistened her lips in response.

She turned... Could she ever be ready for that face? Those determined, hazel-green eyes holding to her own. The strong jaw line and clean shaven face. It wouldn't have surprised her to hear Tanner shaved with a large bowie knife. Or was it what she hoped he did. Blair couldn't be sure anymore.

"Sorry if I made you uncomfortable," Tanner said. "That boy can just be a real pain in the arse."

"Don't I know it," Blair found herself saying. The thought of Jacob somehow got her riled up in a completely different way. Now she was wanting to vent. "He teases me every chance he gets. Never gives me a moments rest. Manipulates information he gives others about me to get his own way. You saw him today. He was in top form..." Tanner's half smile caused Blair to trip over the sentence. The right side of his lips curled up to embrace his face, drawing Blair in in that moment.

"I'm glad you made it through okay." Tanner replied. "I'll see you back her just before 10 and don't worry about the lock. That one doesn't work anyway." With that Tanner swung out the driver's side door. He made to leave but paused a moment and looked back. "It's good to finally hear your voice properly. Like a breath of fresh air. I expect more in the near future."

"Eep..." was all Blair could muster.

Tanner just smiled once more and headed to the show leaving Blair steaming in the Pickup. A knock on the window roused her from her stupor and Blair looked up to see Jacob swaying back and forth.

"Come on, Blair. The fair is in full swing. Let's go," Jacob said. His voice had been muffled by the window but Blair understood the hardest part of the night started now.

With a grunt Blair shifted herself to the passenger door. Reaching for the handle the door flung open and Jacob bowed.

"Milady," Jacob said.

"Don't be stupid," Blair replied. As she moved past him she caught a glimpse of Tanner once more. To her surprise and shock, he now had an arm around another girl. Blonde and thin was all she could see but the picture started to tear apart the fantasies she had been building. "Who's that?" She asked Jacob. Her eyes didn't leave the pair.

Leaning closer to Blair to get a better view, Jacob instantly saw the person who caught his sister's attention causing him to smile. "That is Astrid," Jacob said. He did not elaborate.

The silence between them caused Blair's focus to shift to the young boy. "Well? A name doesn't say much."

"Astrid is Tanner's girlfriend. We don't like her," came Jacob's reply.

This was the answer Blair had feared. Then she found it curious that she felt this way. She had liked boys before who were out of her league. Only days before she hadn't even known this one existed so when had her feelings gotten this far. "The car trip," she decided out loud causing Jacob to raise an eye at her. That would have caught anyone unawares. And then the rest of what Jacob said filtered in. "Why don't we like her?"

"Well for one, those lusty eyes of yours for her boyfriend. It's plain to see exactly how you feel," Jacob said. Blair was about to get defensive, but Jacob cut her off. "And since you have the hots for him, as your brother, I want to see you succeed. Hence, we don't like her."

"I haven't got the hots... and you're not my brother," Blair argued. She was once again focused on Tanner and Astrid.

Jacob ignored her denial on both accounts. Nothing he hadn't heard before and the small hesitation before denying his heritage actually felt like a win. "She isn't that nice of a person when you get her on her own."

Blair didn't look back, struggling to process the

information she had just gained. After a long moment she took the first step to the entrance of the fair. "Come on, Jacob," she called back.

Jacob was looking forward to how this would play out and having a new enemy for Blair would give him opportunities to win some affection. He took a few quick steps to come up beside his sister.

The memories Blair had for the Fair were far outdated and bias through the eyes of a child. When she was younger the lights and sounds spurred on her excitement. Sideshows and random performers kept her gleefully entertained. And the rides... There had been nothing to cause young Blair such thrills to make her scream with giddy pleasure except the experience of youth.

Around the corner and the Ferris Wheel made her think of the last time her dad, mum and herself shared a ride. She sat on her dad's lap as the world opened up about her. Glancing at her parents she noticed they had only eyes for each other at the time. There was such love in those eyes and Blair shot Jacob a dirty look.

The fair she had remembered as a child was now no longer. All around were couples enjoying themselves with the trivial events or friends trying to outdo each other in the side show games. Without good friends or partners around her Blair had little interest in the fair anymore. No doubt Jacob still saw the world through the eyes of a child. He had been on countless rides and gorged himself on fairy floss and Dagwood dogs. He even had a go at the shooting range having the games owner cock the rifle for him. Five dollars to come out with a small keyring of a No. 8 billiard ball. The games owner probably paid barely even 10 cents for it. She wouldn't be caught dead keeping a side show keyring.

Blair checked her watch. 9:30.

How had time slowed again? All night it was continually getting slower and slower until the last what seemed like an hour since she had checked her watch was only 5 minutes.

"Look, there's Tanner," Jacob said. He grabbed the edge of her shirt and pointed over to a ball toss game. Jacob then leaned in close. "And he's alone."

"We shouldn't interru..." Blair started but before she could finish Jacob had dashed towards the stall and Tanner. He had already interrupted the man. With a quick glance around in case Astrid wasn't too far away, Blair made her way over to them to stand just behind Jacob.

As if sensing her, Tanner's eyes found Blair's. "Having a good night? This one hasn't been hassling you too much?" Tanner motioned to Jacob.

The knowledge that Tanner was taken had a rather unique effect on Blair. She didn't feel as shy anymore around the man and she could not feel any blush colouring her face as she looked into his eyes... Well, that couldn't be helped actually. At least she could now speak. "He has been as most children at a fair are. Over excited and rushing to and fro. He has had no moments of true clarity to hassle me." Blair's eyes became distant. "I don't fit into this environment. The fair brings back so many memories of my childhood that always lead back to sadder times."

Tanner had an idea of what she was speaking of having seen the apartment she lived in. "Then override those moments with happiness. You have a lifetime ahead of you too make some fond memories."

Blair gave a sad smile and nodded.

"Come on then let's get you smiling properly. How's your arm?" Tanner asked stepping aside to allow Blair access to the ball toss.

Instantly, Blair started to shake her head. "Nooo." Blair was waving her hands in front of herself. She had no intention of submitting herself to laughter and defeat with her unco hand eye coordination. What she didn't see was Jacob walking around her to stand just behind and with a nudge from his hip, Blair was sent off balance towards the stand. Tanner caught her just in time and Blair stabilised herself in his arms. So warm they were, even as a gentle misty rain began. A soft patter echoing down from the canvas awning above.

Without thinking, Blair took what was offered to her. Her mind finally clearing as she found herself looking down the row of the ball toss game. A simple setup of 6 bottles stacked in a triangle. To win the major prize a player would need to knock them over at two separate distances with three balls.

Blair looked concerned but a glance at Tanner found the man smiling back at her holding a ball of his own.

"You'll be fine, Blair. Just straight down the middle," Tanner said though the encouragement didn't boost her expectations. With a wind up, tanner let fly a ball with almost pin point accuracy. The curve of flight in the last moment saw the ball knock over only half the tower of bottles. He turned to wait for Blair's throw.

Biting her lower lip, Blair mustered up all the courage she could. Never having bothered to even show up at her previous school gym classes she had trouble finding the right way to bring her arm back. In the end, with an awkward throw, Blair was able to launch the ball... Straight up. Looking left and right to determine what happened, the ball connected with the awning to fall straight back onto the confused girl's head.

"Ow," escaped Blair's pouty lips and she reached up to rub her head.

Instantly, Jacob burst into peals of laughter. The loud, rippling noise grabbing the attention of many people around though luckily Blair was not the focal point. One set of eyes that were aimed directly at her were Tanner's. There was an amused look beaming from the centre and he was trying to stifle his own laugh with a clenched fist. This was too much for the girl and Blair made to leave only to be caught at the wrist by Tanner.

"Let me go. I told you I didn't want to do this," Blair said trying to free her arm.

"It wasn't so bad," Tanner said. His voice showed some concern when it was he that pushed her to play to begin with.

"You were laughing at me! Jacob is still laughing at me!"

Immediately, Tanner lopped a ball at Jacob taking him square in the face. The laughter ceased. "There is a big difference between laughing at you and a friend laughing at a shared moment as if the world did hold joy for people. We were sharing a moment, making fresh memories to be viewed with a smile. That smile came forth as a laugh and I had thought you too would share in that moment. I am sorry if you were saddened by it.

Blair looked away.

"Come, finish the game with me," Tanner said. This

28

immediately got Blair's attention and she turned on him, eyes wide in fear. "Let me give you a few tips on throwing at least."

Tanner's hands caught Blair by the hips and started to bring her back to stand before her nemesis, the ball toss game. Standing at her back, Tanner drew her in close, her form curving perfectly down his chest to the... the... Her face went bright red as she told herself it was only Tanners fly that was making her so hot. Her legs were shaking as he ran his right hand up her side and along her arm to rest above Blair's hand. Fingers intertwining he wrapped his hand around the second ball in Blair's hand, her fingers following suit.

"Now, what you want to do is..."

That was all Blair heard. Tanner's voice drifting away into the fantasies of the embrace. There were no clothes in this fantasy. No zipper. She moved with him, her arm coming out and up. Their bodies like two electrical forces merging into one. As their arms came over and forward Blair leaned into the throwing motion, her mind still in the fantasy of Tanner bending her forward. Her arm came down to hold onto the counter for support as she pushed her firm butt back a little.

A light suddenly came on in Blair's mind as she remembered where she was. "Fuck," she whimpered.

"Are you okay, Blair? You lost your balance for a moment," Tanner said, he still had one arm around her holding her close to keep her upright.

"Umm... Yes! I'm alright. Out, up and over," Blair said remembering the movements. As her words came out she draw the second ball in the motion and sent it flying. This time the ball had a little better accuracy as it flew across the tented area to crash into a large stuffed bunnies face.

"Yes, that's exactly it though this time let go only when your arm is lined up with the bottles," Tanner said as he clapped her success.

Blair couldn't look back at him. Not now. She needed calm. And Jacob saw this opportunity. Reaching slowly for the final ball Jacob rushed in and snatched it up himself.

"My turn. My turn," he cried before throwing the ball down the line to send 5 of the 6 bottles spinning to the ground. Reaching into the stall Jacob picked up a 1 Ball keyring to match the 8 Ball he scored earlier.

"You little thief," Blair yelled at him but the agile boy jumped away even as her arm swiped the air. "Argh!"

"It's okay," Tanner said. "You can have one of mine."

Blair found she was back in control of herself again, the anger for Jacob suppressing her own fantasies. "Thank you." Still, she found it difficult to say his name.

Tanner threw first knocking the remainder of his stack over. This triggered a new stack to be built half a metre behind and Blair had one last ball.

"Don't fear the distance. The bunny is further back than the bottles are. It is only accuracy that you should focus on."

Blair nodded and took a deep, steadying breath. She visualised the movement and brought her hand down a few times opening her fingers at the same moment. One last, deep breath and she was ready. She wound up for the throw and brought her arm around as best she could remember. Releasing the ball at the practiced position saw it course through the air to clip the side of the lowest bottle. The bottle shifted slightly but nothing fell. Blair's shoulders sagged.

"Why the pout. You hit them. Congratulations. It was a long way from the awning you took out the first time. Be proud," Tanner said.

"I still missed," Blair returned feeling defeated. She started to walk off in the direction Jacob had gone but only made a few feet.

"Wait, Blair. You forgot your prize," Tanner said catching her shoulder.

"Keep it. It'll only remind me of my failure," Blair said turning to face Tanner only to find a face dangling in front of her. Her eyes focusing, Blair realised it was an emoticon smiley face with an odd strap connected to it.

"It's a phone strap. You can attach it to that phone you have. When you see it think instead of the fun time we shared together and disregard the meaningless parts like success and failure. Success wouldn't have made the moment any more fun for me. Just seeing you smile maybe."

Hesitating a moment, Blair reached up and took the strap. It was a thoughtful pick and Tanner had done so to make her happy. A small smile grew on her face.

Tanner returned it. "Get Jacob and meet me back at the car. We had better be leaving now. I just need to say goodbye to someone."

Shocked, Blair looked to her watch. 9:58. This time, it only felt like 5 minutes had passed.

Looking up Blair saw Tanner standing with his girlfriend. Astrid seemed annoyed and was motioning to Blair. Blair couldn't determine just what was said but she understood the girl was jealous that her boyfriend was enjoying time with another girl. Tanner looked to have gotten the situation under control and started for the entrance. As Astrid watched him go her gaze landed on Blair still standing where she had been. Eyes menacing as if locked onto their prey. A wicked little smile crept across the other girl's face.

Uncomfortable under Astrid's glare, Blair turned to look for Jacob. Seeing the boy taking a large, swirled fairy floss stick from a cart vendor she made her way to him. Leaning in close, Blair felt a small amount of elation as the boy flinched having not seen her approach.

"You're right. We don't like her," Blair said.

Jacob seemed confused only a moment as he thought back to the earlier conversation. Astrid! "If you need me to sneak some old prawns into her car air conditioning, I would be delighted."

Blair considered the boy a moment before turning and heading for the gate. "Tanner's waiting in the carpark. We can't act out in front of him now can we?"

A warm, fuzzy feeling filled Jacob as the walls around Blair started to crack. He would use Astrid well to get closer to his sister. Not to mention help her to smile a little more. Jacob rarely saw Blair smile and started to wonder how someone could be so sad. Ripping a large chunk of floss from the stick Jacob stuffed it into his mouth to have it dissolve into a sweet, sticky goo.

At home and tucked away in bed, Blair held to her mother's phone. Light from a ¾ moon providing enough of a glow to see by. Cradled in her hands the phone waiting patiently for a comment but Blair remained silent. Her mouth opening only to close again just as quickly. She had spoken of Tanner to her mother before, but this was different. It was just an 'I've met a man' or 'there is a man working dad's farm that has an agreeable look about him" before. Nothing like the feelings and events that occurred this evening. It was hard to find just what words to say.

"I think I'm starting to accept Jacob," Blair said. She decided she needed to build up to the main topic on her mind. "Sorry, mum. I know he is the reason our lives fell apart. I know when that woman fell pregnant, dad's honour would force him to look after the child also. I just wish he showed some honour in turning away that woman before any of this happened. I will always hate her but I'm finding it hard to hold that hatred for Jacob," Blair confessed. "Yes, he is a jerk and yes, he is immature but he also comes from a broken family. I may not have paid attention before but the moment we met, he was so excited to have a sibling. Maybe he is just lonely."

"Or maybe it's because he was being immature that I... got closer to Tanner." Blair's face set aflame as she felt the crimson creep across her skin. "On the car trip to the fair he held me close. Protected me from Jacob's antics. That alone had made me come alive. But at the fair, I played a ball toss game with him. It was again, Jacob, that got me over to the stall, but Tanner taught me how to throw better." A soft giggle escaped Blair's lips. "Well, I don't need to tell you how bad my aim was. But with Tanner I actually hit the target. Grazed it would be closer... And I lost myself for a moment in his arms. My mind and body went wild when he held me near. It was like electricity from our souls merged into one. The world became a warmer place..." Blair's mind wandered back to those thoughts for a moment.

"He also got you a gift," Blair said. She suddenly remembered the emoticon phone strap. Reaching over to the discarded clothes on the floor she dug down to find the clutch purse and pulled out the prize. After a moment fidgeting with the chord, Blair had the strap on the phone. "Do you like it? I think of him each time I see it. I guess I won't be seeing too much more of him now though with school coming up tomorrow... and he has a girlfriend. I can't be the other woman. It would be a dishonour to you. I love you, mum. I hope you're having fun wherever you've

32

found yourself."

Rolling over, Blair closed her eyes to drift off to sleep still holding the old phone.

Chapter 3 – Friends and enemies

The knock on the door shattered her dreams. Dreams that would, now, never be remembered from her startled start to the day.

"What?" Blair called. The tone of her voice husky and slurred. Her mind fuzzy as it tried to kickstart itself.

"Good, you're awake." The voice was Jacob's and Blair started to reconsider the nicer things she had said about him last night.

"Go away," Blair said.

"I would but dad has asked me to get you up. He'll drive you this morning and show you what you need."

Blair seemed confused only a moment before the thought of school popped into her head. Throwing the blankets back, she jumped up too quickly. Her mind swam as she clutched the bed head to remain stable.

"Your uniform is hanging on the door handle here. There is some breakfast on the table. We'll be leaving in 20 minutes."

Blair heard the retreating footsteps on the stairs. Stabilising herself, she tenderly opened the door to peer through. Nothing moved in the hall way so she reached around and unhooked the uniform. '*Well this isn't going to be fun,*' she thought to herself spying the tie. It was a forest green pleated pattern that matched the skirt. The shirt was a white button up with a crisp collar that would definitely be poking into the sides of her neck by mid-morning.

Swapping out her pyjamas for the uniform, Blair studied herself in the mirror. The uniform was too neat, and the skirt ended below her knees. It was the tie that troubled her though. She'd never had to wear one before. Her old dress code, on the occasion she went to school, was casual wear. Opting to go without the tie, Blair left the top button undone and headed downstairs.

"Ready for your first day at school?" Bryan asked as Blair entered the dining.

Blair nodded looking at the full table of food. Cereal, toast, eggs, bacon, hashbrowns. There was so much there.

"I wasn't sure what you liked before school so I got you a bit of everything. Your bag with all the books you need is on your chair. You'll be assigned a locker on arrival so the bag will be all but useless after today."

"Thanks... Dad," Blair didn't have the heart to tell him she could barely afford a descent breakfast, if any, most days of the week. It was a hard thing to get used to, being cared for.

Moving her bag, which was far heavier than expected, Blair sat at the table getting two slices of toast and eggs and bacon to top. On first bite, her taste buds went wild. The flavours imbued into such a simple breakfast, from such a simple kitchen were unbelievable. It wasn't long before she'd finished her meal.

Bryan smiled. "Jacob's already caught the bus. It would've arrived about the time you walked into the room."

"You should've woken me sooner," Blair said. A look of apology written all over her face.

"No, I had planned to take you in today. Call it a father's wish to see his girl off to school. I hope it's not too embarrassing. You can catch the bus tomorrow. Jacob will show you which one to take this afternoon."

An odd feeling swept over Blair. A mixture of warmth and love causing the girl to become coy. "Thank you," she said softly.

"Well then, if you're ready, we can be off."

The size of the school was incredible for such a small town. The bus bay alone had room to fit 8 buses and Blair counted another 4 waiting to turn in. The buildings were two or three storeys high with many out of sight, hidden by the large school frontage. Students were walking around the yard, entering buildings or just hanging out with friends. To have such a large school, Blair was sure she'd be able to hide away in the crowd.

"With such a large school I'm sure you'll quickly make friends and stand out," Bryan said, no way close to picking up on Blair's true feelings. "We're lucky, you know. Many of the students come from neighbouring towns and farms. Some even travelling a few hours each way just to get an education and we have it almost on our doorstep."

Blair thought the 20 minutes into town was a little more than on the doorstep but she let it go.

"I know you're going to fit in just fine."

"Thanks, Dad," Blair said. "I'll do my best." Turning

Blair pulled the handle to open her door and was about to get out when she paused and looked back. She wasn't at the stage of kissing the man goodbye. Would he want that? A hug maybe..? Blair reached out and patted the man on the shoulder causing Bryan to smile at the sentiment.

"The bus you'll want this afternoon will be a big blue one parked at the end near the woodlands. It's the first to leave so don't miss it or there'll be a couple hours wait before I can come get you. Have a good day," Bryan said.

"You too," Blair replied. Finally she hopped from the vehicle and walked towards the entrance. There would be signs inside directing her, she was sure. Without looking back she heard the old pickup drive away.

The inside of the building was nothing short of massive even when judged against the city high schools. Wide hallways to accommodate a large flow of students and staff. Lockers abounding every wall with small gaps where classrooms and toilets could be found. It was a rather plain cream colour pallet but that was offset by paintings created by the students whose art pieces won awards or posters for after school groups plastered on the walls. All in all though this school was just one in many Blair had seen. The only difference with this one was that this school should see her out.

A sign above a large open window told Blair she'd found the office administrator and she proceeded over to line up behind three students, each almost a perfect mirror of the one before. Only the facial features changed as their hair style and even colour were very similar. The last of which glanced back and gave Blair a quick up and down with her eyes.

"They're going to chip you for your uniform," she said in hushed tones.

Blair just shrugged at the smaller girl.

"City girl, hey?"

"You could tell just from a half-hearted shrug?" Blair asked.

"Most city folk expect some sort of gesture will end a conversation they don't want. Here in the country it's a bit harder to shake a person than that."

After a moment, Blair just shrugged again but this time threw in a genuine smile. The girl had gotten a good read on her.

Returning the smile the girl nodded and turned her attention to the front of the line now only moments from her turn. "Lillian," the smaller girl said. "In case you do wish to start up a conversation."

"Blair," was the reply as Lillian stepped up to the window.

It wasn't long before it was Blair's turn. The clerk just sat staring at her waiting for some direction but Blair didn't offer any.

"Can I help you?" The clerk asked. Her patience had finally run dry causing her attitude to become harsh around the edges.

"I'm starting at this school today. I need to pick up a timetable and wanted some directions. I didn't expect the school to be so..." A hand was flung up before Blair's face stopping her mid-sentence.

"I don't care about your troubles or how big the school is. I'm sure you have plenty of other things to size up. All I need is your name."

"Blair Thompson. 11," Blair stammered.

"I don't need your mental age. Bryan's kid... ah yes, here it is." The clerk pulled out a few sheets of paper. "This is your locker number and combination. This is your timetable. Don't be late to your classes. Jacob will be over shortly to show you around."

"Jacob!"

"Is there a problem?"

"Jacob will sooner lead me astray than help me out. Isn't there anyone else?"

"Not at this time. I'll organise a student rep to meet you at recess. Until then you're on your own. Thank you. Next," the clerk called looking around Blair.

"Please," Blair persisted.

"That's all I can do for you. You need to move out of the way."

Turning away, Blair was shocked the line was now nine deep. Staring at the class schedule Blair was able to deduce the first lesson would be Math... and the second. A double straight up. This day wasn't turning out to be a good day. Still needing to determine where class Q13P was Blair looked around desperately trying to see some indication of direction.

Nothing came to sight, but sitting on a ledge in front of her, Blair spotted Jacob. He was waiting with a large grin upon his face staring back at her and swinging his legs. She tried to find something better to look at but his face kept coming into view. The grin just getting wider.

"Fine," Blair said. "Show me where my first class is and I'll use your replacement after that."

Jacob slide off the ledge and walked over. The grin never leaving his face. "I knew you couldn't say no in the end."

"Don't make me regret this, Jacob."

"Never. So what classroom are you looking for?" Jacob snatched the timetable from Blair's hands and started to peruse the schedule. "Oh damn. You have Pertouski first up... and second."

"What's wrong with Pertouski?" There was real fear in Blair's eyes.

Jacob just smiled again. "There's nothing wrong with him but I made you worried, hey?"

Smacking him across the back of the head Blair took back her schedule. "I'll find them myself. Don't worry about it." With that Blair turned to walk away.

"Blair, wait. I'm sorry. It's this way." Jacob walked back out the main entrance.

Biting her lip, Blair decided to trust him one last time. It wasn't going to be any worse than her sense of direction. Walking out in the fresh air, Blair could hear Jacob going on about the different buildings. He was pointing and talking rather rapidly though Blair had no care for the trail of words that shot from his mouth. Every now and again she heard the word History or English but Blair decided she would get a proper rundown from the student rep that was to be sent around.

Finally, Jacob stopped in front of a beautifully designed building. The architecture reminded Blair of photos she had seen of Greece and Rome. Large pillars with the squiggly scroll looking things on the top. She had never known what to call them but liked them none-the-less. The building itself seemed to only get wider the higher up you looked and the windows were all circular. This building stood out like an elegantly dressed thumb with perfectly smooth white walls all ending at a rather odd sloping curve of a roof.

"This is where you'll be learning Maths. The building is supposed to show the students just what can be achieved when Math is used correctly. Your room will be the first floor, room 3."

Blair had started to get the idea on how the numbering system worked in the school. Though, she did ignore him for most of the time, Jacob got her to her first class. "Thank you, Jacob, for getting me to where I needed to be."

"I can continue the tour at recess if you like?" Jacob said.

"With a double first up I should have all the time in the world to make friends and get the support I need. Plus they'll be sending around a student rep my own age at that time. Still, I won't forget that you can be mature at times."

With a quick smile, Jacob nodded and took off towards some boys kicking around a soccer ball. He settled in quickly picking up the rhythm of the game.

Turning, Blair settled herself with a deep breath and took in the building. After the initial wonder it held had worn away, Blair saw the large mismatching of design. Yes, the different styles showed how vital maths could be but nothing gelled. Blair started to find the building ugly deep down.

"Beautiful, Isn't it?" a voice sounded behind her causing Blair to jump.

"Umm... Yes. Rather," Blair stammered as she turned to find a faculty member standing behind her marvelling at the building. Tall and thin with glasses. He almost suited the building but for the grey frizzy hair on top. Blair's mind ran to more of a mad scientist type teacher.

"You know, I helped design this," the man said.

Blair looked back at the building and tried to give an enthusiastic wow for his benefit.

"I am Mr Pertouski. I don't believe we've met."

"Blair Thompson."

Mr Pertouski nodded recognising the name. He leaned in closer. "A little more bravery from those in my class is preferential. The building was designed to get that initial wow and then start to fade away. I know you're smart enough to see that right."

"Why design it like that?" Blair asked. She could see the man was a little peculiar and that seemed to help put her at ease.

"Maths is fragile. You could accomplish great things with it. Pair it with the wrong brain and things start to fall apart. This building shows both greatness and despair. Were you heading in? There's still 5 minutes before the bell."

"I'm still getting used to the grounds. I didn't want to lose my way back here wandering off at the last minute."

"Then in we go," Mr Pertouski said. He didn't give Blair time to reply and waltzed right in.

Blair felt awkward just standing still and started moving after him. Inside the halls were just the same as the other areas. Odd classes on one side, evens on the other. Nice wide open halls and only the bare minimum for bins and drinking fountains to give any change to the walkway. Three doors up and Blair found herself waiting in the doorway like a lost, little puppy.

"Come in, Come in," Mr Pertouski said beckoning for her. "Make yourself at home."

Blair wandered in scanning the room. Around the walls were simple posters with mathematical theory, Pythagoras's Theorem and algebraic jokes. She even stifled a laugh as she read a few. The layout of the room was much different to the other classes she had been in before. The tables and chairs went back in two big arcs allowing for more students to be in the front and less to hide away in the back. Seeing as how the chairs were limited back there, Blair made to sit in the one closest to the back wall.

"Where are you going?" Mr Pertouski asked.

Blair froze to the spot. "I was going to take a seat. You said to make yourself at home."

"Yes, but in this class seats are assigned." He pulled out a seating chart. Blair wasn't too far off the mark on where she tried to sit but Mr Pertouski didn't like that. Those that chose to sit behind or off to the side were only looking for an easy out. "You are this seat here," he said gesturing to a front seat two from centre. He couldn't very well move his best students after accepting their requests when designing the seating structure but with some small adjustments he made it work with Blair up front.

Blair gave a deflated sigh. "How often do we rotate seats?"

"It's not a matter of when. My better students can choose where they sit because I know they'll complete their work accurately. I don't yet know your capabilities and when you were just a name I placed you appropriately. Prove yourself to me and you'll earn the right to choose your seat. We will reassess mid-year." Mr Pertouski could tell by Blair's face she wasn't impressed. "If you feel your ability lacking this will be the best seat for you."

Blair opened her mouth to make her case but a loud ringing cut her off. Students started to file into the building and filling in seats after a quick word to Mr Pertouski. Immediately, Blair knew there was nothing more she could do to get a better seat and sat where she must.

"City girl, you made the front? You must have had some good grades at your old school... or made an impression on the Teacher." a familiar voice said.

Blair looked up to find Lillian standing before her. "I sat where I was bid. My preference was in the back."

"And you made this known?"

"I had made to sit in the back when I first entered. That's when I was told of the assigned seats."

"Ah, then an impression was made."

"What does that mean?"

"Let's just say Mr Pertouski expects great things from you."

"Girls. Class is in session," Mr Pertouski said.

Blair and Lillian quietened, and Blair was comforted when the small girl sat next to her. She was proving to be the right kind of extrovert. Friendly, to the point, yet somehow knowing just where the boundaries lay. Blair was starting to think she was about to accept a person's friendship if given. Something she hadn't done in a long time.

The class proved to be harder than expected. Because of the number of days she just didn't go to school, Blair found a lot of the topics to go straight over her head. It was even worse when she was called to work out equations on the board and she stood, chalk in hand, just staring at the numbers and letters until dismissed and another was called to complete what she couldn't.

41

A loud ringing echoed through the halls signalling the end of first period. A glitch in the bell outside Blair's class caused it to sound louder than the rest. It was as if another bell was trying to strangle it and this one could only send out a final shrill cry of pain. A Pain that made Blair's ears ache.

As this was a double, no one in the room made to move. Everyone waited patiently for the sound to die away and any movement outside to cease before the lesson resumed once more. Though, Blair didn't attend many school days at her previous school, she did know that normal lessons wouldn't jump around topics so much in a day. And the amount of times she got called up compared to the rest of the class was annoying to say the least. If Lillian was correct and she had made an impression on the teacher at the start of class she was certain the impression would be all but nothing now.

"5 minutes before the bell. How 'bout we finish the lesson with a race. John, Michelle, Billy, Lillian and... Blair. Could you five bring your chairs out and sit facing the back of the room," Mr Pertouski said.

Blair's heart dropped as she heard her name called. And against Lillian, Blair had spied a bit of the girls workings in her book and knew she was nowhere near the level this girl was. This was just going to be another embarrassment. Seeing the others had already made their way out front and were now looking at her Blair jumped forward and swiftly sat down at the end.

"No one is to look back. I will be writing an easy equation on the board for each of you. When I say, I want you all to turn around, get to the board and write the answer. First to finish won't need to do their homework tonight." This comment caused a number of students who hadn't been picked to moan. Some even gave Blair a dirty look seeing how she'd performed during the lessons and thinking the spot wasted on her.

Blair just sat, eyes down, listening to the chalk scratching across the board. A quick glance around the room gave her the impression the questions weren't as easy as they were described. One girl even sat, eyes wide, as she watched each equation jotted down.

"Okay, ready... Go," Mr Pertouski said.

42

Almost immediately four of the five competitors jumped up and froze as they took in the work. It was only a moment before they all raced to the board. Blair took her time; however, she knew she had no chance. Looking up at the board, though, she was surprised. There wasn't anything big and scary. Just a random number in the hundreds of thousands multiplied by a random number in the millions. The others had started writing in their answers and Blair felt that she had given the race away. A race she realised she had a chance with. If she had been taught one thing by her last math teacher it was the shortcuts in the ways of addition and multiplication.

Feeling deflated at her lose, Blair still walked to the board and wrote her answer. It was over in a matter of moments and she looked across to see who had won, holding a small hope it would be Lillian. But everyone was still writing. Columns of numbers filled the board under everyone's equations and it took a moment for Blair to realise they were using the long handed version to work it out.

"I see we have a winner," Mr Pertouski exclaimed. The other 4 students paused and glanced across, eyes wide in awe at the single line providing Blair's answer. "You couldn't provide an answer to any other question in class but I see you do have some mathematical ability dormant within you. Good job. It would be even more impressed if you could do the same for the other equations."

With a hand rolling in front of her to help her think Blair slowly gave the answers to each of the questions. The last she gave as the bell sounded. Everyone in class scurried out but Blair was called back.

"You have a lot to catch up on," Mr Pertouski said. "Any issues I need to know about?"

Blair shook her head. She didn't want to start getting into the old life she had in the city.

"Be that as it may, I know I said the winner wouldn't need to do their homework but I would ask if you would at least consider doing it for your own benefit."

"I'll see what my afternoon brings," Blair replied.

Mr Pertouski nodded and tilted his head towards the door. Blair didn't wait for him to start talking again and after gathering her stuff left the class.

"Don't mind him. He's just getting a gauge for your ability," Lillian said as Blair left the room.

"It felt like he was picking on me."

"No, he would do that with anyone new to his class."

"You seem to know a lot about him."

"You could say we're close," Lillian said, a small smile crossing her face.

Blair just scrunched her nose in disgust to which Lillian levelled back a glare.

"At home I call him Dad."

"Still doesn't help," Blair returned, eyebrow raised.

"Stop it, seriously!" Lillian playfully shoved Blair's shoulder. "I didn't say daddy."

"You called, Honey?" Mr Pertouski said as he left the class closing the door behind him. Blair stifled a laugh as she watched Lillian's face turn ghostly white.

"No, Dad! Go!" She pushed the man on his way down the hall before turning back to face Blair who was now openly laughing.

"Still hasn't helped." Blair settled down to a smile.

"So you're Blair," a new voice sounded. The tone was dripping with acid.

Turning Blair found herself face to face with Astrid, Tanner's girlfriend. She could see a high and mighty attitude hiding in her eyes.

"What do you want with her?" Lillian asked stepping up. Something about the situation had her visibly shaken

Astrid turned to glare at the girl. "Take a step back, Peewee. Unless you want your time in the school to be made far worse. I don't care whose daughter you *claim* to be. You know that."

Immediately, Lillian backed up a few steps. Blair felt let down by this move but understood bullies better than most. Divide and conquer. Blair turned to throw back a comforting smile. Something to convey she wouldn't hold it against Lillian later.

As Blair turned back a shimmer caught Astrid's eye. Swaying from one of Blair's pockets was the phone strap she saw Tanner give Blair the night before. A dread anger bubbled up inside her and Astrid reached out to snatch the ugly little thing and smash it under foot.

"Astrid, Blair? I see you two've met."

Blair looked up to find Tanner standing in the hall way and her eyes went wide as electricity coursed across her body. Trying to find a reason for his being on school grounds a small voice in her mind was trying to highlight the fact he was dressed in school colours. "You're a student here?"

"You didn't know? I'm only a year above you. I'll graduate this year."

"I thought you were far passed that." A crimson blush heated Blair's cheeks. Her eyes scanned over tanner taking in the information that he was her senior. The uniform looked so... sexy.

"The office sent me over to show you around, get you acquainted with the school grounds..."

Astrid looked at the connection these two shared and was getting more pissed off being left out at the edge of the conversation. Taking Tanner's arm and levelling her eyes on Blair, Astrid's voice changed instantly to a harmony of sweetness and purity. "You don't need to anymore, Tany. Blair was just telling me how she wanted to explore the school with her new friend back there." Astrid motioned at Lillian. "Isn't that right, Blair?"

Pausing only a moment, Blair gave a slow nod. Her eyes set on Astrid's.

"I understand," Tanner said with a smile. "I'm glad you're making friends so quickly."

Before anyone else had time to say anything Astrid whisked Tanner away.

"I... I... I'm sorry I couldn't do more," Lillian stammered. She seemed saddened about the situation.

"Don't be. I've been let down before." Though she had every intention of forgiving the girl, Blair was still hurt and small echoes of her old life had started to creep in. She needed to be alone. "Where is history C7 and Metal T9?" With Tanner gone she now had no one to show her around.

"Come on, it's this way."

Blair could hear the depressing tone coming from Lillian but she still couldn't bring herself to be around anyone. "No, that's okay. Just directions will be fine."

Lillian settled a quivering lip and gave some quick directions for each of the classes and notes on finding any other buildings easily. Blair nodded and turned, walking from the maths block. She heard a sniff and knew the smaller girl was starting to break.

Blair almost made a friend. Almost, but was reminded how much they can hurt you.

The rest of the day became just what Blair had hoped for. Quiet and insubstantial where she hide in the background and flowed through the day. At lunch, she made use of the longer break to really get herself acquainted with the school. She was even able to find her locker and ditch a lot of the books that'd been weighing her down. In places, she spied certain people. Jacob tussling with the boys on the soccer field, Tanner and Astrid hanging with a bunch of other seniors, and even Lillian. The smaller girl was alone, staring at a sandwich with only two bites taken from it. These three areas Blair made a mental note to avoid in the future.

Only one other class of the day had Lillian sitting at the front and as Blair walked in the smaller girl's expression lightened. This sunk right back down as Blair walked to the back corner of the class and took a seat.

And finally the day ended. Blair need only reach her bus and endure the trip home to find sanctuary in her room once more. Blue bus near the trees? Blue bus near the trees? Spotting what she was after Blair's heart sank as she saw a group of girls waiting near her bus line headed by none other than Astrid. To think the older girl would be content with the earlier meeting was an over sight.

Blair just needed to get into line and get on the bus. She was adept at ignoring bullies even when it pissed them off more. And so that's what she did. Without looking Astrid's way Blair made it to the back of the line. Astrid had called out a few remarks but Blair was so focused the words didn't even reach her. Then Astrid was in her face.

"You think you can start hanging around my boyfriend and not get any of the consequences?" Astrid said.

The girl was so close Blair could literally taste the satay Astrid had for lunch on her breath. Her nose retracted in disgust and Blair done what she could to look around Astrid towards the front of the line. Though she had trouble pretending Astrid wasn't breathing down her neck the point got across and rage grew in the other girl's eyes.

46

"Bitch!" Astrid snarled shoving Blair of balance.

Blair landed hard, the pain flowering in a deep rage. A rage pent up from years of ignoring or pretending she was ok. A rage built on the foundation her mother had been stolen from her too early in life, her father had chosen another woman over his own family, and nothing in this world offered the warmth and love she longed for. Her hand flew out, fist clenched. Blair hadn't even realised she'd found her feet once more, let alone was connecting with Astrid's left eye.

Maybe not warmth and love, but the happiness that exploded from her hand at that moment was fulfilling indeed... nope, that was pain. Definitely pain.

Unclenching her fist and shaking it back and forth, Blair was rushed by the other girls around Astrid. They grabbed her arms and held her strong. As much as Blair tried to struggle one way or the other there was always another girl to take up the slack and keep her in place.

Astrid was rubbing her eye but had recovered her composure. "You fucking bitch. That's going to leave a bruise." Her voice was deadly quiet as she approached Blair. Grabbing her by the chin, Astrid pulled Blair's face right in front of hers. "Now you listen to me cos I will only warn you once. Stay away from Tanner." Astrid punched Blair in the stomach. She immediately pulled Blair back up to look at her, ignoring the girl's trouble breathing. "Stay away from me." Another punch to the stomach. This time Blair remained doubled over "And don't pester my boyfriend for silly little toys." With that, Astrid reached into Blair's pocket and ripped away the phone hanger with phone still attached. A dark laughter filled the air as Astrid tried pushing the buttons. "Look at the brick, girls. So ancient it doesn't even work."

The other girls laughed with her as Blair tried to reach up and take back her phone.

"Oh, silly little thing, I can see you're in need of a new phone. I'll help dispose of this one." Astrid spun on her heel and threw the phone as hard as she could into the forest. The phone disappeared high up in the wall of tress and no trace of where it landed could be seen.

"Mum..!" Blair gasped as she tried to take in gulps of air.

"That's enough girls. You've made your point." There

was a man standing just behind Astrid with a stern look on his face.

"She knows where she stands now. And I have no time for little cry babies who call out to their mummies when there's trouble." Astrid tilted her head and the other girls fell in line with her as she walked from the scene, head held high.

"Will you be coming on this bus?" the bus driver asked. He didn't offer a hand or show any compassion towards Blair.

"Why didn't you help me?" Blair asked.

"Get involved with students, especially girls, you get sued... or worse. I need to leave."

"Just let me get my phone."

"You'll be lucky to find the phone with a week up your sleeve. If you're coming you need to come now. Otherwise, I'm leaving to make my rounds. The phone's gone."

Blair looked back at the forest and tears welled in her eyes. This was the second time her mum had been stolen from her and there was nothing she could do about it. As the bus driver turned to walk away, Blair staggered to her feet.

"Bye mum," Blair said, a tear rolling down her face, before moving to the bus.

Why should she believe that this school was going to be any different? Teachers and staff that like to throw their power around, employees who did nothing to help you, people who bullied and worse... someone who could have been a friend immediately letting you down the moment you needed them. Blair decided it wise not to allow herself to be so stupid in the future.

Leaning back against the chook shed, Blair absently stroked Shadows fur. This was such a calming and soothing act and at this moment Blair really needed it. Her dad didn't understand the whirlwind of emotion that stormed through the front door, locking itself away in her room. Any attempts to try and talk to her where met with screams or silence. After a while he walked away under the male programmed thought she must be at that time of the month.

When Blair heard Bryan leave to pick up Jacob from

town, she snuck out to sit with Shadow. And now with twilight darkening the sky and the stars starting to shine Blair's tears had eased. Shadow had his head resting upon her lap as he always had from a pup and she hugged him deeply.

Lights shimmered upon the side of the house, a tell-tale sign a car was coming up the driveway. Then she heard it, the low rumble of her dad's old pickup. Not wanting to alert anyone to her presence just yet, Blair waited by the chook shed as the car pulled up and Jacob and Bryan got out. They were arguing... Well Bryan had his voice raised while Jacob kept his mouth shut.

"I still can't believe you skipped practice on your third day after weeks of pleading to be allowed to join. You know how hard it is for me to leave everything and come get you at this time of the afternoon. You promised me the soccer training schedule wouldn't be too much. Not to mention the large down payment for uniform and sign on. Tell me why I shouldn't just call the coach now and have you removed from the roster. Why?" Bryan yelled. Blair had never seen her dad so worked up.

Jacob stammered as he fiddled with something in his hands. He never met Bryan's gaze.

"Nothing? Not even an excuse to why you skipped practice... Fine then. I'll take your silence as your wish to quit soccer." Bryan turned and walked towards the house. As he reached for the front door he stopped.

"Dad!" Jacob had screamed. Blair could see he wasn't completely in control of his emotions either. He still wasn't looking at Bryan but rather off to the side as he wiped a tear away.

"Well?" Bryan asked.

Blair watched as Jacob walked over to the man and held out his hand. She still couldn't tell what Jacob was holding or hear the words he spoke but almost instantly Bryan's face relaxed. He patted Jacob on the back and sent him inside. Before heading inside himself, Bryan glanced up at Blair's room with a stern look on his face. Blair could only guess at the stories Jacob must've told Bryan to get himself out of trouble.

Not wanting to leave her spot just yet, Blair allowed the heavens to darken completely and the stars to grow in strength and numbers. It had been a long time since she was able to see the stars so clearly if at all. The glow of the city stealing their beauty. In fact, the last time was when her parents split for good. Blair could remember being upset as her mum yelled at her dad and raced out to the comforting touch of Shadow. Growing late in autumn with winter snapping at its heels, Blair snuggled closer to Shadow for warmth, falling asleep. Her mum found her then and packed her into a car to leave the farm. There was no goodbye possible for her dad.

A shiver ran up Blair's spine causing goosebumps to rise upon her skin. She felt it time to head inside and took the quickest route to her room. Luckily no one was lurking in the hallways but rather at the dining table allowing Blair to make it to her room unencumbered.

She paused at her door. Resting before it was a plate of beef and gravy with a side of vegetables and beside that was... Her phone! Even as she scooped it up into her hands, Blair couldn't believe what she was seeing. There were some dirty marks on the body and phone hanger but all in all seemed undamaged by the flight. It took more than a moment to realise what'd transpired.

Jacob!

Blair picked up the plate of food and walked back to the dining room door. She stood tentatively unsure how to enter but Bryan rose and bade her come in. He pulled out the chair for her.

"New schools can be hard," Bryan said as Blair sat down.

Blair nodded, smiling over at Jacob. "Coming home to family helps."

"Hi mum, thought I'd touch base," Blair said. She was lying on her bed with a lamp lighting her immediate vicinity. In her hand she held a piece of paper filled with handwriting. "I haven't said much since the incident with Astrid. Nothing much has really happened. I've been keeping to myself around the school and letting the days go by. I hear talk of Astrid looking for me. I wouldn't know why. She made her point. Still, I've been able to avoid her for now."

"I haven't seen much of Tanner either. As school has

started, he doesn't help on the farm during the week. It's only going to be the weekend when I can perve." Blair giggled. "Not like anything would happen. Tanner and Astrid seem tight and the closer I get to Tanner the more jealous Astrid gets. Still..." Blair blushed. "No, no, no, no, no, no, no, no, noo. Let's not go there."

"Then there's this letter. Lillian poured her heart out to me. Can I just ignore it? I'll read it to you."

Hi Blair,

5 minutes ago it was 9pm and now its 10pm. An hour lost to my thoughts is enough time wasted without writing anything down. You don't seem like the type of person I could walk up to and talk things over with. I don't even know if you will read this but I like to think you are generally nice. I gave you reason to doubt the person I am. I showed myself to be flaky when a situation became dicey like I may not have your back. I have history with Astrid. I know what she can do, what she has done, and yes, I was scared. Scared enough to react as I have done for a year or more. Flee as there has never been anyone I needed to stick up for. I left you to fend for yourself and I have felt horrible about that ever since. Especially when you were someone who I was hoping to make a genuine friend. I don't have any in this school after meeting Astrid. I'm sorry to have already hurt you but I want to be your friend. I want to be able to have your back and know someone has mine. If that's not something you want to be, I understand. I'll leave you be. Give me the chance.
Lillian

"If it was me, I'd be happy for people to avoid me. But she isn't me. She longs to have friends. She is kind and I liked her up until Astrid got in the way. Do I do this? Do I try one last time to make a friend in this world...? Yeah, you're right. I've known pain enough to take a little more if it should come to that. I guess I have a new friend."

Chapter 4 – For the chips and chocolate, of course

The week was coming to an end and Blair was looking forward to the final lesson. She'd kept to herself for the majority of the day not causing any trouble. A small run in with Tanner around a corner and he said *see you tomorrow* like he was looking forward to it. That smile...

But Lillian was to have her attention now. Maths was about to begin and Blair entered at the last moment taking up her seat next to Lillian. She was sitting stiff and didn't look her way. A posture she had taken on since hurting Blair. A smile crossed Blair's face. Once she had gotten past the negativity created by Astrid, Blair could see just how affected the smaller girl had been and how much she wanted this friendship. Blair placed a note on Lillian's desk.

As Lillian unfurled the paper her brow furrowed. In rather large letters was the word chance and it took her more than a few moments to realise the implications of this word. Eyes wide she looked to Blair to confirm the hope that she'd just been given the chance she asked for. Blair just shrugged with a smile on her face before turning her attention to the front as Mr Pertouski started speaking. For the rest of the lesson Lillian couldn't keep the smile from her face and was more relaxed now than she had been in days.

The dying bell screeched as school ended for the week. Students started to file out of the room and Lillian would've walked out with Blair too but she hesitated as Blair made no move to leave. In fact, Blair had risen from her chair and walked over to where her dad was packing away his things.

"I only have a moment before I need to leave to catch my bus, but do you need your daughter tonight?" Blair asked.

Mr Pertouski eyed Blair a second. "An odd question."

"What I mean is, will it be alright if Lillian joins me for a sleepover tonight?" Blair said. She could hear Lillian blanch behind her.

"It's alright with me," Mr Pertouski said hesitantly. "Why does my daughter look so surprised?"

"Oh, she doesn't know yet," Blair replied swishing her

hand in front of herself. "I thought I'd be pragmatic and get my ducks in a row first."

Blair saw Mr Pertouski's eyes narrow as if questioning Lillian. Blair glanced back and saw Lillian tap her wrists together to make a quick cross. She thought this was odd but all families had their own personal quirks.

"I have no issues with it. Clothes?"

"Dad's given me a whole trunk of clothes I may never wear. There's plenty of spares. It'll be ok." With a smile Blair walked to the teacher's desk and jotted a number on a bit of paper. "Dad's number if you need it. Thanks sir."

Blair turned and grabbed Lillian by the wrist dragging her out the door. Lillian's head was spinning as she chased her friend down the corridor and out to the bus... Her friend! It had been too long since she could say that about someone.

"I see Lillian's found herself a little girlfriend. Look at the pair of Dykes," a voice sounded close by.

Lillian's heart dropped as she recognised it as Astrid's and more than this her whole being seemed to plummet. Blair noticed the change and a fire ignited in her. She turned to look Astrid in the eyes.

"Hell yeah!" Blair slapped Lillian on the rump causing a yelp to escape the smaller girl's lips. "Who could resist an arse like this." Not giving the stunned seniors a chance to respond, Blair ushered Lillian up and into the bus to sit closer to the front.

Blair watched as the seniors shook their heads and wandered back to whatever things they do after school. It was a good feeling to undermine their jeers but as she turned back to Lillian she doubted her actions. The smaller girl was sitting hands on knees staring down. Everything shouted she was definitely not okay.

"What's wrong, Lillian?" Blair asked, cocking her head sideways to try and get an angle under Lillian.

"Why...? Why did you do that?" Lillian's voice was barely a whisper. "People are going to talk. People are going to say we are a couple and that we are lesbians."

"What does it matter what others think. We know what we are. That's the only two opinions that I really care about. And it wasn't about you anyway. Astrid's been looking for me all week. She was gunning for another fight.

I don't know the reason for it but stealing the power in her words was my best option to stick it to her."

"You don't know Astrid like I do. She'll use any flaw you have to bring you down. People are going to shun you. People will hate you."

"Do you hate me, Lillian?" Blair asked suddenly.

"Well. No," Lillian stammered.

"That's all I care about. I've made about all the friends I'll need in this school and from your own words you already had trouble with the students here. We can have each other's backs. Whatever's thrown at us we can support each other. Words are just words. You are my friend, Lillian. We've got this."

Lillian blushed a little and looked up at her friend. Those strong blue grey eyes lifting her spirit instantly. "You've changed, Blair."

"Oh? I don't know if we really had the time to get to know each other well enough to notice change."

"I don't need to know you too well to see it. You were held back all week. Today you've been very outgoing."

Blair thought for a moment. "I guess with how long I've been alone the dam wall finally burst when I accepted you as a friend. There is so much emotion and excitement at what's ahead."

"I feel the same," Lillian replied.

The half hour bus trip to Blair's house went by so quick Blair almost missed the stop. The girls had been talking about themselves, their interests and hobbies, types of music they liked and what they aspired to be when they grew up. Blair was surprised at the smaller girl's interest in everything professional bull riding while Lillian didn't seem surprised at all when Blair didn't have any real aspirations ahead of her. Collecting their belongings, the girls got off the bus.

"There is still a bit of a hike up the driveway," Blair said slapping Lillian's back and making a run up the dirt road.

"Hey!" Lillian remarked chasing her friend.

Blair had felt confident in her running speed but as she glanced back Lillian was closing fast. Too fast, it seemed, to even be natural but there was nothing helping her along. Suddenly, Blair's world turned upside down as she ankle tapped herself and went sprawling to the earth.

Giggling, Lillian slowed down and softly slapped Blair on the back. "Gotcha," she said through the laughter. "Oh wow..."

Blair had looked up at Lillian as she made the last comment. Lillian's eyes were wide a moment before her laughter almost doubled. A big smear of mud ran down the right side of Blair's face and uniform which was made obvious to Blair as she got to her knees and could see her clothing and feel her face.

A loud horn hooted behind the girls causing them both to almost jump out of their skins. Neither one had heard the pickup creep in behind them.

"Do I need to wrestle you two off each other or are you happy playing in the mud?"

"Tanner!" Squealed Blair as she tried to hide herself behind Lillian.

Jumping from the pickup and approaching the girls, Tanner stifled a laugh. "The look suits you, Blair."

"Doesn't it just?" Lillian pitched in. She stepped out of the way of Blair.

"Lillian, you're supposed to be my friend." Blair pouted.

"And as such need to be truthful at every chance," Lillian replied.

Blair shot her friend a dirty look. "What are you doing here, Tanner?"

"During the school weeks, I work the farm Friday afternoons, Saturdays, and part of Sunday. It works out better for me that way."

"Doesn't sound like you have a lot of time to yourself," Lillian commented. She surprised herself at how easily she was talking to Tanner but seeing her friend was having a little difficulty doing so helped push her along.

"It does seem like I've given a lot of my own time up but honestly, I enjoy the work. I want to run my own farm one day. I know at that time I'll have a lot less down time then now."

"Well, the day isn't getting any younger. We won't hold you up more than need be," Lillian said. She wasn't too sure what more to say at this point.

"Actually, I would normally be here a lot sooner, but I missed you at school, Blair, and had to drive at the pace of the bus. Because I'm heading here anyway, Fridays you can get a lift with me if you'd like. Also, if you need a lift to the house now, there is room in the pickup... unless you're happy to keep playing in the mud."

Blair puffed out her grubby cheeks and pursed her lips. "I can walk just fine, thank you," Blair said stubbornly. She made to walk away but Lillian caught her arm. There was a cheeky little smile growing on her friends face.

"Please Blair, that run tired me out and the house still looks some distance ahead."

Blair just glared at her friend. "Fine... but we can ride in the tray." Taking a few steps towards the truck, Blair grasped the sides of the tray and vaulted up into the back. As she did, her grip gave way causing her to tumble awkwardly into the back. Blair rose quickly with a stern look on her face holding a finger up first at Tanner and then at Lillian daring them to say anything.

As Blair settled against the back of the cab, Lillian and Tanner glanced at each other. It was Lillian who cracked first, a crumbling puff of air escaping her lips. It was enough for their walls to tumble and within moments loud streams of laughter filled the air. Blair just sat with a grumpy look on her face, her arms crossed.

Lillian vaulted easily into the back of the pickup. Having been on a few horses she had no issues getting up to high places. Sitting down next to the grumpy Blair, she waited for the engine to start. Blair was emphasising her mood by looking away from Lillian so the smaller girl leaned in close to Blair's ear.

"You like Tanner."

There was no question behind her words and Blair turned, eyes wide. Her face had grown beet red, mouth fidgeting much like a fish.

"Don't worry. I won't let on," Lillian said. "I just understand a little better why Astrid has been gunning for you."

Letting out a sigh, Blair settled some. "I really haven't done anything to warrant it. The other night at the fair Jacob got me involved in a ball toss game against Tanner. Tanner ended up giving me the prize he won. Astrid saw this."

"That's plenty enough for Astrid to get jealous," Lillian replied nodding. "But there's more you may not have

56

heard. Being alone in school means I can get around unnoticed. Hear things that I normally shouldn't be able to. There are rumours that Astrid and Tanner are on rocky ground after an incident that occurred between Astrid and another girl at the bus lines on Monday. Was that you?"

Blair only nodded. She hadn't heard anything like that around the school but then she hadn't been going near anyone gossiping either. She looked up through the back window of the cab at Tanner's profile. A small feeling of guilt touched Blair's chest thinking she may have caused trouble for him.

"Honestly, Tanner is a nice guy and could do a lot better than Astrid... But I guess we all love who we do. There are many reasons for why people are brought together," Lillian said. She reached over to put a comforting hand on Blair's shoulder as the pickup came to a stop outside the house.

"A little late," Bryan called from the veranda.

Tanner just motioned to the back of the pickup and Bryan nodded seeing Blair.

"Just got a call about a possible break in the fence out A12. It's a bit of a hike and will see you out today."

"On it," Tanner said heading to a nearby shed.

Bryan walked over to where Blair and Lillian were getting out of the vehicle. "Welcome home, Blair. And whose your..? Lillian?" Bryan said recognising the girl.

Lillian's eyes narrowed while Blair cocked an eyebrow at him.

"Sorry, your mother and Blair's mother were close friends. Karen was your godmother actually," Bryan said.

"Mum was?"

"I've heard mention of her name," Lillian replied after a moments surprise. "I never thought to link the two names."

"It's good to see you again. Last time you barely fit in my arms. Will you be staying for dinner?"

Blair cut in. "If it's ok, I asked Lillian for a sleepover. Was kinda a spare-the-moment thing. Could we drop her home tomorrow?"

"That'll be fine if she doesn't mind waiting for Tanner in the afternoon. We have a big day tomorrow. Keep it in mind when organising these kinds of things."

"Dad won't mind. There're no plans for tomorrow as such," Lillian said.

"Thanks dad," Blair said before grabbing Lillian's wrist. She didn't want to get stuck talking all day. "Come on. I'll show you my room."

As Blair led Lillian into the house, Bryan called after them that he'd be gone on dusk to collect Jacob. Waving over her shoulder Blair raced up the stairs ahead of Lillian. There was a quick pitstop at the bathroom to clean up before heading to the room. Blair paused outside her door.

"This is my room," Blair said as she ushered the smaller girl inside. "Best view in the house."

Lillian looked around the spacious area, mesmerised by the open views in every direction. She could do so much with this area and was a little envious of Blair. Then she saw the queen bed.

"This room is gorgeous. It'll be a pity to camp out elsewhere in the house."

Blair raised an eyebrow. "I was planning on using this room for our sleepover?"

"Oh, I just thought it'd be awkward getting another bed up her."

"The bed's big enough to share," Blair responded now understanding the confusion.

Furrowing her brow, Lillian continued to stare at the bed rolling her top then bottom lip in and out of her mouth. She started to bite a nail. "Blair, can I tell you something?"

"Of course," Blair replied. She saw her friend visibly pale.

"Um, well... I was going to tell you. Umm... It's not like I was hiding it. Well... umm." Lillian's mind was spinning.

"You wet the bed?" Blair asked suddenly.

"Wha... What! No." Lillian took a moment to register what'd been said.

"Snore?"

"No. Blair I..."

"You roll around the bed kicking others off it in your sleep." This last one Blair said as a statement.

"Blair, stop." Lillian had started to get frustrated.

"Are you afraid I'll do naughty things to you when you're vulnerable?"

"I like girls," Lillian blurted out.

Blair paused a moment. A stern look crept across her

58

face as she digested what Lillian told her. She found it didn't affect her in the slightest and a cheeky smile grew across her face. "So, you're the one that'll be getting handsy?"

"Blaaaiir! This is serious," Lillian said.

Blair calmed down. "Do you like me, Lillian? I mean, more than a friend?"

"Well... no. You're not really my type," Lillian replied.

"Ouch." Blair feigned sadness a moment before smiling. "You have nothing to worry about. I would've been sad for you if you did like me. Unrequited love is never fun."

Blair watched the mix of emotions roll around Lillian's face but couldn't gauge how her friend took the answer. This was until Lillian's eyes started darting around as if she was thinking of many different things at once and her lip started to quiver. Watching the small girl break down in front of her almost caused Blair to break. Closing the space between them, Blair drew Lillian into a firm embrace as great sobs ran unchecked. Blair could think of nothing to say and just held Lillian close, stroking her hair until the tears ran their course.

It was more than a few moments before Lillian had finally gotten control back. She had remained quiet, head resting against Blair's chest, sniffling softly. Let's see if I can spark her up, Blair thought in a bid to lighten the situation.

"Bursting into tears isn't always going to work, ya know?" Blair said.

Lillian pulled back to look Blair in the eyes. She seemed confused. "What do you mean?"

"You're going to need to come up with better tactics to get at these boobies next time."

Eyes wide, a warm crimson filled Lillian's cheeks. "Blaair! I didn't," she squealed.

Blair just walked over and sat on the bed motioning for her friend to join her. Lillian sat down tentatively nearby.

"So, tell me, what happened just now?"

Lillian was quiet as she tried to get her thoughts straight. "I've told people who I trusted. Family mainly. I did open up to one other person about it on a year 10/11 camp." Lillian went quiet.

Blair could only imagine what could be bothering her

friend so much before a dark thought manifested itself. "What did Astrid do?" The thought was shown to be true as Lillian turned sharply, eyes wide, mouth agape. "It's the only thing that would explain her hold over you."

When Lillian could finally speak, her voice came out soft, the words fragile. It was all she could do to hold back more tears. "It was all the little things that combined, evolved, consumed. It started with Astrid believing that I wanted to be with her. All I wanted was advice from a senior. I wanted to be open about it and was looking for a way to tell my friends. Astrid spread this news around faster than wildfire with a strong backing wind. She made it sound like I was diseased and that I could infect those around me. The friends that did stay became targets themselves. Astrid peppered them with ridicule, called them names and isolated them also. In the end it was easier for me to leave them behind, save them the grief. It was the only way for Astrid to give up on them and move on, leaving my life in pieces."

It all made sense now and Blair's heart was breaking for her friend. Instinctively, she reached out and pulled Lillian in to hold her as long as needed. There was no words Blair could think of to relieve her friend's pain but letting her know Blair would be there was a start... Then the words she needed came to mind. "I see you worked out some better tactics," Blair said softly into Lillian's ear. Blair felt Lillian flinch before settling down again, and then she felt something more. A hand was slowly tracing up Blair's stomach lightly caressing as it went while a second was reaching around to her bra strap. The first hand stopped at the base of Blair's bra slightly tucked under the cup. "Lillian!" Blair squeaked.

Leaning back, a little chuckle escaped Lillian's mouth. "I didn't think so," Lillian said as she brought her hands back. "Are you ever serious, Blair?"

With a smile, Blair realised Lillian was just teasing her. With a slight scrunch of the nose Blair just shrugged.

Narrowing her eyes, Lillian's smile grew. "How 'bout just this once, city girl, you tell me what you're thinking."

"What I'm thinking comes from the emptiness and lack of experience with people than anything concocted about you. The moment you told me, I knew it changed nothing.

60

No. More, it made us closer. Through your fears and doubt, you still proceeded in telling me something really personal about yourself. For that, you are my sister." Blair thought a moment. "God sister, even."

Lillian considered this. "I like that."

"I'm not sure how to help those who're crying or feeling down and sorry for themselves. I know I can show you I'm there for you. My mum used to hold me when I was feeling sad. That always helped. Other than that, I only wanted to lighten your spirits. To get you back to the cheerful girl I know. Jokes and a little light teasing were my weapons of choice. Worked a bit too well," Blair said with a wink. Her seriousness vanishing.

"You were being rather open about me molesting you I thought I may as well call you out on it and push your boundaries," Lillian smiled.

Blair took on a cheeky smile. "You hadn't reached my boundaries yet. Just my lack of experience in... things."

"You're a virgin?" Lillian asked.

Something about the tone of her voice stuck with Blair. "...You're not?"

Lillian only smiled.

"Boy or girl?" Blair asked.

"I've always known what I liked."

"School?"

"Well, we didn't do it at school if that's what you're asking."

"You know what I'm saying," Blair said. She was becoming rather interested. "Is there another girl at school..? Who likes girls, that is?"

Lillian smiled again. "Plenty, Blair. A number of students are either bi or lesbian. I'm the only one that's out. Everyone else is scared to be after how I was treated. I was always going to let people know. I just didn't get that chance. Being out though, I'm a beacon to those who are holding back. I've talked to a few in secret, boys and girls. Just, I could never be their friend. They were more afraid of being branded gay by association than saying it themselves."

"Yes, all that," Blair said impatiently. "Who took your flower?"

Lillian genuinely laughed at that comment. "Mary, from

history class. A few times now."

Blair's mouth hung low with a sharp intake of breath. She leaned in close as if others were listening. "Mary," she repeated in hushed tones.

Lillian nodded.

Blair looked to the side thinking of the pairing. "She's cute. You're full of surprises."

"I didn't think it'd be that surprising. So many people our age have had sex. Didn't you feel the urge to go further with a boyfriend?"

"I..." Blair looked lost in thought. "Haven't had a boyfriend."

She could see there was more to it, but Lillian didn't push the subject. "And now you've chosen to chase a taken man." The sound of a quad bike filled the room. "Speak of the devil." Lillian jumped from the bed and raced to the window. "Come on, Blair."

When Blair shook her head, eyes wide, Lillian insisted and reluctantly Blair followed. She gazed from the window and her heart pulsed with excitement. Tanner looked no different to how he had been in the pickup but that was enough to reel Blair in. She watched him navigate the quad into a stop near the house. Raising his arm, he made three big circles in the air and rounded the quad to head back out into the fields. Blair saw Bryan jog over to the shed and moments later was following on another Quad bike. There was a large load of gear on the back.

"You have to take even the small moments when they arrive," Lillian said. "Wasn't that worth getting up for?"

Blair smiled still looking out after Tanner. "Yes and no. It's like my body awakens each time I see him but also knowing he is taken really puts a damper on it."

"Well, let's hope that won't be an issue much longer," Lillian replied. "Tanner'll wake up to himself soon. Especially when he's got this arse to look at while working. May have a few more accidents on the farm." Lillian lent over and tapped Blair's butt for emphasis.

Jumping, Blair pushed her friend with a giggle. "I wonder what's going on." Blair changed the subject.

"Cow in the fence. Tanner was motioning to your dad to gather gear," Lillian replied confidently.

"That reminds me. When I asked your dad about you

62

coming over, there was some unspoken words between you too before I got an answer?" Blair left the obvious question hanging.

Lillian laughed. "Yeah. He was asking if you were a love interest of mine. That something may be starting between us. I told him it wasn't. If I scratched above my ear it would have been a different story."

"Ah, that makes sense but I'm little offended."

"How so?" Lillian asked, one eyebrow cocked.

"You'd written me off before you even knew if I was chasing you or not."

"John or Billy from maths. How are you going to choose between them?

"What? Eww," Blair said.

"But you don't even know if they're chasing you yet."

Blair's eyes narrowed. "Okay, okay, I get it. Still, I hope it wasn't an eww for me."

"You have some looks about you, I will admit, but red hair and freckles just..." Lillian trailed off, a look of glee filling her face.

Blair shook her head, a smile rising on one side of her mouth. "Mary sure fits that."

"Even more so that the freckles run down her body."

"Hey, some details you can keep to yourself," Blair said.

Lillian gave a cheeky wink.

"So what do we do now?" Blair asked. It was a long time since she had a friend stay over.

Lillian shrugged. "Raid the cupboards for snacks and start getting to know each other enough to be true sisters. You've heard a lot of my personal life. Tell me of yours."

Blair was uncomfortable about her life but knew it was going to come out this afternoon. "Snacks then."

And of the girls ran through the house to reach the kitchen. They opened the fridge and ransacked the pantry but found nothing suitable for a girl's night. The only thing close were a couple of muesli bars that Jacob takes to school and a small bag of plain chips. Lillian suggested a raid on Jacob's room. If there was ever going to be a hidden stash it would be there.

And so, the journey continued taking the girls to a room Blair never thought she would ever have need to step into. A typical boy's room with clothes strewn around the floor, random gaming posters on the wall and a mess across his desk. The typical places were checked first. In drawers and under the bed. As Lillian checked the cupboard she stumbled across a notebook.

"This is a journal," Lillian exclaimed.

"What? I never would've believed Jacob to write a journal... even so, that's private isn't it?" Blair said.

A wicked little grin crossed Lillian's face. "Just a quick peek at his latest entry. May get to see what he really thinks of his big sister."

"I don't know, Lillian." Blair's brow furrowed. "I don't need any negativity."

Lillian smiled once more and opened the book where Blair couldn't see. Her eyes started tracing the lines as she read and soon a whimper escaped Lillian's lips. There was a sadness to her look that spoke of someone feeling sorry for another.

"That bad?" Blair asked.

Lillian started to read aloud. "I couldn't do anything to protect her. My sister was being bullied and I couldn't protect her. Astrid and her gang were too much. They stole her phone and threw it into the bush. It was all I could do to make it up to Blair to find the phone. I didn't think I would but at the last moment when a branch whipped my face the phone was found to be sitting on a fork in that branch. Dad yelled at me for ditching training, but Blair is more important. I was forced to tell dad what happened. He went easier on me, but I hope he won't hound Blair about it. She seemed happier after finding the phone again. I hope it was enough for her to forgive me. I love my sister and am so happy she could live with us..."

Blair was quiet a moment. "Let's find those snacks," she said unable to voice her emotions.

Lillian understood and continued the hunt. It wasn't long before they found a variety of chocolates and chips. The girls had to remove the bottom drawer in the bedside table but there they were. Lillian started to pick them up, but Blair stopped her.

"Just... one chip pack, one choc pack." Blair said.

"The words got to you too?" Lillian said with a pout, placing a number of packets down.

"We just don't need to take them all," Blair said before

leaving the room and heading back to her own.

Lillian smiled as she snuck one extra chocolate pack.

The afternoon was filled with idle chit chat and gossip. Blair had yet to talk about her past with Lillian but on mention of Shadow the smaller girl was almost running down the stairs to meet him. Blair literally lost Lillian on the stairs and by the time she made it to Shadow's kennel Lillian had the dog rolled over giving him belly rubs and making coy little noises at him. And Shadow was lapping up the attention, leg pedalling in the air and tongue lolling from his mouth.

Blair walked over and looked down at her dog. "Traitor," she said before giving him some ear scratches. Shadow felt 10 years younger under the fading sky.

The sound of quad bikes filled the air and both Tanner and Bryan rode into view. They didn't look so happy and little was said when they got back. Tanner packed up and left while Bryan called out, he was off to pick up Jacob and some dinner.

"Everything okay?" Blair called back.

"Next doors cow got caught up in the fence. Had to put her down," Bryan replied before getting into the car and driving off.

"Don't worry about them. Farmers take that sort of thing to heart but it's all part of the job," Lillian reassured Blair who was still watching the cars drive off. "Let's head back in."

Back inside Blair walked over to her dresser. "Let's get more comfortable and get into some pyjamas. I've been sorting out all mum's old clothes and everything we need will be in this drawer here," she said opening one at the bottom. Blair picked out her favourite set of a flannel pink 2 piece. "They may be a little baggy for you though."

"I like baggy. Oversized shirts are incredibly comfortable." Lillian bent over and started sifting through the collection. She found the perfect large white shirt with a band motif on the front. The length would almost be a dress for her. Lifting it high as she turned to show Blair, Lillian's breath caught in her throat. Sub consciously she brought a hand to her face to softly bite the skin of her finger. "Blair," she whispered stunned.

With her head popping through the flannel neck, Blair

pulled the top down over her bare chest. Hearing Lillian, Blair looked over to find her friend frozen, eyes wide and locked on her. Her eyes narrowed. "All good?"

Lillian shook her head. "I just wasn't expecting to be greeted by such a view," Lillian admitted.

"Didn't think you liked what you saw." Blair smiled.

"...Technically," Lillian tried to find the right words and decided to just be direct. "I said you have some looks about you but not my type. Still, a body like yours is arousing in its natural form."

Blair laughed gleefully. "Then be aroused... or not. I have no issues changing in front of you. You can look away or find a comfortable medium. If you aren't as confident with yourself, I can step out or there is a bathroom one level down."

"It really doesn't bother you at all? Who I like?" Lillian asked. There were still reserved feelings that screamed Blair was only being polite. That she would slowly back out of the friendship they had formed. These now vanished.

"Why should I be worried? Many girls have boys for friends. You've been open with me. I trust you to get handsy only a little bit before stopping."

Lillian chuckled as Blair winked. "I'm so glad I met you, Blair. You've made such a difference to my life. You can't even imagine."

"I know the pain of loss and being alone," Blair replied with a deep sigh. She went silent a moment gathering her thoughts before going into detail about her parents, Jacob and the reason she had issues with him at the beginning. Blair then took a moment before diving into her past schooling life, her mother's death, and how she tried to survive living on her own. The weight that seemed to fall away as she spoke made Blair feel as if even life itself could have a warm and loving nature. That it wasn't something to struggle through before being thrust into darkness at its finale. Blair had never believed she could feel this way again. To feel as she had when her parents were together and all was sunshine.

Lillian listened intently, her face a mask of steel. All the while her little heart broke more and more as Blair welcomed her into the world of turmoil. When Blair concluded her story and turned to Lillian for her thoughts

66

or maybe just an easy comment, Lillian could hold her pose no longer. Her face drew long with a pout at its epicentre. Lips downturned and locked together. This just seemed to widen her eyes which were again teary. As the sobs started she reached over and drew Blair into an embrace this time.

"It's ok, Blair. Let it all go. Cry until you can't cry anymore." Lillian had not realised that Blair was actually smiling for how good she now felt. She didn't realise she was the only one teary eyed. That was until Blair acted up again by nuzzling her face in between Lillian's breasts.

Lillian slowed in her tears and glanced down at her friend who was looking back at her acting like a little kitten. Lillian pushed her away.

"You're having way too much fun at my expense." Lillian turned away puffing out her cheeks.

Blair wrapped her arms around Lillian cuddling from behind. "And you're being far too serious at mine. Speaking about my life for the first time has lifted a load off my shoulders I never thought would leave. You've given me the first light breaking through a sky of clouds and darkness that hasn't been pierced in years. Thank you, Lillian."

"Girls, dinner," Bryan called up the stairs.

"When did he get home?" Blair said, jumping as another voice sounded in the house.

Lillian just shrugged imitating Blair and took off out the door.

"Oi, get back here," Blair called, giggling as she chased her friend. Part way down the stairs she crossed paths with Jacob. Pausing a moment to look her step brother in the eyes she hugged him thinking of the comments he made in the journal and continued down the stairs.

"What was that for?" Jacob blushed. He was caught off guard by his sister's sudden act.

At the bottom of the stairs Blair swung back on the railing. "For the chips and chocolate, of course."

"What!" Jacob started before rushing off to his room to check the damage.

Predawn light broke through the eastern window giving substance to the objects of the room. Blair had woke early not used to having another sleeping in her bed let alone wrapped around her. Looking down at her friend, a soft warmth flowed through her. A warmth born of love and friendship. Lillian was, it seemed, a snuggler. Any object that bumped into Lillian while she slept was caught up in a web of arms and legs to be drawn in much like how an octopus ensnares its prey. For the past half hour Blair had been the latest victim. A leg was laying lazily over her own and a hand that not only had found its way up onto Blair's chest was also under her shirt. It was innocent and concerned Blair not at all.

All that Blair felt in this moment was empowered. Her life was now beginning. She'd made a friend, talked to a boy, and stood up to a bully. Yes, her life was starting now. And Lillian's...? Would it be fair to meddle? No, it wasn't meddling anymore. It was having the back of, standing up for, and protecting a friend. Lillian's life was going to be all the more brighter soon too.

Stroking the smaller girl's hair, Blair gently called her awake.

"Is everything ok?" Lillian asked with a start. A little drool had trailed down from the edge of her mouth. Realising where her hand was she pulled it away quickly. "Blair, I'm sorry," She said.

"I didn't wake you to remove the hand that was keeping my breasts warm this last half hour."

Lillian blushed.

"Put it back and settle down again."

Hesitantly, Lillian settled back to where she was. She wasn't sure what was going on or if she may even be dreaming.

"We're going to take back the school," Blair said, an arm around her friend. "We're going to build a world where we don't need to be afraid of bullies or judgement or rejection. We're going to take back our lives."

Groggily, Lillian snuggled into Blair's side once more. "I should have more dreams like this," she whispered before falling asleep once more.

Blair chuckled to herself. "This dream will soon be real, my friend." Leaning down she kissed Lillian's forehead before drifting off herself.

Chapter 5 – Picnic by the falls

Brows furrowed, eyes locked to their prey, Astrid watched Tanner drive through the main street. After a day decompressing from a horrible week by way of shopping, Astrid was starting to feel herself once more. Starting to feel like she could let hers and Tanner's relationship get back on track. But now that was a ways off. The sun's reflection was slowly rising up the shop fronts to disappear into twilight, so it was understandable Tanner would have finished work by now. The reason Astrid's hackles rose upon seeing him was the little dyke in the seat next to him.

So, Lillian had stayed out at Blair's house overnight. Blair was going to be finding out just what spending time with Lillian meant to her social life. Tanner though should know better. He was hers. That rug muncher had come after her, tried to make Astrid as sick and twisted as Lillian was. It was already obvious she messed up Blair. Tanner, though, should know to stay away and stand up for his girlfriend. Astrid would need to put a stop to this nuisance once and for all. Get Blair to stay away, Lillian to stay away. They need to know their place in society.

Tomorrow then, Astrid thought. I'll show Blair that Tanner is mine and how close we are. That Blair has no chance in corrupting him. Astrid would show Blair just who was in charge.

The sun had just peeked over the horizon, bringing light and warmth. An open curtain gave a path to gently caress Blair awake. With a yawn and a smile she embraced the new day, then rolled over to bid it 5 more minutes before she would admit the embrace. The noise of an engine drifted through the room and Blair recognised Tanner's vehicle.

"5 more minutes, I said," Blair moaned over her shoulder. The words of Lillian crept into her mind. You have to take even the small moments when they arrive... Blair made a note to chip her friend for the comment as she threw back the blankets. Catching a glimpse of herself in the mirror, Blair laughed at the frizzy hair protruding from the left side of her head while the right remained flat.

Taking a seat by the window, Blair kept her silhouette

from view. She rejoiced in her decision to where the baggy shirt to bed. It was so comfortable. Lillian had been right on that front too. A little breezy underneath, but she thought some wider underwear would fix that.

Stepping from his pickup the world exploded before Blair's eyes for that was what Tanner was. Blair clutched at the window frame floating in space. Galaxies and nebula rushed by all around as if she was a comet in the heavens. But through this one window the world that was Tanner remained constant, warm, and beautiful. Bringing a finger to her mouth, Blair couldn't help but sigh as she bit the edge. Her whole body becoming fuzzy and disconnected in the most perfect way.

"EEEP!" Blair squeaked. She had been complacent in how she sat and now a full view of all her morning glory was on display.

Tanner had noticed and turned to give an over embellished bow. Hat from head, he swept it under himself as he bent low. Coming to stand erect once more, Blair was nowhere to be seen and Tanner shrugged continuing to his job.

"Oh, I'm definitely having words with Lillian after this," Blair said in a huff. She dove back onto her bed leaving the blankets scattered.

It was longer than the initial 5 minutes she wished before Blair could calm herself with hot, heavy breaths. Her legs were like jelly as she wobbled across the room to find some fresh clothes. A long flowing yellow dress took her fancy and she pulled it over head. Blair didn't bother with a bra this day as she was planning on remaining in the house and the mirror was telling her everything looked fine either way. Turning she picked up the oversized shirt she wore to bed from where it landed in the corner of the room earlier and placed it in a wash basket.

"Sorry," she told the shirt, a shy smile touching her face.

Her body still on a high, tingles running over her skin, Blair took off to the kitchen. She was starving and the clock on the wall told her it was closer to lunch than breakfast.

"Geez, you look like you've just run a marathon," Jacob said as he walked in from outside. "Get ready for some yelling."

Seeing Jacob motion out the door, Blair walked over to

spy Astrid standing in the driveway. She held a wicker basket in her hands and was leaning against a small silver hatchback. Turning back to Jacob she looked a little confused. "Why yelling?" she asked.

"Well, I may have told dad about how you lost your phone the other night," Jacob said after a moment's hesitation.

"I know. I was sitting a few metres away in the chook shed patting Shadow," Blair smiled.

Jacob's eyes went wide a moment before he shrugged it off. "Well, I may have just mentioned to him moments ago who it was that caused you trouble. Dad just got that look in his eye like he was about to run someone down with his tractor."

As if on cue the sound of a tractor started near the house and seemed to be getting closer. "Oh, shit, Jacob," Blair said and dashed to the door. Outside, Tanner had reached Astrid and they seemed to be having a heated discussion that Blair just couldn't make out over the tractor. Finally, the incessant motor stopped a few metres away aimed at Astrid.

"Mr Thompson won't mind. Will you, sir?" Astrid called over to Bryan.

"Actually, I do mind, Astrid. Tanner is needed on the farm and it's not yet time for his break. You can take your car and leave."

"Excuse me?" Astrid said taken aback. "This is my boyfriend and if I want to have a picnic with him, I will. He won't be away long."

"I will say this only once more..." Bryan paused as Tanner held up a hand.

"You can leave, Astrid. As Bryan has said, I have work to do here. I will see you after work," Tanner said. His tone gave no room to argue.

Astrid's eyes came ablaze with fury as she looked from Tanner to Bryan. Each returned the stare. Then Astrid's peripheral caught a flash of yellow and she looked at the house to see Blair standing on the porch. She had a cheeky little smile and gave a patronising little wave at the edge of her face moving only her fingers. Astrid turned back to Tanner. "You don't need to work under these conditions."

"I like this job. And these conditions are my choosing,"

71

Tanner replied.

Astrid softened a moment and stepped in close to Tanner. "Baby, come with me. We can head out to that little spot you like. I can... you know," Astrid bit her lower lip.

"Best to be on your way," Bryan said.

"Are you going to let him talk to your girlfriend like that?"

"Astrid, leave," Tanner's voice became stern.

Brows furrowed, Astrid locked onto Tanner's stare. "Come with me now or we're through."

"Goodbye, Astrid." Tanner turned and walked away leaving the shocked girl floating.

Blair saw Astrid glance at her once more before screaming and throwing the food basket at Tanner. Getting in her car Astrid spun the tyres on the dirt and took off down the driveway.

"Guess Tanner never gave her throwing lessons," Jacob laughed and motioned to the basket that had missed its target by metres.

"That was rather fun to watch. Thank you... Brother." Blair said without looking down at the now blushing boy. He was too stunned to move for a moment. The title catching him off guard. Finding his sense once more Jacob ran over to where the picnic basket still sat.

Blair was intent on watching the outcome of the event. She heard her dad apologise to Tanner about the relationship, but she didn't hear the reply. Tanner had leaned in and whatever he said must have been significant. Bryan had slowly made a fist as if he was about to hit Tanner before finding himself once more and patting the boy on the back. Bryan had nodded once before jumping back in the tractor.

Tanner called out seeking what needed his attention so urgently.

"Just didn't want to ruin your morning routine," Bryan replied.

Blair was surprised when Tanner genuinely laughed and continued on his way with a smile. He possibly just lost his girlfriend and didn't seem to care. Did he really not care that much for the girl's he was with?

"Blair, wanna join me?" Waving his arms and holding

72

the basket high, Jacob was trying to get her attention.

"Anything good?"

"Plenty," Jacob grinned.

"Well, set it up then," Blair said and jumped down from the deck.

"Not here," Jacob replied. "I know you've yet to eat today but if you could last another half hour or so, there's a nice little spot near the waterfall."

Blair thought a moment. "I know the place. Give me a minute and I'll be out."

Jacob stood waiting for what seemed a half hour in itself. He was beaming on the inside having gotten so close to Blair. He almost died when she called him her brother. It wasn't something he expected anytime in the near future.

Finally, Blair wandered from the house. A juicy red apple partly eaten in her hand and flashes of red from the shoulders of her dress. Swimmers, Jacob thought before looking to see what he put on. These shorts'll do, he conceded.

"Sorry, I don't think I would've lasted had I waited to eat," Blair said raising the apple for Jacob to see.

"All good. Shall we?" Jacob asked motioning to the forest edge.

"We shall," Blair replied.

The trek out to the waterfall was quiet and even relaxing. The forest embraced the pair as kin. There was no true pathway but both Jacob and Blair had walked these woods excessively, grew up in these woods, and imprinted these woods in their mind that they would never be lost. Sure, for Blair it was more a nostalgic trek, remembering all the little details as they went along but at no point did she lose her way.

Soon, over the rocky hills and passed the empty cave where Blair had believed was the entrance to the Forest King's realm, the waterfall came into view. Crystal clear water tumbling 5 metres to touch down in a deep pool of smooth rocks and swimming sunbeams. To lay face down on the water's surface, one would feel as if they were flying far above the land. Blair had never made it to the very depths of the pool, being too dark and too cold for one so young, but she decided she would give it another shot after the picnic.

Jacob picked out a spot in one of the clear areas on the bank and set up lunch. He was enjoying the day far more than he ever imagined he could. He had gotten to stick up for Blair, recover a rather fancy meal, be called brother, and spend time with his sister where she actually wanted to be there.

Finishing setting up he called Blair over from where she was still gazing at the small gem this farm held. Jacob watched as Blair's face lit up surveying the platter of food spread out over the red and white rug. An arrangement of cheeses and dips surrounded a supply of crackers and cheddar biscuits. Strawberries, mango, watermelon, peaches and a number of other exotic fruits Blair had never even tried let alone Jacob could name, filled the central area. Chunks of chicken, ham, and... Blair tested a meat.... Marinated Lamb was in small containers with brioche buns ready to be filled. There was also a pot of gravy that was keeping a nice, warm temperature nearby. It was amazing nothing was ruined from the flight across the front yard but Blair didn't doubt the tight packing had something to do with it.

"Astrid went all out. Almost feel sorry for her not getting to eat this herself," Blair said still amazed by the spread.

Jacob scoffed.

"I said almost. Then I remember who she is and what she has done to me and the people I have come to love. She had this coming. Still, I was surprised and a little put off with how Tanner reacted," Blair said.

"In what way," Jacob replied.

"Astrid was in love with him and tried to do something nice for him, spend time with him. Sure she pushed the point in a horrible way but Tanner threw her away so easily. It was like he felt nothing for her at all. That he just uses girls for his own enjoyment. That is an ugly attribute for a guy."

Jacob smiled.

"What?" Blair's eyes narrowed.

"You know I was recovering the picnic basket straight after the fight. Fairly close to where Tanner and dad were talking."

"Yeah..?" then a light bulb turned on in Blair's mind.

"You overheard what Tanner said."

"And I see you didn't." Jacob's smile grew.

"What was said that could change my view of the situation?"

"I won't repeat it," Jacob said seriously. "But I will say this. Tanner did love Astrid for a time. Recently, things have changed for him and the relationship was already heading towards this end. It was time."

"So I'll just get my answers from your diary later? Is that what you're telling me?" Blair said and giggled when Jacob blushed.

"You... You read my journal?"

"Well, technically, Lillian read one page... out loud... within earshot."

Jacob blushed harder. "What did she read?"

Blair leaned in all serious like. "I won't repeat it. But I will say this. The page she read was the difference between us raiding your whole supply of goodies and taking just a minimal amount."

Eyes darting back and forth, Jacob shook his head. "No! You'll have to get the words from Tanner himself."

Pouting, Blair turned towards the food. "Fine, keep your little secrets. And here I thought we were growing closer."

"Not going to work," Jacob said before stuffing his mouth. "Huffing fluffington balijerun."

"Eww, Jacob. Cover your mouth," Blair said as she wiped a projectile chunk of chicken from her dress. She sighed having not gotten her way. "What you wrote really touched me. It broke through some walls I had in place against you. Walls that were set in place for my hatred of your mother and what dad did to my family. For years I watched mum break down. In the end, when the accident happened, she had not the strength or even the will to fight through it. I bundled you into the world of hate I had created. I know now you were just like me. An innocent victim to the actions of our parents."

"Gruffimberadjeris," Jacob said placing a hand on Blair's knee and being rewarded with a look of disgust and a shaking of Blair's head. He was still chewing and finally gave an over exaggerated swallow.

"What were you trying to say?" Blair asked.

"Oh, I was only letting you know you had a little

marinade on your cheek," Jacob grinned touching his own face as if he was a mirror to her.

"You little bum," Blair said and threw a chunk of Mango at the quick-to-his-feet kid.

Jacob giggled and dodged easily. "Guess it wouldn't hurt to get a few more lessons from Tanner." He was acting extremely childish, tongue out, moving his hands back and forward beside his ears.

It was when Jacob turned around to wiggle his butt at Blair that Blair acted. Grabbing a handful of fruit, she sprung to her feet and was about to stuff it down Jacob's pants when she tripped. A rogue root in the path snagged her foot sending Blair sprawling to the ground.

Jacob turned and for a moment only seemed amused by the situation. "Are you okay?" He asked.

Pain was racing up Blair's leg from a rolled ankle and she was doubled over holding her foot.

"I'm sorry. I'm sorry," Jacob started saying while hovering around Blair not knowing what to do.

It was a few more moments before Blair could recover enough to talk. A large egg had formed on her ankle showing how good a job she'd done on it. "I'm not going to be able to walk back on this," she said. "You'll have to get dad."

"Okay, I'm on it," Jacob said instantly and made to set off down the track, but Blair stopped him.

"We have a lunch to finish first. No rush. Let's just settle in and eat a little. Help me back to the rug." Blair told him.

There was real despair in Jacob's eyes, but he did as he was bid. Helping Blair to her good foot, Jacob took the slack from the other and helped his sister hobble back to their picnic. Nestling her down and making sure she was comfortable a low rumble stopped him in his tracks. Both Blair and Jacob locked eyes not wanting to believe the sound they'd heard could be thunder. The day had not a cloud in the sky so far.

Climbing part way up the waterfall, Jacob confirmed their fears. "I think I need to get dad a far sight sooner than expected." On the horizon over the trees a dark mass of clouds and erratic lightning was forming quickly and heading there way. Torrential rain was falling in sheets along the underside of the storm.

76

Racing to the edge of the clearing, Jacob paused a moment. "I'll get dad back here as quick as I can. At least enjoy the food and sun while it's here."

With that Jacob was gone and Blair was left to worry about what was coming. Her stomach however, greedily pushed for her to eat her fill. And from worry and stress and the pulsing pain Blair ate far more than she normally would. It was while she sat basking in the last of the sunlight, bloated from an amazing meal, that the dark storm clouds came into view above. The thunder had been getting louder and now a lite sprinkle of rain had begun. The wind suddenly grew in intensity sending a gale through the treetops. Blair was protected from the wind where she sat but the sheet of rain she could now see was not far off. She could do nothing but wait to be rescued.

Ten more minutes and a voice echoed passed the torrential rain.

"Over here," Blair called trying to pick the voice. Pulling back tendrils of wet hair from her soaked face, Blair squeaked seeing the form of Tanner tracking her.

"Are you okay?"

Blair could only nod... and shiver having not dressed for the occasion.

A look of genuine relief crossed Tanner's face. "I'm glad. Come on. We'll leave the picnic here and find some refuge." Tanner pulled off his full length, leather coat and wrapped it around Blair before scooping her up in his strong arms. Until now, the coat had kept most of the rain from Tanner but the white of his shirt was fading, and the outline of Tanner's muscles could be seen. The muscles Blair's head was now resting against.

"We need to find a place to ride out the storm," Tanner called over the rain. When no answer came, he looked down to find Blair daydreaming. Bouncing her in his arms, Tanner called again.

Shaking her head, Blair blushed. "The only place I know is a cave nearby. Empty except for... umm, no, nothing."

"Tell me, Blair. It needs to be safe."

Blair internally berated herself for even bringing up the silly fairy tale. Now, she was to look really dorky. "It's the Forest King," Blair mumbled.

"What," Tanner said, his voice rising higher to pierce the

weather.

"It's the Forest King," Blair said loud enough to be heard. She made sure to keep her eyes lowered.

"Is he still around? Guess we should see if he will accept us for dinner."

There was only a small smile on Tanner's face when Blair looked up expecting a mocking expression. After a moment's hesitation, she talked Tanner to the aforementioned cave. It was warmer inside and the deep rock structure halved the sound of the rain. Blair couldn't believe she'd never come inside. The backs of the cave, though deep in shadow when looking in from outside, weren't deep at all. Maybe 5 metres at most. A vein of quartz must have had access to the sky as a luminescent glow filtered down into it. The earth was soft almost like the beaches from exotic locations, smooth and delicate. It was a beautiful world once Blair's eyes adjusted.

"Shall we see if his lordship is home?" Tanner asked standing before the quartz in the back. Blair had been about to protest but Tanner's voice rippled out, strong and direct. "Good King of the forest, your subjects seek to share your home with you while this storm passes by. My lady is hurt and needs rest before we continue. Will you grant our request?"

Of course, nothing would come from this, Blair thought to herself. She watched Tanner's hypnotic smile turn back to her. Thankful she currently wasn't on her feet; the smile alone would have sent her to the earth. Then his eyes seem to lock on something behind her. Swivelling she saw a small squirrel had entered the cave mouth and was currently regarding them. Tanner bowed and the squirrel seemed to do the same before finding a warm secluded area of the cave.

"Thank you, Lord, for your generosity," Tanner then said to the squirrel.

The play acting on Tanner's part and the actions of the squirrel were too much for Blair. Growing from a low rumble into a rolling laughter, Blair's lost it. One of those laughs that were made to eat away everything worrying you, everything that had you tense or uneasy about a situation. The type of laugh that when Blair finally started to get herself under control a quick glance at Tanner's confused and judging face brought it back two-fold with tears and trouble breathing. And on this went with Blair unable to get her glee under control. 5 minutes... 6... 7 before her body could take no more, before her body finally said enough and reversed the need to laugh. When Blair could finally see again, the tears wiped away, she found Tanner sitting against the opposite wall. The squirrel was curled up in his shirt and he was lightly scratching it behind the ear.

"Didn't take you long to make frie..." Blair finally realised Tanner's shirt was now on the ground as a bed for the squirrel. A fire filled her face as her eyes betrayed where she was looking.

"I like squirrels. Always have a nut somewhere for them." Tanner moved across to where Blair sat and slumped down next to her. "You over your little fit?"

Nodding furiously, Blair was only just now trying to act like she was looking away.

"Cold? I can warm you. I've been told I have a warm body," Tanner said pulling back an arm for Blair. Her eyes grew wild, and he shifted back a little. "Sorry. Maybe I'm coming on a little strong. I'm having a hard time fighting these feelings I have for y..."

I loud slap rang out about the rain echoing from wall to wall. Blair had moved instinctually and was now standing above Tanner, hand still at the end of its flight. Her shoulders were rolling as she breathed to calm herself.

"Why!?" her voice dangerously low.

Stunned, hand holding his cheek, Tanner tried to piece together what just happened but was drawing a blank. "Why, what?" he asked.

"You and Astrid, you were together for a long time from what I heard. Yet, you gave up on her so quickly. She only alluded to breaking up and you held no emotion for it. You didn't try to keep her or make some kind of compromise with dad to show her you loved her. You acted like she was a piece of meat you were finished chewing and spat out. Now you're already chasing the next closest piece of arse. What is wrong with you? I actually liked you. You filled my waking moments, my dreams, my nightmares even. Why would you try to do this to me?" Blair demanded, adrenaline pushing her on.

Tanner settled a little, knowing where Blair's thoughts lay. "How is your foot?" He asked simply.

As if by magic, the pain grew instantly. Losing her balance, she fell forward into Tanner's arms. "No, don't touch me," Blair was saying, punching his chest softly in an attempt to get away. "You don't get to touch me."

"Blair," Tanner's words were soft as he cradled Blair in his arms. "You have me wrong. The relationship Astrid and I shared was already at an end. It had been moving this way for a few weeks now. I had suddenly found myself at a crossroad where I had to choose to mend what we had or let it come to a final resting place. I chose the latter."

Having calmed to the soothing words of Tanner, Blair laid still. "There's nothing that couldn't be mended."

"In a loving relationship that would be true. But in time our relationship had gotten darker, more lecherous. Well, I can say this but the truth of the matter above all else was that I didn't want to fight for her. My heart belongs to another. I couldn't play the charade any longer."

"So, what am I to you? Just some little game you wanna play until you can run off and be with the one you love?" Blair gave up trying to beat the man to a pulp and was just laying her head against his bare chest. She was both being angry with and getting comforted by the man. It didn't help when Tanner laughed aloud at her comment. "Just leave me alone, Tanner. Go find the girl you want to be with."

A hand came up to cup Blair's face. It was large and strong and rough from days out on the farm yet flowed along the contours of her cheek and chin perfectly. Her whole body awoke to the touch. Supernovas exploded in her chest making her breathing ragged at best. Her stomach rolled in anticipation and nervousness. It wasn't sickly but giddy, like a new fowl learning to walk. Skin, tingling with fresh goosebumps, craved more than the hand was providing. Her mind already active, she turned with Tanner's hand to look him in the face as she let another booming slap slingshot into Tanner's cheek.

The man ignored the pain, eyes still soft, loving... closer than normal. Blair's being melted away as Tanner's lips touched her own. An electrical circuit was now complete, pulsing through the two glowing bodies. Worlds collided in that moment sending ripples across the universe centred on these burning souls.

Blair rocked back a moment, the last will to fight fluttering like a candle under water. There was no will to be anything less than his. Blair's eyes held his emerald green eyes for the eternity of this second, before leaning in to continue the kiss. No memory of cold could survive in this moment. Tongues dancing, hands exploring... Blair had noticed his hands congregate at the edge of her bikini when they should of been coming inside. *Did they know they were welcome?*

Reaching back, Blair let go the clasp holding the material to her body. As the tension left the barrier, strong, welcome hands slide inside moving the bikini further out of the way. Hands that traced around the base of Blair's buxom breasts. They caressed and teased enticing small whimpers to escape Blair's lips.

Feeling the hands jagging on the dress, Blair ripped the clothing covering her top half away and threw them accidently at the squirrel, missing by millimetres. Tanner allowed the sight of this goddess's true form to settle upon his eyes and sink into his mind, filling each dark and unsettled area held within. Tanner lent forward, lips nibbling up Blair's neck to tease the lobe of her ear.

"AHHIIMMM!!! Take me... Everything I am is yours, Tanner" Blair moaned into Tanners ear, her pelvis thrusting into him of its own accord. Feeling the tiger pushing against his cage, Blair got an idea at what was ahead for her and became worried. Taking Tanner's face into her hands as he did her own she stopped him. Tanner paused in her gaze worried she may wish to stop.

"Please, be gentle... Everything I am includes my first." Like the birth of a new galaxy, exploding, expanding, Blair couldn't stop what was to come. She was merging into Tanner, wanting him to explore inside her, her body wetter than the moment Tanner found her in the rain.

Tanner looked worried as if in two minds on how to proceed and Blair gave in to her desires. With a hand tracing down Tanner's chest, Blair lost it in the top of his pants. Fingers caressing the pelt of hair before finding her target. The tips of Blair's nails traced up the protruding shaft to curl over the top of Tanner's throbbing member. With a gasp of excitement from Tanner to spur Blair on she grasped as well as she could the entirety of the shaft to thrust down to the base.

Standing, Tanner brought Blair's fingers up to tuck them into the waistband of his pants. Taking the hint, Blair ever so slowly dragged the clothing down. Pausing at the point of greatest resistance, Blair put a little more force into the manoeuvre. As the pressure built, the pants finally gave way and like a springboard, Tanner's hidden delicacy made itself known. Blair wrestled the penis to be still and as she pulled back the foreskin Blair kissed the very tip sending a shiver through Tanner.

"Take care of me," Blair whispered to the one eyed snake and leaned back against the cave wall. Holding out her hands Blair lead Tanner to the same position he had a moment ago, placing his hands in the band of her red swimmers. These disappeared faster than her baggy shirt this morning. And if the impossible could be made true, Tanner became harder, growing another inch to the 6 inches Blair desired. She needed him now, his warmth ploughing into her. She dearly needed him to make her cum. There was nothing else.

And Tanner responded. Kneeling down between Blair's legs, she drew them up and out in anticipation. Kisses rained down upon her neck slowly moving southward. The kiss upon the collar bone was tantalising. Never had Blair been kissed there and the reaction was like a meteor hitting the moon. This continued to multiply as Tanner reached her breasts. Lightning strikes touched down on each kiss racing around the breast to travel between Blair's legs. Tanner's tongue tracing around her pink areolas but staying just clear of the nipples. With a strong agonizing moan, Blair grabbed Tanner by the hair and pulled him to her erect nipples. They had waited patiently as he teased them but no more. With gusto, Tanner sucked the first nipple into his mouth rolling it with his tongue. His free hand was kneading Blair's other breast in similar motions.

She had not thought it possible, but her body was starting to act with familiar feeling, feelings Blair would take a half hour of heavy petting to produce, and Tanner had almost brought her there in moments with just her breasts. It was the switch that tipped Blair over the top. Tanner's tongue trailing from one nipple to the next ready to relieve her yearnings.

A soft kiss to the tip and the small draft from Tanner's mouth, Blair's back arched as her body tightened in every direction. Raising his head, Tanner watched the waves of the orgasm pass through Blair's soul. Her eyes, rolled into the back of her head and shockwaves scorched her body as Tanner blew little whirls of wind over her skin.

Settling into the soft earth, Blair took in a calming breath. A breath Tanner had been waiting for. Forgetting her flower was completely exposed, Tanner dived in with his tongue. He caressed her outer lips, drawing down the blood, enhancing the feelings before he let himself go further in. Blair's mind tumbled like a sheet in a hurricane, and she had no control over the words 'Do me' continually rolling off her tongue. But Tanner kept her in suspense. Blair's body was positively floating in mid-air as all her feeling was focused on one point. The small tingling of her cherry tucked away in the top of her honey pot was slowly building in intensity. Though Tanner hadn't come close on purpose that only accelerated her lust for him to eat her wholly.

A secret kink of Blair's had always been to make herself squirt. She knew boys blew with the intensity of a volcano but when she heard that a woman could do the same with the longevity women are known for, Blair needed it. But it was not to be. She had tried a number of times in many different shapes and forms to bring on that extreme climax yet always had it eluded her. That was until Tanner's tongue grazed around her pulsing clit. That one touch and the flood ways opened. Like a dam releasing thousands of litres of water Blair exploded. Her whole body convulsed in wave after wave of climactic bliss. She was in nirvana as her thighs locked Tanner's head at the entrance of the heaven, she crafted for him. If the squirting worried him he didn't show for his tongue continued to dive in and out, tasting and licking all that was Blair. And Blair in turn could take no more. It was the 8th orgasm that tipped her over the top pushing him away. With her legs when he wouldn't budge. She could barely breathe as she tried to find all the pieces to her soul that were scattered around the room. Nothing had prepared Blair for this voyage to pure bliss.

"Are you okay," Tanner asked gently. He sat beside her drawing the beautiful, naked form that was Blair, into his arms.

"Yeah... Just catching... My... Breath," Blair panted. "I'm not about to... stop yet."

Tanner turned Blair to look him in the eyes. "We have all the time in the world."

Blair just shook her head. "If I stop now, I will step aside for the girl you love. I just couldn't stay away."

Tanner smiled once more. "Blair, you are the girl I want to be with. From the moment I saw you in the alleyway, the moment our fingers sparked at the touch in the car, you started something within me. Something building out of control like a forest fire under a strong wind. I can think of no one other than you in my arms. It's you, Blair."

The words flowed over Blair, ephemeral as to reach out and grab them, to simply acknowledge their existence, they would fall apart. But they didn't. They melted into the skin, a warmth of love that filled her being. Never had Blair known such joy in the words of another and her body set alight. Reaching up with a gentle hand she pulled Tanner in for a kiss. Soft and sweet with her own nectar, the kiss was the perfect first kiss with the man she loved and that loved her.

"I'm ready," she said, a strong blush enhancing the enticing gaze.

A gaze that stole Tanner's senses leaving nothing but themselves and stars all around. Gently shifting Blair to a comfortable position Tanner moved to sit between Blair's legs once more. His penis swinging just above the moist gateway.

Blair stole a final look taking in just how large his cock was. Never had she used anything of such length, such girth and knew she was about to be stretched in more ways than one but she desired it with such intensity the initial pain wouldn't matter. The last sight she had was as Tanner's balls grazed her slit, the head of his penis sitting just above her belly button.

Head tilted, shoulders inwards with a nervous, giddy jitter running down her spine, Blair locked eyes with Tanner. He had given her time to adjust and be ready and for this she silently thanked him. "Always, shall I be in your arms. Even at the moment this life ends and our bodies are shed, my soul, my eternal being, will forever circle yours."

As if a lock broke, as if the hidden door to all the ancient secrets of the world opened at these words, Blair and Tanner froze. Eyes upon each other, images, pictures, motions, feelings... ... memories flooded in. Drifting through a distant nebula to be attacked by energy erasing mites. To be saved by a greater energy. To flow into and be consumed by... to share an existence with this energy before her. Seeing stars born and worlds collide. To pass into a black hole, to be reawakened and thrown into the underflow of Aether. To write books with, for lives to be lived... for her world to be stolen from her and darkness given in its place.

A single tear fell from tanner's cheek. His eyes damp. "You found me, Sigrún. Against time, destiny, and the fates of this world, you found me," Tanner said. His voice boomed like a thousand suns.

"I will always be with you, my twin flame, my love, Airyck." Blair's voice echoing Tanner's.

And as quickly as the doors opened, they slammed back shut again. Not a trace of what happened had reached Blair or Tanner.

"You're crying," Blair said, touched by the emotion in the cowboy.

Tanner wiped his eyes clear. "Just happy." Shifting himself to sit at the opening of Blair's paradise, Tanner lent down for one last kiss.

Blair could feel his penis rocking up and down over her opening as it covered itself in her juices. With a sigh, she braced herself for the force that was about to come down on her but Tanner didn't act forcefully. Gently, with great care he slowly worked his way inside. With each centimetre gained, millimetre made, Tanner realised the barrier he was expecting had already been dealt with by Blair and he could move a little more freely.

At each moment, Blair felt different parts inside her stretch, get touched, tingle, and on occasion moan out ecstasy.

Early fun made this so much easier but she was still adjusting to just how big Tanner was. She loved him all the more for going slow but now he reached her cervix. With a glance down, Blair was expecting to see Tanner's balls crashing against her but to her shock there was still inches of the man that needed to be accommodated. She felt terrible that she couldn't fit the man she loved, that she wasn't made for him.

But the pounding had begun and Blair's mind went fizzy to the thought. Pounding that Tanner was feeling intimately and without warning there came a thrust sharper than the rest. This thrust opened its way through her cervix and buried Tanner all the way to his balls.

Both Tanner and Blair moaned together as everything in Blair clamped tight. Electricity like lightning striking the same point continuously ran up and down Blair's spine, spreading to all her limbs. With Tanner in her deepest depths, she couldn't relax and so held Tanner in a vice, velvet grip. Each minute movement, sending 100-fold bliss in every direction. Her mind filling with the euphoria that was Tanner.

Tanner started moving in and out to the length of his throbbing cock. It was still slow but constant, taking the complete length of his journey in every thrust. Everything was set alight inside Blair. Every inch of her fleshy, squeezing interior sent overloading messages of everything pleasurable imaginable and Blair flowed into the river of absolute rapture to drift and tumble where it would. The river turning into a strong rapid as the thrusts got faster... harder... and somehow deeper.

Blair lost control when the rapids came to a waterfall. Eyes rolling in the back of her head, Blair started shaking uncontrollably as the orgasm hit her harder than any other in her life. Her body didn't work as it normally should, but she didn't realise. To lost was she in the rolling waves of pleasure that minutes passed before she returned once more. A smile crossing one side of Tanner's face to the next.

"Are you back?" He asked, nibbling Blair's ear.

This caused Blair to tense as echoes of pleasure continued to surface. "I... I think so." Blair replied.

"Good," Tanner said. Flipping Blair over, he worked her backwards until she naturally raised herself up onto hands and feet. Tanner moved behind to place himself once more at her entrance.

"What am I, a fucking dog?" Blair growled over her shoulder to see Tanner just smile. With a thrust he was inside. The slight bend in his cock hitting new, intense locations in Blair and she almost lost the support of her arms to the exciting new feelings. "O... Ohhoo... oohoiiieeee. Fucking Woof!" Blair moaned causing Tanner to slap her arse.

It was far quicker this time to arrive at her orgasm. Tanner was hitting every mark inside her she'd spent years finding herself and he would not relent. Even as Blair lost control, slumping to the soft ground below, Tanner continued. Wild, unutterable, moaning bellowed from the cave mouth as Blair continued a blissful process of orgasm, partial recover, and repeat. It was only when Tanner made her aware of his building to explode that Blair's lustful nature resurfaced.

"If you're... mmm... If you're going to cum I want to eat you. IF YOU'RE GOING TO CUM I WANT TO EAT YOU!" she screamed.

Tanner rolled her around and brought himself to her lips. Eyes rolling and tongue lolling Blair took as much of Tanner as she could. Saliva running down her cheek, she started thrusting her mouth on him, her hand taking the rest of his length. She was grateful that he didn't go too deep allowing her to make most of the movements.

Soon, Tanner reached round Blair's head to hold her firm and she prepared for his release. And what a release it was. Load after load filled Blair's mouth, some breaking out the seal of her lips. Tasting and drinking as it came through Blair sucked the last pulse of semen from Tanner and swished it around with her tongue. The taste was extraordinary and unlike anything she had experienced before. She would be dining here again she thought as she swallowed the last mouthful.

Tracing her tongue over the eye of the penis, Blair was rewarded with the last few drops as Tanner's cock spasmed. Slumping back to the earth Blair was exhausted. Tanner lay down beside her, arm around her and gently kissed her neck. This sent little shockwaves through her but Blair went with them. Her butt bouncing every so often.

"Are you okay?" Tanner asked having recovered his

general thinking including the ability to realise others have feelings too.

"You need to do that to me every single day for the rest of our lives. I'll take nothing less," Blair said seriously.

"Done,' Tanner smiled and drew Blair into a deeper more comfortable hug.

"I really like you too, Tanner. I felt that same spark when our hands touched for the first time. I have dreamed of nothing but you since that moment. I want to be yours," Blair said. After the last few moments there was nothing to be embarrassed about around Tanner, nothing to be shy about. She was completely open.

"Then be so for I am already yours." Tanner's smile was like a warm summer day that Blair could remain in, encompassing and full of joy.

"There is probably something you need to know before we go back to school."

Tanner cocked his head in question.

"I'll be helping Lillian with something. You may see us kiss, hold hands, act like a couple." Blair noted as Tanner's penis bounced a little and Blair reached over to stoke the slowly engorging member. "You don't get to join in on this. She needs to break away from public encumbrance. I'm helping her. Nothing more."

Tanner smiled as his penis came fully erect again. "I don't mind and that is a future matter. For now..." He glanced down then with a cheeky grin that matched his eyes, Tanner looked to Blair.

Returning the smile, Blair climbed upon her lover. As she impaled herself, Blair's back arched in the pure ecstasy entering her. She took the whole length in one blissful movement. The pain in her foot completely forgotten. This was a future matter and all Blair needed now was Tanner charging into her.

"Aww, Mum. Did I have a day," Blair said holding her phone. She was lost in the memories leading up to Tanner carrying her home and placing her in bed. The bed she desperately wanted to drag him into but for other ears in the house. Tanner recovered a towel for her from the linen cupboard as his final job for today and Blair sent her love after Tanner's vehicle traveling from the home. Blair shook her head.

Blair brought the phone close to her lips. "I may have lost it... It. Me and Tanner had a... big moment today after I twisted my ankle at the falls. He... I... We... clothes came off and we let our feelings for one another take over. He likes me the same as I like him. He left his girlfriend. Something he had wanted to do so that he could pursue this relationship with me. I was blown away to say least but, mum, my life is starting to come together."

From the corner of her eye Blair saw a shooting star streak across the sky. The darkness in the room enhanced the light of the heavens. "Did you see that, mum? A shooting star. I can make a wish."

Blair opened the window wide to view the heavens as she wished to spend every day with Tanner as happy as this day had been. Another star fell. Then another. Blair couldn't believe the display that suddenly unfolded before her eyes. The Western sky started firing star after star over to the east until it looked as if the whole world was moving in reverse.

"What a way to end the night. A meteor shower at this time of the year. Today has been the very best of days." Blair stayed up another half hour watching the sky dance across the night until she couldn't keep her eyes open anymore. "Goodnight, Mum," Blair said before curling up in her bed and dreaming such perfect dreams of Tanner.

The sun had just peeked over the horizon, bringing light and warmth. An open curtain gave a path to gently caress Blair awake. With a yawn and a smile she embraced the new day, then rolled over to bid it 5 more minutes before she would admit the embrace. The noise of an engine drifted through the room and Blair recognised Tanner's vehicle.

"5 more minutes, I said," Blair moaned over her shoulder. The words of Lillian crept into her mind. You have to take even the small moments when they arrive... Blair made a note to chip her friend for the comment as she threw back the blankets. Catching a glimpse of herself in the mirror, Blair laughed at the frizzy hair protruding from the left side of her head while the right remained flat.

Taking a seat by the window, Blair kept her silhouette

from view. She rejoiced in her decision to where the baggy shirt to bed...

But she hadn't worn this shirt to bed. She almost destroyed this shirt the day before when Tanner arrived for work. Tanner shouldn't be working today. Could he be taking me to school? Blair pondered as she walked to the window.

Seeing Tanner step from his vehicle, Blair was lost in the warm and fuzzies of the moment before he noticed her. He turned to give an over embellished bow. Hat from head, he swept it under himself as he bent low. Coming erect once more, Tanner thought it odd Blair was looking around the grounds of the farm. Suddenly, the normally shy girl pulled her shirt high exposing her soft, supple, inviting breasts. Breasts he could only dream of tasting. Tanner tripped hard in a tangle of rope and wheat bags.

With a laugh Blair retreated into the room to prepare for school. She could get used to this back and forward around the farm and if Tanner was going to pick her up each day, then she may need to get up a little earlier to be able to spend more time with him.

Dress on, tie done up, bag ready, Blair mounted the stairs to see her lover. She was part way down when Jacob blocked her way.

"Blair? Something's wrong," he said, a troubled look upon his face.

"Not now, Jacob. I need to see Tanner." Blair said shoving passed.

"Blair, please, something's terribly wrong." Jacob tried again.

"Not you too," Bryan said from the kitchen. "Are you kids so gung-ho to get back to school you'd give up your weekend?"

Blair slowed. "What weekend?"

"It's only Sunday. Go get yourself out of the school clothes and into weekend attire."

"It's Monday, isn't it?" Blair turned on Jacob who only motioned to follow him up the stairs. "Sorry, dad... I must've gotten confused."

Bryan laughed aloud. "You and Jacob are more alike than you think."

Blair followed Jacob into her room before he shut the

door behind them. "Is dad okay? Is he having a mental breakdown or anything serious?"

"So, you believe it's Monday too."

"Of course, it's Monday. Lillian was over Saturday and you and I had a picnic yesterday."

Jacob burst into tears and hugged Blair tightly.

"Jacob, what's going on? You're scaring me."

"No one else believes it's Monday," he sobbed. "Even Tanner."

Blair shrugged her way out of Jacob's embrace and walked from window to window until she saw Tanner. "Tanner," Blair called to get his attention. "What day is it?"

"Sunday... You all good? Not quite yourself today." He was clearly blushing.

"What happened yesterday?" Blair tried again now deeply worried.

"Not too sure what you and Lillian got up to. I was working the farm until Lillian got a lift home in the afternoon."

Blair turned on Jacob. "What's happening? Is this a prank of yours? Did you rope dad and Tanner in on it...? Ha... Ha... very funny. Knock it off." Blair demanded.

"I'm not doing this, Blair." Jacob's tears fell anew.

Brows furrowed Blair was at a crossroad. Either the boy was telling the truth and was just as scared as she was, or the prank was being executed well and needed to be played through to the end. Either way, Jacob needed to be comforted. With open arms she pulled the boy in realising for the first time just how small Jacob really was. "I can't say I know for sure what's going on nor whether this is one of your elaborate pranks but there is one thing that will without a doubt tell us if the day is playing over or you need to fess up. Astrid... There is no way she'll be coming over again if it's Monday. Still, she is an hour or two away and if this is going to get me a day off school I need to change."

Jacob didn't move.

"Get out," Blair's voice held daggers.

"Oh... yep, sorry," Jacob said and made his way to the door. At the last he turned back. "If you're going to be praising the sun as you did this morning, maybe choose a different time when I'm not feeding the chooks."

Watching Jacob leave, Blair sat a moment trying to work out what he was talking about. Suddenly, she remembered her greeting to Tanner. "You little bum!" she yelled after him.

The thought occurred to Blair that if the day was repeating and yesterday didn't happen Tanner wouldn't know what she was doing. She knew he'd be happy having come to learn his true feelings but nevertheless copped an eyeful before he was ready. Blair blushed furiously.

And so, the day wore on detrimentally slow until finally the noise of another vehicle could be heard from the yard. Pleading to any of the Gods that may be happening by and listening in for it not to be Astrid, Blair peeked over the sill... Astrid!

Jacob burst in causing Blair to jump.

"See, I told you it wasn't my doing," Jacob said.

"I know. I'm sorry for that. Picnic to make up for it?"

Jacob grinned and the two turned to watch things fall apart. Only, this time, Tanner and Astrid wandered off to have a lunch. It was Bryan that insisted Tanner take the moment that presented itself while he could as there was nothing else happening.

"No!" Jacob exclaimed.

"What? What happened," Blair asked, upset with how things turned out.

"I wasn't there to word up dad today. He doesn't know Astrid's a bitch." Jacob sniffed sadly. "I'm so sorry, Blair."

"Don't be." Blair was feeling disappointed at how a little change destroyed everything. "We've both been put out by what's happening. You got it right the first time. We'll work it out again. For now we need to accept the reality we've found ourselves in. If it happens again, we get our picnic. Okay?"

Jacob wiped a tear away before nodding.

"Now go get some of your stash and we can have a day up here."

Jacob's eyes grew bright, and he raced off to his room.

Blair's heart ached to see Tanner walk away with someone he didn't want to be with. To walk away at all. "I'll fix this," she said.

Chapter 6 – She is truly one of a kind

The pen dug deeper into the soft wood of the bench. Other names and crude remarks had been etched into the forgiving surface, but this was different. The pen was only moving back and forward, digging deeper and deeper with each movement. The wielder didn't take care in what they were crafting; this was an act of rage. An emotional attack, lashing out at whatever could be found. Well, the table had had enough. The tip of the pen came upon a harder point getting jagged underneath. The wielder, too caught up in their own mind, exerted extra force to push through only for the pen to bend and snap in the centre.

"What's got you all worked up, Lamby?" another asked seeing the first staring at her pen in regret.

"Nothing, nothing," Mary replied. She waited for the attention to be off her once more before glancing across the school yard. Lillian was there... and so was the whore of a girlfriend stealer, Blaaiir. Their actions at the bus stop made that clear. Scrunching up her nose and sticking out her tongue, Mary ripped her attention away.

A friend leaned across the table to trace the line of sight. "Oh, eww. Don't pay them no mind," Francesca said. "It's bad enough we had one little dyke in the school but now she's found a fellow rug muncher to flaunt her disgusting nature with. Just ignore them."

Mary nodded. Her heart was pounding from her chest. It was no secret the school looked down on anyone that was different. But how could she. She was... different. Not different, not different. But when it came to standing up for Lillian and going down on her sinking ship or save face and live a better... less harassed life, she corrected, Mary took the latter. She saved herself and this ate at her every day. It was all she could do to comfort Lillian under the shadow of night.

She was already infatuated with Lillian before they got together. Even before it was made general knowledge Lillian liked girls. The small, curvy girl with the striking smile. It was because of Lillian that Mary had to accept she was gay. Yes, she tried to fight it. She even dated a boy or two but nothing filled the hollow part of her soul. And when one of these boys came on too strong at a cinema causing Mary to flee into the night it was Lillian that found her crying on a stoop.

The moment their eyes met the world stood still. There were no words spoken. Lillian just moved in closer and before acting, asked with a determined stare if Mary wanted to be comforted. With a nod Lillian wrapped her up in warm arms, her touch, each movement, loving and soothing. The boys were a distant memory and as the tears subsided and their eyes locked once more in such a close vicinity it was Mary that acted. She leaned in, kissing Lillian on the mouth, the smaller girl's eyes going wide in such a surprising moment.

Lillian had rocked away, trying to piece together what was happening, looking around for those that may be in hiding. A hand pulled her face back front, and Lillian couldn't mistake the lust and longing in Mary's eyes. With a shy little smile, Lillian accepted the courtship, something she secretly longed for herself. Those freckles...

Slamming the table, Mary got to her feet. Chaos rippled across her face. No, she couldn't just come out as gay now. But she desperately wanted to fight for her love. "Fuck, fuck, fuck!" Mary yelled slamming the table on each word. Her friends were shocked by such an outburst from their Lamby, sitting back in case they became collateral damage.

"Look out, Mary's gotten the attention of D2" Francesca said referring to the shorthand for Dyke 2. And sure enough, Blair was walking the yard, eyes locked on Mary.

Bracing herself, Mary couldn't be sure what was about to be said. Anyone else and she would be safe but the new girlfriend of her ex holding all the cards... This couldn't end well.

Blair held out a hand with some folded pieces of paper held within.

"What's this," Mary asked uncertain.

"Your geography notes, you silly ingrate. Heaven forbid you come over and ask a girl for them that may check you out while giving them to you. Can no one take a compliment these days?" Blair made an obvious, over exaggerated look up and down of Mary. "Nothing much to look at anyway. You're all the same."

Blair threw the paper into Mary's lap and took off to the sound of the first bell.

"No wonder, Lamby," Francesca laughed aloud. "You have no luck in class pairings."

Mary, still no idea what was going, on sifted through the papers. Yes, a lot of them were geography notes which were gunna be good for first period, but one page was different. *Dear Mary,* it began, and Mary hid it away quickly.

In class she was able to score a seat to herself in the back corner and pulled out the papers Blair gave her. Her teacher approached.

"You okay, dear? I saw your little outburst in the yard and you don't normally sit here"

Mary just shrugged her shoulders and nodded. It didn't quite say she wasn't but should be enough to get by.

The teacher returned to the front of the class and started the lesson as Mary read the letter.

Dear Mary,
My name is Blair. Lillian and I are...

Mary pushed the page to the desk taking in a few deep breaths. She needed to steel herself for what was to come. It was one thing to be dumped without a word, but quite another for her ex-girlfriend's new mistress to dump her in a letter.

My name is Blair. Lillian and I are fast becoming close friends, God sisters on my mother's side. I just wanted to introduce myself and state my intentions to you before you heard too many rumours. This place is terrible for that. I am 100% straight... I am 100% straight... I am 100% straight.

Mary continued to read the line over and over again. She was having a hard time computing what was read, already expecting something else.

"I am 100% straight. I like Tanner Anderson. Though I am comfortable around your little love muffin, I have no desire to enter a relationship with her. I need you of all people to know this because you may see or hear a lot of things about Lillian and I that would speak of the contrary. I am on a mission to change people's perspectives of other people's sexual preferences. This may include a kiss or two and naughty talk or hands in places they would not normally be. I seem to be making it sound worse than what it is. We won't be having sex in or

out of school. It would just look like we are in a relationship. I want people to become comfortable if not just able to ignore what doesn't concern them.

Lillian loves you dearly. I think she will hit me for that comment but will definitely hit me for saying she doesn't shut up about your "delicious" freckles. She does say delicious. I don't want to know.

Mary let out an audible laugh then covered her mouth. The whole class turned to stare at her including Blair who was wearing a cheeky grin. The teacher just raised an eyebrow.

The deep, crimson flush that burned the girls face suited her and she just turned away in the hopes everyone else would. They did.

I don't want to cause any issues for you or out you as gay. I just want to pave the way so that if you wanted to come out you could with no negative effects in the aftermath. Also know, at any moment you can walk up to me and without a word I would step aside for you and Lillian. Also, also know, if you hurt her, I will be coming for you :)

With your blessing, I will begin.

Blair

It surprised Mary at just how much Blair's letter affected her. The rush of emotions including relief, surprise, and how much she did not want to lose Lillian all bubbled around in her throat until it overpowered her and caused her eyes to tear up. Soon, she was crying openly and again had every eye in class on her. Quickly, the teacher moved to where Mary was and got an arm around her getting Mary to her feet.

"I knew there was something wrong," the teacher said as she started to escort Mary out. "A little time in sick bay may help and if need be, we can call your parents. Young women these days don't need to act so tough all the time."

As she just passed Blair's desk, Mary paused. "Miss," she said to the teacher. "I give you my wholehearted blessing." Mary said before continuing out the door.

"We love you, Lamby," some of the students called. "Be strong."

96

Mary was one of those girls that everyone adored even if she didn't come across as popular. There was no student that could say a bad thing about her... except Lillian. Lillian could tell you exactly how bad a girl Mary could be.

At no point did Mary look at her, but Blair was the only person in the room that knew exactly what just happened.

"I think I broke Mary," Blair said to Lillian at morning tea.

Lillian's brows furrowed in, and she looked at Blair as if the taller girl had moments to live. "You did what?" Lillian raised a daring eyebrow.

"I think I broke Mary. I wrote her a letter and she read it in class. Afterwards she burst into tears and walked out."

Lillian licked her lips. "A letter? And what perchance did this letter say?"

"There was a bit about how you and I will be getting all kissy face and about stepping aside etc." Blair waved a dismissive hand acting nonchalant.

"Blair! That's not what we discussed. If you've ruined..." Lillian was burning red with anger and paused only long enough to realise Blair held a copy of the letter up in front of her. Snatching it away, Lillian started reading.

"I thought you'd want a copy."

No response. Then Lillian turned and punched her in the arm. "They are delicious." she pouted causing Blair to laugh. "So? What happened then?" Lillian asked having finished the letter.

"Well after exciting a giggle from her, I'm guessing at how delicious she was, she broke down into tears. When the teacher escorted her out, Mary gave the "teacher" her blessings."

Lillian looked down. Looked back up. Looked down. Looked back up. With pursed lips she waggled a finger in front of Blair. "That could have ended terribly, Blair. She may have walked away for good."

"Then you didn't see her giving us the stink eye this morning. In her mind you already had," Blair said.

"But I hadn't. I would never," Lillian replied worried at what she had just learned.

"You better make sure to give her some snuggle time. Make her the focus, let her feel special. The rumours would have knocked her around good, you're what she needs to be able to come alive again," Blair said with a smile.

"Thank you, Blair," Lillian rocked up against her in a cheerful manner. "Tonight, I'll do all the things..."

"That's disgusting." Both Lillian and Blair glanced up to find Astrid and her little possie standing before them. "It's been bad enough seeing this little queer running around the school this last year, now I have to be subject to hearing your dirty talk."

"Don't be upset, Astrid," Blair replied acting coy. Rising to her feet, Blair started to give a sway little walk as she approached Astrid. "We can talk dirty too. We didn't get much of a chance yesterday when you came over. Your mouth was otherwise occupied." Blair said with a wink as she reached out a hand.

A hand Astrid hastily slapped away. "With Tanner... It was with Tanner, I was occupied."

"Don't protest too much, Astrid. Your *friends* may start to question."

"Shut up!" Astrid screamed and pushed Blair to the ground. "You stay the fuck away from me."

"Gotcha," Blair said with an exaggerated wink from her seated position.

Astrid's eyes came ablaze, and she was about close-in to attack when another figure came from around a corner.

"Lillian, Blair, Astrid," Mr Pertouski said as he looked to each girl. The rest huddled behind didn't seem fit to be named. "It's not often I see you together."

"Just passing by, Sir." Astrid's change was so quick it was frightening. "I only just mentioned how Lillian must have had a wonderful upbringing to turn out as she has. I start to worry sometimes with the people she may end up hanging around."

"Thank you for such concern but the praise should all go to Lillian. Even from a young age she knew what she wanted and wasn't afraid to go for it. Sometimes, I hope she may make a mistake or two. At least then I can be there for her. Still, I'm so grateful she's found a friend in Blair. I can see what a positive impact she's had on my daughter."

"Very positive," one of the other girls said, underlying meanings dripping from each syllable.

Mr Pertouski's eyes narrowed. "Girls these days are all

the same. Mindless, travelling in packs, never going against the flow, never truly happy. I'm glad my daughter was able to steer clear of such girls." On the last Mr Pertouski levelled his gaze on Astrid.

"Let's hope such girls leave her alone in the future," Astrid said. She kept the teacher's eyes with equal intensity.

"It would be wise... Anyway, I seem to be eating up your morning tea. I'll let you take your leave." Watching the students go, Mr Pertouski turned on his daughter. "Having fun picking fights."

"Trying something new. You can trust the end justifies the means," Lillian said.

"That's just it. With you, I know it will. Still unsure about you." He turned on Blair.

As innocently as she could, Blair replied. "Then I will prove myself and make sure your kind words about me ring true... Even if they were said only to oppose Astrid."

"At least I hit right when I saw your intelligence potential." Mr Pertouski turned back to Lillian. "Just take care. I don't mind picking you up from detention. Just not the hospital."

Thank you, Daddy." Lillian smiled warmly as her dad walked off. Turning back, she was met with a mocking smile from Blair. "What?" Lillian asked cautiously.

"You said Daddy," Blair replied.

"Ah, fuck off." Lillian turned away to the sound of Blair's laughter. The smaller girl glanced back. "You still haven't told me the big event that happened after I left."

Around the school a bell signalled the end of morning tea. Blair leaned in close to whisper into Lillian's ear.

"I slept with Tanner." Blair leaned back blushing and spun on her heal to race off to the next class.

"What! Blair, wait! When!" Lillian called to no avail. "You can't just leave it there."

"It all sounds so surreal. Like out of a fantasy novel," Lillian stated. Blair had spent lunch telling Lillian everything from the moment she woke the first Sunday to... She thought a moment... Blair had spent lunch telling Lillian everything from the moment she had retrieved her shirt from the corner of the room to when she saw the second coming of Astrid and its outcome. Now with a free period and no one else in the playground the girls continued the conversation. "There is absolutely no way you had a nice... dream? Or maybe Jacob slipped some strong drugs into your food? We know how Jacob likes to deal drugs."

This only got a half-hearted grin from Blair. "I would honestly believe that theory... I would be convincing myself of that and only giving you a detailed point by point of my dream in the cave right now. I want to believe it was just the drugs but for one thing. Jacob. He experienced everything I did... What's that look for, you sick minded, little girl. Jacob also experienced a second day." Blair was shaking her head. "And well..."

"Well, what?" Lillian asked.

"My flower isn't what it used to be."

Lillian glanced down at Blair's thighs. "Can't argue with that. So, what now?"

"I actually feel blessed. Blessed in the knowledge of where Tanner's heart lies. Blessed for the experiences only I remember. Blessed to have flashed Tanner yesterday."

"Why the flashing?" Lillian looked confused.

"Something for him to think about. It'd be playing on his mind even now working against thoughts of Astrid. I still have hope we'll be together."

"Cheeky, but I meant what are our next steps. Will you be moving in on Tanner? Playing it safe? What?"

"You know how most romance novels go. I'm about at the stage of finding something that would continue to push us together and keep us together without choice of exit."

"But this isn't a romance novel. Fantasy at best. What activity could you do to have a senior and year 11 get paired up."

"I'm not quite sure yet but there'll be something... there needs to be something."

Lillian wrapped a comforting arm around Blair and drew her in to lay with her back against Lillian. Thus, they stayed in the middle of the playground, in view of many classrooms, until the bells rang signalling final period.

The day rolled on and Blair was none the wiser to what she could do to spend more time with Tanner. She rarely even got to catch a glimpse of him until the weekend unless she went out of her way to find him. That had its risks with Astrid always on watch and now a known enemy to both Lillian and herself. She was doing everything she could to make life miserable for them and therefor keeping Blair and Tanner apart was part of it.

Lying in bed at night talking it out with her mum didn't help either. Blair hoped there would be a little clarity from it, but the action bore no fruit. No spiritual enlightenment sent from above. Even while she was dreaming, Blair got no ideas. Sure, she did get to spend some interesting and memorable moments with Tanner but nothing for the waking world.

Still thinking she was dreaming, the sound of Tanner's car echoed up the driveway to catch Blair's ear. She drifted a moment longer, body not ready to come awake until her conscious mind caught onto what was happening. Eyes firing wide, Blair looked around the room. There was no engine roaring, no sound of a bouncing tray back, metal clanging from the loose equipment. There was only the empty air. It was too early, Blair chided herself seeing only the predawn light barely highlighting the mountains. Even on one of his work days, Tanner would still be an hour or so from arriving.

With a sigh, Blair found she was now too awake for anymore sleep this morning. Too awake, too worked up, and too lazy to do anything about it. Throwing back the blankets, she wandered to the bench chair next to the front window. It would give the best view to watch the coming sunrise now starting to paint the sky with deep crimsons and oranges. The weather not getting too cool yct, Blair comfortably remained in the oversized shirt and swung the windows wide taking in the crisp fresh air. Nothing in the city could compare to such a beautiful place.

Such a beautiful atmos... Tanner!

Standing below with his attention drawn to the opening windows, Tanner was watching Blair. When he knew he had her attention he started slowly turning his head from left to right, eyes locked on the girl. Blair thought it an odd motion as if he was warning her of something, but she couldn't understand what. Moments later, Bryan walked into view holding a large sheet of paper and understanding dawned. Tanner was thinking I was about to flash him again! Blair couldn't hold back the smile and when Tanner glanced up once last time, she sent him a little wink. The man turned to a boy in an instant. Face red, knees buckling, and small jerking movements. Blair knew she still had his attention and settled on the seat to watch her love while she could.

Undetermined as to why he was here so early, Blair watched Tanner and Bryan running around the yard gathering odd bits from different sheds and throwing them into the back of the pickup. Nothing really made sense. Still, the electricity that ran through her each time Tanner glanced up, eyes sparkling like the rising sun, was nothing short of ecstasy.

But as always, the morning grew old and Tanner had to leave to prepare himself for school. Blair raced downstairs to catch her dad as he entered the house. She was now wearing her uniform having changed close to the window when she knew her dad was in back and Tanner at his pickup.

"What was that about this morning?" Blair asked. "We don't usually get company on a week day."

"Sorry if he woke you, Blair. Have an event coming up for the farm soon and Tanner is helping out," Bryan said.

"Do you now?" Blair started considering the options. "What sort of an event?"

"Just a yearly farmers market. Biggest around but nothing to worry yourself about. Can you make the bus this morning? I need to head out."

"Sure," Blair replied. She really didn't want to walk to the bus stop but it couldn't be helped. At least Jacob would be keeping her company.

"See ya, Blair." A whirlwind that was Jacob sped down the stairs and made for the front door. Pausing he doubled back, collected the piece of toast on the table and ran out the door with a quick wave. Bryan's old ute then came to life and took off in a rumbling orchestra of pistons and gears.

With pursed lips Blair just stood there a moment cursing her mind for thinking the "at least" statement. A quiet house to herself, Blair prepared for school and took off to catch the bus. Missing it would mean she would miss

102

the chance of running into Tanner at school or catching up with Lillian. She especially didn't want to leave Lillian open for any abuse from Astrid. Even leaving early Blair needed to run the last 50m to make it as the bus pulled up.

"I might have something," Blair told Lillian as she got to school, seeing the smaller girl just arriving herself.

"Something... by which you mean Tanner?" Lillian said.

"Is there anything else? There's a farmers market thing coming up and Tanner's going to be popping into the farm most mornings."

Lillian pouted. "I see."

"What's wrong?" Blair asked picking up on the lack of enthusiasm. "You can't always have me to yourself."

Lillian giggled. "Mary may have come up with the same solution for you."

"Mary?" Blair asked, her eyes questioning deeper than the spoken word.

"She came around last night. She's never been to my house. Never met my dad on a personal level. And I've never actually told him of our relationship. Mary was happy to let him know."

Blair's grin deepened. "And how did our big, hunky, Daddy take it?"

Lillian just levelled a glare at her.

"Wanted to try out the title... see why you liked to call him that." Blair reached out a hand to place it on Lillian's shoulder. Her voice became husky. "I can see exactly why."

"Fuck off." Lillian slapped the hand away. "Do you want to hear or not?"

"Please," Blair turned serious.

"Dad invited Mary to stay for dinner... then left us to our own devices half the night." Blair raised an eyebrow. "Uh uh, no kiss and tell from these lips. Not this time anyways. Too special. It was about 2 in the morning when Mary and I were actually discussing what was going on. I told her how you were trying to get Tanner's attention and she told me she knew just the thing."

"Farmers market?"

"Well, harvest festival," Lillian confirmed. "She's putting herself in a rather awkward position to get the information to you so please act surprised like the information is new."

"Why put herself in that position? She could have just

given the info to you."

"I asked her the same thing and she told me that you've light a fire under me. That Mary had never seen me so happy on the school yard. She wanted to show you just how much it means to have you in my life."

Blair's lower lip popped out. "I hope you thanked her for me."

Lillian smiled and with a wink replied. "She got home after 5 at least."

"Good girl."

And as if she was aware they were talking about her, Mary made her way across the school yard. She seemed really nervous keeping her eyes low. Before a massive yawn broke the silence. A yawn that caused her to squeal uncontrollably through its entirety. Immediately her hand came up to her mouth and face started burning red.

Blair let out a loud, rich laugh. "Sounds like you haven't been getting enough sleep, hey Lillian?"

This only caused Mary to burn hotter. She held forth a bundle of paper as Blair did the day before. But Mary seemed to be muted. As Blair took the bundle Mary turned and took off back across the yard.

"Damn, I can't help but find her shyness cute," Lillian smiled sweetly watching Mary's butt sway to and fro.

"You're a lucky girl, Lil. She's so sweet, so innocent," Blair said as she sifted through the paperwork. Mostly, it was the school work that Blair had used the day before, but a number of sheets were on the harvest festival. The cover sheet went into detail about where and for how long the event spanned. Blair smiled. It was everything she needed to bring Tanner back to her path away from Astrid.

Looking up, Blair considered gesturing to Mary to show she got the message but stopped instantly. The table of girls where Mary sat had all levelled dirty glares their way.

"Must have been how Mary looked when she got back," Lillian said.

"If nothing else, those girls have Mary's back," Blair replied.

"But will that change if they knew the real Mary. The person Mary desperately wants to be known for. Accepted for."

"I don't think there is a person in this school who would

104

say anything bad about your Lamby. She is truly one of a kind."

"She really is," Lillian said watching the group of girls comfort and bring a smile back to Mary's face.

The look on Lillian's face brought on the warm and fuzzies in Blair. She couldn't help but feel the aura of love surrounding her friend.

Chapter 7 – I want to be like you

"Umm... Exc... Excuse... No, don't worry," the young girl mumbled to Blair and Lillian at lunch. Turning, she made to leave.

"Sophie, wait. What's wrong?" Lillian called but the girl was already off and running.

"Who was that?" Blair asked still watching the girl.

"Sophie Berrum. Year 9. Lives on a farm three doors over from you. You possibly even catch the same bus."

"I hadn't noticed but I've never been the best at interacting with or taking in the people around me," Blair said. "I might keep an eye out this arvo."

Something about the moment stuck with Blair. Something she couldn't put a finger on. Something that kept her thinking all afternoon. Something that was made all too obvious at the bus stop. A group of girls surrounding another. Inarguable signs of bullying. Blair could tell names were being called but was still too far to hear the terms. It was Sophie that found herself in the middle taking the brunt of it. Then the pushing and shoving started. All of it was one sided and finally Sophie ended up on the ground, her bag's contents exploding everywhere on impact. The girls took off and Blair ran over to help.

"Please, just leave me be," Sophie said to the shadow of a figure next to her. As she looked up her eyes went wide and mouth shut.

"You catching the bus?" Blair asked and Sophie nodded. "Good. You're going to be sitting next to me and will be telling me what this was about."

"Okay," Sophie said softly, eyes downturned.

Blair couldn't help herself. She knew just how Sophie felt having been at the end of Astrid's bullying lately. Thankfully, not today though. Walking to the bus, Blair decided this girl had already gained her protection.

"So, where do you want to begin?" Blair asked as she sat next to Sophie near the back of the bus. This only brought a shrug from Sophie. "This is your journey, your life. If you can't find the strength to seek help how am I to truly help you. You tried at lunch. I can see that now but still; you need to be the one to put your troubles into words."

For many minutes Sophie was quiet. She sat staring at

her thumbs catapulting over each other in constant twiddling. "I *%&$^ $(#(= $**$ you." She mumbled ever so softly.

"I'm sorry but you're going to need to be more vocal. Trouble hearing in my old age," Blair said causing Sophie to look at her, one eyebrow raised questioningly. "If this is the effort you put into helping yourself, I'm not going to be able to do any better."

"I want to be like you," Sophie said. There was more determination in her voice now.

"Good. This is a good start," Blair said with a reassuring smile and a nod. "Now let's clarify just what that entails. Do you want to be in year 11?"

Sophie shook her head.

"Shoulder length hair? Ravishing good looks?"

Sophie shook her head.

Blair feigned thinking with a finger on her lips. Eyes shooting wide, Blair looked around and leaned in close. Her voice lowered so only Sophie could hear. "You want to dance naked around a fire under the full moon with ritualistic chanting and rubbing against your fellow sisters."

Sophie shook her head... her face suddenly went red as her eyes traced up and down Blair's figure. Looking away quickly, Sophie became still.

It was in that one look that Blair understood just what was happening. Placing a comforting hand upon Sophie, the younger girl tensed. "I'm not a witch. I was only trying to be funny but you're going to need to say what it is you want. I can't put these words in your mouth. You can trust me."

It was a long, straining moment before Sophie could muster the courage to speak. "I want to be open, like you. To find a girl I can love and not be shunned for these feelings I have."

With the biggest smile Blair could muster, she embraced the now embarrassed girl. "I'm so proud of you for how brave you just were, but you can't be like me."

Sophie's fragile world shattered into a million pieces hearing the last statement. A look of distress and despair spread like wildfire across her face and Blair believed she was about to burst into tears. "You can be like Lillian,

107

however," Blair stated. "You can be free to love anyone you want and have love returned. To be free to live your life in whatever way you decide without the need to fear others. I'll protect you as best I can. Lillian will protect you as best she can. If you find it hard to be in the school yard, come sit with us. You just can't be like me anymore. Your confession just now sent you from my path."

Sophie looked confused at just what she had done, and Blair was finding out that the girl's main form of communication was these facial expressions.

"I'm attracted to males. I know it looks as though I like women, but that is only a ruse. Lillian on the other hand can't get enough of them. We've put up this front for people like yourself. People who don't feel they can be who they want to be. We're putting this image into the school so that people can become more accustomed to it. Maybe even accept it once they get past the fact we are different to them but in the most important parts the same. We still want to be loved. We still want to enjoy our time on this earth."

It took a moment for Sophie to process and fully understand what'd been said but Blair marked the moment of apprehension with the smile that crept across Sophie's face. "Thank you," Sophie said.

"You're most welcome," Blair replied. "Can I ask who knows?"

"I told dad yesterday. We'll be telling mum together this afternoon. The girls at school only think they know because..."

"Your hormones let you down?"

"I stared a little too long at someone's swimmers at the pool. The swimsuit was so cute."

"Possible to recover from but you've shown yourself to be strong enough to walk your own path. We can try and help."

"I don't want to give up my friends," Sophie said. She had a look of fear in her eyes.

Blair thought hard a moment on how to answer. In the end she thought to prepare Sophie for the worst. "The bullies for one are not your friends. They show this in their actions. Still, as much as you want to keep the friends you have; your friends may still leave. It isn't just about your position on things. Lillian lost her friends because they were also treated badly by bullies for being just that. A friend. It was Lillian who finally stepped away to protect them."

"I would protect them too if it came to that," Sophie said sternly.

"Then you are the strong, kind-hearted, beautiful person I believed you to be. We'll get through," Blair said before flicking her head towards the front of the bus.

Sophie looked around and was surprised they were coming up on her stop. "Tomorrow?"

"I'll be on the bus and we can sort the bullies out first thing."

Sophie smiled and seemed to be floating as she left the bus.

"But how shall I do this?" Blair asked herself.

"Here we go, mum. Wish me luck," Blair said before kissing the phone and placing it on her dresser. She'd gotten up early to be dressed and ready to infiltrate Tanner and her dad's plans. Now, the sound of Tanner's pickup was coming up the driveway. Heading downstairs with the intent of timing her entrance as Bryan met Tanner, Blair got it perfectly. Walking out to the chatting pair she positioned herself beside the two.

"Oh, sorry, Blair. Did we wake you again?" Bryan asked.

"No, I heard about the harvest festival coming up and..." Blair turned to give Tanner a cheeky smile. "...I'm interested."

"There's no need, Blair, but thank you anyway," Bryan said.

Blair knew it wasn't going to be straight forward. "If you're going to wake me each morning you may as well let me help." The words at least got her dad's attention. "And you need me more than you know."

"Tanner's had no issues in the past two years he worked our stall. In fact, business has increased from years prior."

"Increased, but only to a point," Blair said. She'd been thinking all night about how to talk her way in and all she could think about was how hot Tanner looked. Then it hit her. Tanner was hot. "Tanner is hot," Blair said. Eyes bulging, Tanner almost spat at the comment and Bryan

109

shifted nervously. Blair turned and took on a shy little smile. "You are. There's no denying that. And the female side of the crowd will be attracted to the stall because of him. They would even drag husbands along. That's when they'll see your good work." Blair turned back to Bryan. "Sorry, dad. It's not all about your farm."

"So you fit in..?" Bryan started twirling his hands to get things moving. They didn't have a good amount of time this morning.

Tanner smiled. "Blair's hot."

It was Bryan's turn to scoff and Blair smiled at how this was playing out.

"She is. There's no denying that. Blair's looking to tempt the male side of the crowd to the stall. The men that may be there on their own. Am I correct?" Tanner asked Blair who simple nodded.

"I can't allow that," Bryan said sternly. "You'd be putting yourself at the mercy of the men there. I'd hate to see anyone take things too far."

"They won't," Tanner assured him. "I'm there. If need be, I'll treat her as my own partner. No one will dare treat her poorly then. I do see the merit with her proposal. I've always had a hard time getting the cockies in."

"I don't know..." Bryan said scratching his head.

"Come on, Dad. At least let me in on the prep work. I'm going to be woken each morning anyway."

Pursing his lips a moment as he thought Bryan gave in. "Alright, but if I see that you aren't capable you'll be staying home. And you..." He turned on Tanner. "This is only because I trust you like a son."

Tanner bowed. "I won't let you down."

Blair became so excited she could barely contain it. After bouncing around a little with a few shouts of glee she settled back to find Tanner and Bryan staring at her like she was 'special'. "Sorry, let's get into it."

From her vantage point in her room Blair had watched Tanner and Bryan moving around the farm performing different tasks. Even yesterday, watching Tanner preparing for this festival, everything looked so easy. Now that she was actually involved with the work she was horribly mistaken. For most of the morning Blair felt as though she was more of a hindrance than a help and this was only made clearer when Tanner was asked to come over in the afternoon. Bryan said he would pay regular holiday rates, being time and a half, as this was time out of Tanner's personal life. The reason being, Blair needed to have a training session and Bryan would be busy with Jacob this afternoon. Tanner said he was going to need to juggle some things but would see it done.

Blair was still smiling at the outcome when she boarded the bus this morning. Right up until she saw Sophie. Well, until Sophie sat next to her. Blair being too caught up in her own little world she still had yet to determine the best course of action for Sophie's bullies.

"How did your mum take the news?" Blair asked in the hopes of keeping the topic from the bullies. At least Sophie was smiling this morning so it couldn't have gone too bad.

"We sat mum down, me and dad that is. We sat her down and she started to stress out. The mood in the room was already tense with dad and myself. I knew dad was going to be fine. He once sat me down for a talk and said. Sophie if you want to bring home a boy, a girl, a donkey, go right ahead. I won't care for their sex but for the person they show themselves to be. Don't bring home a donkey. He told me this. So I knew he was going to be okay," Sophie said before Blair placed a hand on hers.

"Sophie you're starting to ramble a little. Take a few breaths. Calm. Just tell me what happened," Blair said with a smile and Sophie calmed herself.

"Mum burst into tears," Sophie said after a time. "I had been sad then. I was sure mum wouldn't want me but she pulled me into a long hug. She stroked my hair to console me. It was only later I realised I was crying too."

"So it was good?" Blair asked.

"Mum apologised for the tears saying they were selfish. She had grown up looking forward to watching her daughter walk down the aisle to be with the man of her dreams. To watch and help her daughter bring children into the world made with the man she married. To have secret women's talks about their husbands while the men watched football. She had longed for this all her life and her mind was on the verge of disowning me but for one thing. Me. She loved me dearly and her little daydreams were nothing to watching me truly be happy living the life I wanted." Sophie's eyes had started to dampen again.

"I'm happy for you, Soph," Blair said and Sophie's brow furrowed as she shook her head. "Not... happy?"

"Phia, if you want to use nicknames. Soph is what Elise and the other girls use while they tease me," Sophie said.

"Phia it is," Blair replied happy in the fact she hadn't hurt her and now she even had the head bullies name. This was valuable indeed. "And the rest of your night?"

"Mum and dad really made it about me. Had my favourite food, watched my favourite movie. I got to sit snuggled up between them. We all talked about fun memories. It was just a night where I truly felt loved. No matter what happens here on out, how much we may fight or be put off by one another, I know they love me regardless."

Sophie looked so happy in that moment that Blair felt a little envious. She would never have the chance to experience that with her broken family. And this was the headspace Blair was in when she got off the bus behind Sophie, when she saw the group of girls start on Sophie almost immediately, when she heard one of the girls mention Elise by name. It was clear that she was in charge.

It was in that moment Blair's instincts took over. Walking past Sophie and straight into the thick of it, Blair started to hear a sentence from Elise along the lines of 'was she Sophie's girlfriend' or some such. Blair's hand snaked out with such force that the slap sent Elise to the pavement causing grazes on elbows and knees.

Blair could see Elise about to cry but she bent down right in her face, the fear pausing the younger girl's tears. "If you ever even try to come after Sophie again, I will do far more than bitch slap your horrid little face. You'll know just what it is to be fucked by a real woman and it won't be the fun kind." Blair's voice was so low only Elise could hear, but the strength and ice behind her words stilled the other girl's heart.

Scrabbling to her feet, Elise burst into tears as she took off in any direction she could that wasn't towards Blair. Some of the other girls ran after Elise but some of the more game girls stayed to turn their attention on Blair.

"What did you say to Elise?" one girl said approaching Blair and shoving her in the shoulder.

Fast like a snake, Blair's hand shot out to grab the girl by the throat. She gained complete control over the girl with now bulging green eyes. If the girl tried to move one way, Blair just dragged her straight back into place. "I will say this one more time and one more time only. Any girl who decides that Sophie should be a target just for being herself they will have me to deal with. I will not go easy on you. I will not care just who is watching. If you are teasing or bullying my friend then you are my enemy and I will plough you the fuck down." To emphasise her words, Blair threw the girl she had to the ground.

The girl started wheezing and struggling to take in great gulps of air. Her friends came in and half picked her up, half dragged her away.

"Thank you, Blair," Sophie said. There was a little fear in her voice but Sophie knew she was safe. "I fear you may have attracted the wrong attention though."

Blair looked back and found the eyes of three teachers on her. One raised a hand and motioned for her to approach. Nodding, Blair turned back to Sophie. "I hadn't planned any of this but I'm not sorry for what I've done. Find Lillian if you need anything." With that Blair turned and started off to the staff. Behind her Sophie called out that she would let Lillian know what happened to which Blair was grateful. Blair stood tall in front of her judges.

"I assume you know where you're going?" One teacher asked.

Blair nodded. "To see the principal."

"Mr Pertouski here has elected to escort you there to give an account of what was seen and ensure you arrive."

"Then shall we?" Blair bowed her head to her friend's dad.

Mr Pertouski took his place beside her and the two started off on the walk to the other side of the school. "Should I be worried that my daughter has you as a friend?

"It depends on where your morals lie. I understand that there are better ways to deal with things but I needed a quick, harsh solution that would be remembered. I am sorry for my display but not my reasoning."

A smile crept across the man's face. "Don't worry. I know what you're trying to achieve and am honestly relieved you know there are better ways to do things. I would be a hypocrite to reprimand you any further. I believe in the good person you are outside some rash choices."

"So... I'm free to go?" Blair asked hopefully.

"Well, no. I still need to do my job and all choices have consequences. Remember that. Also remember Mr Henderson doesn't like controversy in the school."

"I will." There was nothing about the moment that scared Blair or made her think twice about what she did. She truly believed she'd done the right thing.

Unlike most books or movies that Blair had seen, the principal of this school had a rather normal and even boring name, Rodney Henderson. The room was behind a glass wall so that no rumours could be made up after students had entered putting the Principal's job in jeopardy. The furniture was basic and a picture of his wife was on the table.

As Blair was motioned in and took a seat in front of the Principal, Mr Pertouski gave an account of what happened.

"Thank you, Cooper, you can go," Mr Henderson said. Waiting for Mr Pertouski to leave, Mr Henderson continued to try and intimidate Blair, staring her down. "Anything more you wanted to add?"

"I only acted as I did to defend my friend who was being bullied."

"There was no talk of bullying."

"No. The teachers here wouldn't have seen it, but it's been going on for days. The girls were getting ready for another round so I acted pre-emptively to put a stop to it for good."

"By beating these younger girls up? It doesn't seem like a good enough reason."

"Then what about the school allowing discrimination for a minority."

"Sophie Berrum? She is a Caucasian girl from a prominent farming family. How can you call her a minority in this region. Maybe back in the city?"

"Sophie's sexual alignment is towards the female gender. To reprimand me for defending my friend, after she came to me for help mind you, from a bunch of girls that had targeted her for being gay will not go down well in the papers."

114

The principal's eyes grew wide as this news came to light and he seemed to physically shrink back. Swivelling on his chair he weighed his options. "You believe what you have done will be the end of it?"

"Yes," Blair replied confidently.

"As this is your first offence and we have no real way to determine who was in the wrong, I will overlook suspension. You'll have a weeks' worth of detentions after school but know this..." He leaned forward pointing a finger. "This school has a zero tolerance for violence. If you enter my office again over a physical offense it is an immediate suspension. Am I clear?"

"Yes, sir. I am sorry, sir," Blair said as she stood and bowed low. "And just know that me missing the bus is going to upset my dad, having to pick me up each day. He won't let me off so easy.' Blair added this to sound like she still got the raw end of things but knew that most days Bryan was picking Jacob up anyway.

Mr Henderson nodded. "Get off to your class."

Taking in a deep calming breath as she left the office, Blair realised she was shaking. She'd never been one to play up in school and had never been sent to the principal. Rubbing her hands together to gain some calm, she took off to... maths. "Ha," Blair said aloud. At least those close to her would find out her fate quickly.

Reaching the maths block Blair arrived as Lillian was entering. The small girl looked so low and as she entered glanced across to see Blair just smiling at her. Pausing in her tracks Lillian was knocked clean over by the person coming up behind. After taking the curses that were grumbled her way, Lillian came running out and dove on Blair in a massive hug.

"You're still here! What happened with Principal Henderson?" Lillian was almost squealing.

"Let off with a warning. I see Sophie found you?" Blair asked.

"Yeah, she told me what you'd done for her and why." Lillian looked so proud of Blair at this moment that Blair actually blushed. "I'm so thankful to have a friend like you in my life, Blair."

"Stop, I still gotta get my head through the doors."

Letting go, Lillian led the way to their class and seats.

115

There was a bounce in her step that Blair rarely ever got to see. Blair felt blessed to have a friend such as Lillian also. Entering the room, she stopped a moment to give a quick, respectful bow to Mr Pertouski for his advice. It was only a tilt of her head, eyes closed but the emotion was all encompassing.

"You'll be fine to stay this lesson?" Mr Pertouski asked.

"And any other this week." Blair took her seat, and the lesson began. A number of notes passed between Blair and Lillian was overlooked as they also managed to complete their work.

"Guess it isn't over," Blair said.

The day had a rather slow pace to it. Lessons were boring and the teachers seemed to drone on. Even recess, there was very little happening that got time flowing. Sophie was with her friends who had even accepted her with all the rumours flying around. Sophie did confirm the true facts with them.

Now, mid lunch and Astrid was marching straight at her. There was such determination in her face that Blair knew an argument was about to break out. Behind, a smaller figure was following with a smug smile on her face.

"That Elise?" Lillian asked.

"The one lurking around behind Astrid? Yeah. Why's that?" Blair said.

"It's Astrid's younger sister."

"Why doesn't that surprise me? Okay let's get this over with. I may be taking a few days off after all."

"Understandable. Need help?" Lillian asked.

Blair smiled. "No need for us both to get suspended. And our hunky Daddy may get upset."

"You're on your own..." Lillian said with a level glare before sitting down and making herself comfortable.

Several students were following behind ready for a showdown. Blair was always astounded at how even the chance of a fight could get around the whole school within moments. She needed to use this though and there was only moments... well laughing is always a good start.

A ripple of laughter burst forth from Blair as the sisters got near. Astrid began to slow and Elise looked confused. "Look everyone. Look at the sisters afraid of a little girly

116

love," Blair said with glee. She needed to keep this light. If she came off as the aggressor at the beginning, Astrid would come off as the good guy. A number of people in the crowd began to look from side to side unsure what was happening.

"That's not why we're here. Is it true you beat my sister for no reason this morning?" Astrid said, ignoring Blair's odd outburst.

"No," Blair said simply. The girls had given away the upper hand having gone straight into questioning.

"Liar!" Elise screamed.

"No, I'm not," Blair remained calm.

"You did so!" Elise was getting out of control.

"I can't see how that's possible." Blair walked over to the nearest muscly guy and leaned against him casually. May as well have a little fun while I'm at it, Blair thought. "Sure, I slapped Elise this morning. I even did it with as much force as I could muster..."

"See!" Elise cried but the crowd was focused on Blair.

"Yes, yes, Elise. Calm your farm," Blair waved a hand and turned back to her spunky little stand. "As I was saying, I did slap this girl but only in defence of my friend, Sophie. You here, Phia?"

A hand shot up in the crowd and started waving.

Blair motioned to Sophie. "Look at this little thing. Not a bit of muscle or even flab to defend herself and she was targeted and bullied by a number of girls all because our little Sophie here prefers girls."

Sophie blushed as all eyes turned on her.

"You would understand that, wouldn't you, my muscly friend? You can see the allure of a sexy woman?" Blair started tracing her finger over the guy's chest.

"Nope," came the reply.

Blair's eyes shot up. "What?'

"I like my women as men."

Blair was stunned a moment before laughter bubbled to the surface spilling out everywhere. "I was under the impression that the gay community in this school was almost non-existent." She pointed questioningly at the geeky looking guy next to them and muscles just shrugged. "You like girls right?"

The geeky guy went as red as Sophie. "Will you hug me

117

if I do?"

"He likes girls," Blair tussled the geeky guy's hair and walked into the middle of the ever growing crowd. "So we have one guy that likes guys, one guy that likes girls, and one girl that likes girls. Lillian?"

"I like girls," Lillian called.

"How bout I pick people at random and we find out just how different everyone really is." Blair pointed at guys and girls around the circle and one by one they started calling out what they preferred. It hadn't surprised Blair that most preferred the opposite sex but a small handful had called the same sex, and there was even one bisexual. Well, Blair couldn't be sure for one answer but liked to believe it helped her cause.

Spinning on her heel, Blair reached out pointing at another person only to quickly shift away from Mary to the person beside her. Caught off guard by the quick change, the next person awkwardly tried to say males and stumbled over her tongue twice.

"GIRLS!" Mary yelled and Blair's heart skipped a beat.

"Lamby, what are you saying?" her friends looked worried.

"I LIKE GIRLS!" Mary calmed a little and looked over at Lillian. "I... Love Lillian."

"Oh, Lamby, why didn't you tell us?"

Blair's heart almost melted for the freckled girl but not as much as Lillian's when Mary told the whole school it was her that she loved. In two beats of a moment, Lillian was in Mary's arms, the embrace so warm and full of love; a wave of aww ran around the school.

"That's fucking disgusting! You people are all sick!" Elise was screaming at everyone. She looked up at Blair as she approached. "You fucking wh..."

A loud, sickening crack echoed across the yard as the slap sent Elise into a dive for the second time today. Rubbing her palm with her thumb, Blair didn't have time to relax as Astrid closed in.

Talking a handful of Blair's hair, Astrid started to throw her around. Head aflame in pain, Blair shot out a foot to hook the back of Astrid's knee sending her aggressor off balance and tumbling to her back. As she was holding Blair's hair, Blair fell with her to land on top, head pulled into Astrid's poor imitation for breasts.

"You know, I like it when girls play rough and force my face into their tits," Blair said trying to sound turned on.

As a reaction, Astrid gave up her only advantage by throwing Blair's head back. Recovering quickly and straddling the older girl, Blair punched Astrid in the face knocking her clean out.

The geeky guy came over and helped Blair to her feet, ignoring Astrid and Elise. It wasn't easy to determine where it began as the students crowded in closer but a slow clap had started and was soon taken up by everyone there. Blair stood rubbing her head half from pain, half in embarrassment for being the focal point of such a commotion. She saw Lillian smiling at her, head still resting against Mary's chest. They looked so happy to finally be free to love each other openly.

A hand rested on Blair's shoulder. "Such a strong right has gotten the attention of the principal. He has asked for your presence in his office. I'll tend to the two on the ground," Mr Pertouski said. He leaned in close to Blair while looking at his daughter and girlfriend. "And thank you."

A simple nod and a smile was enough. She waved to Lillian before heading over to the Principal's office also for the second time today.

"You didn't even last half a day," Mr Henderson said. He, in no way, looked pleased to find Blair in his office once more. "I don't need you to say a word. Your dad's already been called and is on the way to pick you up. Your belongings are being brought to the office. You will be waiting on the seat just out there until collected. Blair Thompson, you are being suspended for multiple counts of violence at school. You are not welcome to return for four school days. If you do you could face more harsh punishments. This is why there is a zero tolerance rule for violence. It always creates more. Go."

Well that was easier than expected, Blair thought as she made her way out to the corridor lounge. She believed there would be yelling or at least a raised voice but no. Principal Henderson just laid out her punishment and sent her on her way. I guess he must've felt a small part responsible having let Blair back into the playground after

119

the first incident. What was more surprising was when Lillian and Mary came bounding down the corridor with her belongings.

"Oh my god, Blair. The whole school is going nuts," Lillian said dropping Blair's things and pulling her into a hug. "You've really made a difference. When you told me you were going to take back the school after we slept together I didn't quite believe it."

"Slept together?" Mary cocked an eyebrow.

"Oh yes, after she watched me changing she just couldn't keep her hands to herself," Blair shot Mary a wink.

"I was asleep," Lillian argued and turned to Mary. "I was asleep."

Mary held a stern look a few moments longer before breaking into a heavenly smile. "You're just lucky I love you and trust you completely. Trust you both, actually." Mary turned to Blair. "I haven't had the chance to properly talk. Thank you for all you've done and if you would have me, I would love to be as close a friend as you are with Lillian."

Blair just held out her hands. Mary took the hint and embraced Blair warmly before jumping and slapping the hand that was working its way down to grasp her butt cheek. Her face went crimson red almost hiding her freckles.

"You wanted to be as close a friend as I am," Lillian slapped her lovers butt. "I'd take that as a yes. You'll come to find she is harmless... now if you're quite finished groping my girlfriend," Lillian said turning on Blair. "The school's changed. People've been coming out left, right, and centre since you were sent to the office. It took so little to break through the dam. Standing up to the oppressor and having someone as loveable as Lamby here to find the courage to announce herself out."

"That was really brave, Mary," Blair said.

"My good friends call me Lamby," Mary said, still steamy.

"Everyone loves you... Lamby. You changed everything today. Without you it was still 50 50 whether it would be remembered."

"I don't know. You were making your point well."

"I was throwing others under the bus. Can you apologise to Sophie. I know she'd come out to her friends but it wasn't my place to out her in front of the school."

"Girls, there's still classes going on. Just drop off the belongings and leave," Mr Henderson said having come to his door.

"Sorry, sir," Lillian and Mary said in unison. They each turned and hugged Blair one last time, Mary groping Blair's butt cheek. "I'll let Sophie know," Lillian assured her. "We'll see you in a few days, yeah?"

"Of course, Lillian. I'll see you both then." Blair then winked at Mary.

Laughter escaped Blair's lips as she heard Mary comment *Oh, we don't grope her?* After Lillian reprimanded her. Laughter that was cut short as Bryan stormed down the hallway.

"In the car," Bryan growled. He said no more as Blair gathered her stuff and got into the car. "Fighting, Blair! How long's it been? A couple weeks at this school and you're fighting?"

"Defending," Blair corrected.

"You knocked a girl out and sent a number of other girls flying. Where is the defence in that?"

"Jacob told you about the girl that was bullying me, correct."

Bryan's eyes narrowed. "...He did."

"Yesterday, I met another girl that was being bullied. I comforted her and got her to tell me everything that was happening. This morning when her bully and the bully's group confronted her I defended her. I talked this over with the principal and was allowed to stay."

"And the second incident?"

"It seems Sophie's bully is the sister of my bully. Sophie's bully mustn't have enjoyed getting a little of her own back and got her sister to confront me. I was handling it without violence this time until Elise got fed up and came at me. I slapped her down once more causing Astrid to feel obliged to fight."

"Tanner's girlfriend?" Bryan asked.

"The same. I think she targeted me because Tanner works at the farm and she was jealous. Same reason she came over the other day to show me she has a strong hold over Tanner that I couldn't hope to break."

"And she had always been so nice to me. Do I need to let

Tanner go?" Bryan looked worried.

"Heavens no, Dad! Don't punish the dog for his bitch."

A held breath was released as Bryan got his answer before realising what Blair said. "Just wanted to call her a bitch?"

"Yeah," Blair smiled.

"She won't be welcome to the farm again. Well, the story you tell and the story the school has given are rather different. Just know that Mr Berrum came round to see me this morning with nothing but praise for you regarding Sophie. I have an idea which version of today's story is accurate. I can see you've dealt with your issues as best you could though violence should never be the answer. You know you can come to me with anything."

"I know, dad, but I've lived on my own long enough that I'm used to persevering."

Bryan fell silent a moment. "Since you're home it'll give me the chance to help get you up to speed for the weekend. You're going to have to deal with Tanner as he may be angry with you and you'll be working together a lot more."

"I don't think that'll be an issue," Blair smiled inwardly.

"Meaning?"

"Nothing dad. I'll smooth things over with him."

The sound of Tanner's pickup was unmistakable over the noise of the tractor. Butterflies started to multiply in Blair's stomach, and she started to become fidgety. She knew Tanner's feelings for her but could that've changed having decked his girlfriend. Maybe his feelings shifted back to Astrid after their picnic. She'd had a long day of worrying thoughts niggling away at her confidence.

"You made your bed, now you'll have to lay in it with him," Bryan said noticing Blair's shift in attitude then paused. "Not... you don't need to be in bed with Tanner... I only meant."

"It's okay, dad. I understood." Blair giggled then shot her dad a wink. "But he is hot."

Looking flustered and still not used to the ways of teenage girls, Bryan walked away to occupy himself in something he was better equipped for. This left Blair alone with no backup or support should Tanner prove to be hostile. Intertwining her fingers to keep them still, Blair watched the pickup come into view then park close by. As Tanner stepped from the vehicle, Blair's heart sank. The look on his face spoke a thousand words, all curse words, all directed at her.

"Tanner. I'm... I'm sorry for what happened today," Blair stammered.

Eyes like jagged metal shards pierced her soul, but Tanner remained still. Blair stood, shifting from foot to foot. She had been so confident that Tanner's heart was hers, that his true feelings had her at the centre of them but was that rewritten too like the first Sunday she shared with him?

"I never wanted anything to affect our relationship. I know Astrid is your girlfriend, but I still needed to stand up for myself and my friends. I'd hoped you could distinguish a difference in the matter of our relationship and mine and her relationship," Blair's lip had started to quiver, and a lump was forming in her throat.

Hard as stone, Tanner stood staring at Blair. Nothing in his manner gave away his thoughts in that moment. A crack in the stone appeared. A small twinge at the corner of his lip that couldn't be held back. I smile formed on Tanner's face and his eyes became soft and endearing. Laughter like the warm promise of summer broke through her sad wintery world.

"A guy just cut me off no more than 100m back up the road. Sent me off into the dirt and kept going. Didn't care if I was hurt or not. You seemed to take the brunt of my anger against him." Tanner walked over, seeing Blair was on the edge of breaking down and brought her into an embrace. "Sorry if I worried you. Still, you mentioned Astrid. Has something happened? I've been on prac today, though she has been calling no stop."

Realising Tanner didn't know anything about what occurred earlier she took the moment to hug into him. If it was to be the last hug she got then she needed to make the most of it. Finally, gathering the courage to speak, Blair spoke in soft tones. "I punched her."

"Sorry, what?" Tanner didn't quite hear and Blair broke into a deluge of information. Her mouth was running at a hundred miles an hour and when she finished, Blair looked up with her sad puppy dog eyes. The embrace continued.

123

Again, a warm, light laughter filled the farm. "Blair, you really know how to warm my soul. Thank you for punching Astrid."

"Umm... You're welcome." Blair was completely confused by this reaction and Tanner saw it.

"Astrid has a darkness in her heart she tries to hold back. I don't condone bullying of any sort. Normally, she is kind, considerate... Shy even, but when you get targeted by the darkness, she becomes relentless. I've talked to her many times about it but she doesn't always listen. That you have stood up to her and come out on top may help to curb her mannerisms. So, yes, I thank you."

Astrid, shy? Blair couldn't help thinking they were talking about two different people. Maybe there was a different side to her she hadn't seen. "I guess everyone has a time and a place where they can smile. Even one such as Astrid. Then yes, you are welcome for my help. I will '*help*' any chance I can get."

They were both smiling now and at some point, Tanner must've realised they were still hugging. He took a step back causing Blair to pout, internally this time. "So, you'll have plenty of time to get ready for the festival then," Tanner said.

"Dad's gone over a fair bit already, but I'm still ready to learn and help as need be," Blair replied.

"I'm glad to hear. I was starting to think I was going to be doing my regular workload and be tidying up the mess you'd be creating." There was a smile backing the comment telling Blair he was in a cheeky mood.

"You just want more time to flirt around with all the women," she replied.

"Whatever gets the money rolling," Tanner said with a wink.

"Hey, don't think your little winky winks will work on me Mr."

"But I'm hot remember," Tanner said with a smirk.

"As am I if I recall. Playing field remains even," Blair said not missing a beat.

Eyes narrowed and at a stalemate Tanner walked past scruffling Blair's hair. In a moment of silly stupidity and feeling like a little puppy getting a pat from her master, Blair let out a little bark. Immediately, her face went bright red.

Pausing Tanner glanced back. "Did you just bark?"

"No," Blair squealed louder than she meant to.

Tanner just stared a few moments longer. "Come along, little pup. We have work to do."

An embarrassed smile touched Blair's lips as she bit the lower one. She knew she was already too far in. "Woof," she said and fell in behind.

Chapter 8 – To the festival

It was a surprise to be so close to Tanner for hours and be disappointed. Blair had fantasised of cute little trysts ending in a stolen kiss or... more. Tanner though was all business. Sure there was flirting and jests before the work began or one or two at break but in all Tanner was professional.

That, though, is where the disappointment ended. Watching her love working hard at his job was joyous in itself. Seeing Tanner lifting heavy objects, feeding the farm animals, sneaking Shadow a slice of bacon... Sweating. Blair blushed. Just the overall enthusiasm and care he showed in his work was amazing. He was still beautiful even when he was reprimanding her for getting something wrong. She was normally getting something wrong because he was beautiful.

And so, Blair spent her suspension in disappointed bliss. Working hard, close to the man she wanted to spend her life with. Her favourite time though was right at dusk when the sun was setting. With Tanner silhouetted against an orange sky, time would freeze as if heaven was here on earth. Then the sun would sink into the earth beneath and darkness would start to set in with the promise of Tanner's departure. That may be the harshest time of the day.

The mornings with Tanner were different. As the week dragged on and Blair continued to persevere in getting up early she became more and more tired. The mornings became a blur and very little stuck in Blair's memory. Suddenly, her dad would take over and the rest of the day was harder still having no eye candy around.

Once more afternoon and the sound Blair longed for reached her ears. Tanner was here. She raced round the front and stopped in her tracks. The passenger door was open. She would need to share her afternoon with him. And after she snuck herself a sleep in the hay shed to be more alert.

Getting a glimpse of the passenger, Blair's eyes went wide. She would need to share Tanner with another girl...

"Blair!" Lillian ran over and dove into her friends arms.

Still recovering from the shock of Tanner bringing over another girl Blair pushed Lillian back to get a look of her.

126

Her face exploding into lines of love and joy... A squeal really set the mood and Blair brought Lillian back into a strong embrace. The girls bounced around for a few moments.

"Sorry, Blair, but I'm stealing you away for the afternoon," Lillian said.

Turning, Blair caught the eye of Tanner as he was shaking his head at the girls. "Sorry, my little bonbon sugar baby, got a better offer for the night. Guess I'll be seeing you in the morning."

"Understandable. Maybe at the bonfire if you girls make it down."

"We have a bonfire," Blair cocked her head to one side.

Tanner laughed. "Oh puppy, just look for the light after dark." Tanner continued to his work.

"What?" Blair had turned to find Lillian with a cheeky little smile on her face.

"You've gotten far more comfortable with youuur... Little Bonbon Sugar Baby."

"Oh," and Blair blushed hard. "It sorta just came to me."

"But the fact you can say it so easily with him."

Blair leaned in close. "It's easy to do after you've slept with a man. Being a little silly is nothing after exposing your inner soul to someone."

"But he doesn't know that. He's never seen you so vulnerable," Lillian pointed out.

"I know. It's more that when I had that wonderful afternoon, I gained the confidence on the first time. I know it happened and now I can't lose that confidence, if ya get me. I know what he's like and the oddities in his nature. It's like I've known him since the birth of time."

"I do know what you mean," Lillian said, her mind drifting to her love.

"Lamby?"

"There could be no other."

Blair smiled warmly at her friend. She felt so lucky to have found Lillian. If it was up to her she would have been late to school that first day but Jacob needed to be in earlier. Another thing she needed to thank Jacob for. "Let's go raid Jacob's room."

"My thoughts exactly," Lillian said.

"Pfft, your thoughts were freckles and tits," Blair said

127

with a nudge.

Lillian paused and let out a sigh. "Yeah."

With a giggle Blair took off into the house, Lillian close behind. Lillian diverted off into Jacob's while Blair waited at the base of the steps.

"Blair," came a shout from Lillian and Blair rushed back to the room. She knew Jacob wasn't home until morning. Entering, she found Lillian standing over Jacob's stash.

"What? He start sneaking in nudey mags?"

"It's this." Lillian pulled out a small parcel of sheer, purple cloth. It was folded in a way that all the sides met at the top of the basketball sized sphere. A gold ribbon secured the cloth so that it remained shut. On one side was a small yellow card.

"Blair," Lillian read holding the card open. "You've changed my life. You've given me a sister to fight with and tease. To love and protect. I knew you and Lillian would be back." On the side it had a little *'Hi Lillian'*. "And so, I prepared this for you in the hopes I wouldn't lose my favourites again." Lillian suddenly threw the card down, a look of disgust on her face.

"But the card was so lovely?" Blair said looking at it lying where it was discarded.

"You can keep it if you want," Lillian said.

"I think I might." Blair bent over and picked up the card running her eyes over the words one more time, finding the sentence Lillian had omitted.

'P.S. I farted on this card.'

"That little shit. He would've too," Blair said, also throwing the card. "If you see any Turkish Delights, take them. I don't like them, but Jacob can't get enough."

"Daddy..." cough, cough. Lillian made the pretence of clearing her throat. "Dad loves them at least."

Blair let that one slide and they took off up to the room. "I wonder where the fire is that Tanner was talking about."

Lillian cocked an eyebrow. "Seriously? I don't live here and already saw the prep work for it."

Blair just raised her eyebrow right back at the girl.

With a 360-degree view Lillian walked the room until she reached the desired window. Raising a finger, she nudged it outside a few times.

With pursed lips, Blair walked over to the window.

"That? But that's a pile of old fence posts, broken furniture, and other random bits and pieces. There're even a large amount of barbed wire. There're barely any tree trunks or anything in that."

"Is it wood?"

"Well, mostly."

"Will it, *mostly,* burn."

"Yeah?"

"There you go. Bonfire. You're still a city girl at heart."

"I thought it was rubbish to take to the tip."

"If it burns, we like to have fires. Whatever's left can go to the tip."

Blair decided it was time to change the subject. "I never asked, how did you talk Tanner into giving you a lift out here? Astrid surely would have flipped her lid."

"I just asked him straight out. He looked me in the eyes a moment then shrugged and said *'Blair's ready so sure.'* I didn't quite grasp his meaning."

"He and dad have been training me for the Harvest Fes... He said I'm ready?" Blair's face lit up.

With a nod, Lillian smiled at her slow friend. "You have such a funny tunnel vision sometimes. I love seeing your mind start catching the intricacies in what is said."

"Oh, shush, you," Blair pushed the smaller girl by the shoulder.

"Mary wanted to come too but I'm guessing there'd be only one seat spare in Tanner's car for the return trip early tomorrow."

"She could have come and got all snuggly this time," Blair said with a smirk.

"She thought it'd be too awkward on the first sleep over to be alone with you." Lillian's face was somewhere between angry and pouty. The edge in her voice though...

"I know you love your Lamby. I'm not going to steal her from you... much." Blair let out a little giggle as she threw Lillian a wink.

"She's grown very fond of you very quickly. She was the one that suggested this little night out here. Had her own motivations, I think." There was a cheeky smile behind Lillian's words, but Blair didn't catch it.

"I'm sure it's only to create a closer bond with her lover's close friend. Nothing sus."

"I know," Lillian's smile deepened.

"Looks like they're getting ready to light the bonfire," Lillian said as she watched Tanner retrieve the petrol tin and Bryan retrieve the matches. Several neighbours had come for the event. Camp chairs had been set up with a BBQ cooking steaks and sausages and a table with other food and drink. There were a lot of voices reaching the room and Blair and Lillian found plenty to tease and amuse themselves with in other's conversations.

Coming to sit beside Lillian, Blair saw her dad wave up at them.

"You two coming down. We're lighting now," Bryan called.

"Nah, we're hap..." Blair started.

"We'll be right down, Mr Thompson," Lillian cut in. She jumped to her feet and offered Blair a hand up. "Come on. If you haven't seen a bonfire lit, you really need to experience it up close. And anyway, it'll give you a chance to get closer to Tanner."

With a pout Blair reached out and took Lillian's hand. She really didn't want to mingle with so many people and as the hosts daughter they were going to ask her a lot of questions. Lillian was rather enthusiastic though so there was possibly something good to it. As they reached the first landing down the stairs, however, Lillian turned back.

"Sorry, just gotta get something from my bag. Wait for me?"

Blair seemed shocked she would even ask. "I'm not going out there alone."

Racing back into the room, Lillian went straight to the nightstand. Blair's phone was just sitting there, and she picked it up looking it over. "Oh well, guess I'd better take it." And with that hid it in her bag before heading back out to see Blair.

"Get what you needed?" Blair asked.

"Wasn't there. Left the torch at home," Lillian replied evenly.

"Tanner took you home to get your things?"

A little giggle bubbled from Lillian. "Nope. Had my bag packed before heading to school."

"Well now, it really was planned ahead."

"Of course," Lillian replied and raced down the stairs.

Giving chase Blair reached her just after exploding out the rear entrance to the house. All eyes turned back to the girls and they paused with Blair half wrestling Lillian.

"Blair, Lillian," a voice from the small crowd called and Sophie came bounding over. Everyone lost interest and turned back to the fire.

"Sophie! I didn't know you were here. You should've come up. I'm at the very top," Blair said turning and pointing up to the highest windows.

A nervous sway started in Sophie's posture. "I didn't want to intrude," she said coyly.

"Never," Lillian replied. "You're our friend and as such are welcome to see us anytime you want. Especially when you're over and alone in a crowd."

"I'll remember that next time," Sophie said.

"Everyone ready!" Brian called and a loud cheer came from the crowd. Tanner was walking around the stack pouring fuel before he made a long ignition trail. "Now that I have your attention, I'd like to say a few words. The Harvest Fes..." Bryan began to the moaning of the crowd.

Leaning in to Blair, Lillian nudged her side. "Now's your chance. Tanner's gunna be all alone lighting that fire. Go."

"But I..."

"Go!" Lillian repeated pushing her friend along.

Walking only a few metres, Blair turned to retreat but found Lillian already standing with her arm out pointing at Tanner.

"What do I even say? I haven't been to a bonfire before." Blair was flaring her arms in a questioning stance.

"Don't say anything," Sophie said. She seemed happy to be able to give input. "Walk over, stand next to him and he'll do the rest."

Blair didn't move.

"Go," both Lillian and Sophie said in unison.

With a pout and completely defeated she turned and walked over to where Tanner was standing in the dark facing the bonfire. Standing near him a moment he pulled her closer to stand right beside.

"The petrol line was right where you were. Stick with me and you'll be safe," Tanner said is soft tones. Bryan was still taking in the background so Tanner didn't want to speak over him.

"Thank you," Blair said just as softly. For her though, she found herself to be extremely embarrassed. She couldn't quite pinpoint just what it was but her hands had started to shake. She stood trying to think of something smart or funny to say to break the ice but her mind was full of fuzz.

An arm reached out and took her by the waist causing Blair to suddenly go stiff. The arm drew her across to stand just in front of Tanner before another arm reached around to hold her. The warmth that flowed over her, the sweet, intoxicating smell of a working body, the tingling, curling waves of the breath on the back of her neck. This was what forever felt like and Blair was slowly falling into it.

"I wanted to watch the stars with you tonight but soon the fire will steal them from the sky," Tanner whispered in her ear.

The words sent electricity through her body bringing on goosebumps. She looked up and was amazed at just how bright they were tonight. The new moon gave strength to the stars and they crossed the sky like a river of white silk. The moment was perfect up to the second Blair's brain became active once more. Astrid? Blair started to pull away.

"What's wrong?" Tanner asked still trying to keep a tentative hand on Blair's side.

"We can't do this. You're taken."

Tanner just smiled. "So, Lillian hasn't told you? Astrid told me it was her or the Harvest Festival. It was a big thing in front of the whole school. I walked away. My heart was already on this farm."

Blair, having already had this conversation, melted right back into his arms. She knew the way he felt for her and with Astrid out of the way, her conscious could be spared too. "The stars truly are beautiful tonight. It's crazy just how much we forget they're there."

"And where's my daughter? Blair?" Bryan said looking over at Lillian who directed him to where she stood wrapped in the farm hands arms. "Ahem, moving on." The speech continued another five minutes before they were ready to light the fire.

"Squat next to me, okay Blair," Tanner said as he got

lower to the ground to light the fire. Blair followed suit and after the match was struck and the flames touched the fuel she was glad for it. Had she been standing she would have thrown herself backwards and off balance. Even still she needed to grab Tanner's arm to stabilise herself. Fire shot like a bullet across the grass straight at the bonfire. The speed at which it travelled was actually rather terrifying to Blair, thinking what she would do in a burning building. And like an explosion the flames found the soaked wooden pile and burst into a massive fire ball that could've been seen for miles around. The flaming ball of light raced into the sky higher than the house before dispersing into the cool breeze. Heat reached out its forgiving hand and whole heartedly embraced the onlookers with a tender caress. Blair was having difficulty deciding just which heat was better, the fire's or Tanner's until she felt movement across her butt cheek. Movement that could only be from Tanner's... "Ahh, that's the heat I like most."

"What's that?" Tanner asked.

Blair knew it wasn't the time or place to experience again what she alone had memory of and spun in Tanner's arm to face him. The bulge in his pants nestling right into her honeypot meant that Blair was soon going to lose all control.

Reaching up a tender hand, Blair caressed Tanners, fuzzy, stubbly face. Their eyes lost to one another, they each moved in unison, the kiss so soft and sweet. It was love, it was life, it was the beautiful colours bouncing off each droplet of water in a sudden sun shower. This moment stood still as if time itself had been struck by the moment forgetting how to time.

Blair pulled back ever so slightly. Enough that their lips, still trying to hold on, parted ways. "Show me a day like no other tomorrow and maybe we can continue what was just started," Blair said in a raspy voice. Her hand still cupping his face.

With a kiss to the forehead, Tanner stepped back and bowed. "On the morrow then, my lady."

The smile almost held Blair in place. Almost, but she mustered just enough willpower to spin on her heel and speed off to her friends. She was blushing as she got to them and they took her into a close packed circle to hear all about it.

"In the room," Blair said before racing to the front door with Lillian. She turned back. "Sophie, dad will come and get you when yours is leaving."

With that Sophie let her resignations fall and followed her friends into the house and up to Blair's room.

Immediately, Blair chided Lillian for not warning her of Tanner's single status to which Lillian laughed saying it was better this way.

"It just would have been good to know, is all," Blair grumbled.

"Hey, I just found a card in the bottom of the sweets basket. All it says is '*And here*'," Sophie said looking a little confused.

Both, the other girls, however, knew exactly what it was about and cursed Jacob excessively.

And soon the night was coming to an end. Sophie had left an hour before leaving Blair and Lillian to sit watching the dying fire. The low embers crackling as the cool breeze touched them sending sparks like fireflies into the night sky.

"I feel my life is working out just right," Blair said.

"If there was anyone that deserved it more I couldn't think of them," Lillian replied. "You're a wonderful, kind soul, Blair. I'm glad you've found your twin flame."

"And I'm glad you've found yours. It warms my heart to see how deeply in love you and Lamby are."

"I love you, Blair. Thank you for coming into my life."

"I love you too, Lillian. Thank you for giving me the time I needed and not letting me sneak off into my own solitary world. Thank you for fighting for me."

With a smile the two girls hugged.

"Bed?" Lillian asked.

"Bed," Blair confirmed.

And this time, with no worry, hesitation, or doubt at how it would be taken, Lillian had changed in front of Blair. True friends they were.

Chapter 9 – The fates giveth

There were only a handful of hours that had passed when Tanner ventured to open the door to Blair's bedroom. He stayed in Jacob's room for a few hours of sleep so they could leave early. A small flutter of light paved it's path from the hallway into the room.

"Blair, Lillian, It's time you girls woke and got ready," Tanner called but the snoring continued. Tentatively, he stepped inside to make his way over to the bed. He was cautious in crossing certain boundaries. Cautious until the sight of the girls caused his blood to boil. The blanket had been thrown away during the night showing the two sleeping beauties clad only in oversized shirts. Blair's, while on her back, had ridden up her silky thighs to just hide the special and sacred world all her own. Tanner was worried even his breath would be enough to expose her.

Lillian on the other hand was laying with her head on Blair's shoulder and arms snuggled around her. Her body twisted down to a very exposed butt and lower back, her leg resting over Blair's. It was only shadow that held her modesty intact.

Shaking Blair's shoulder, Tanner started to see her stir and moved on to Lillian. In a sheer act of adolescent stupidity, Tanner slapped Lillian's butt causing her to wake.

"Blair, that wasn't nice... Well, it was but I was having a good dream," Lillian grumbled as her eyelids fought against opening. When they finally did, it wasn't the Blair she thought it would be leaning over her but rather a large silhouette of a man. She let out a shrill scream causing Blair to fully wake.

Seeing the figure, Blair struck out, knocking Tanner to the floor and rose to her knees in front of Lillian, arms wide, protecting her. "Tanner?" She said realising just who was intruding all the while remaining in a defensive stance.

"Sorry, I was trying to wake you," Tanner replied sheepishly.

"He slapped my bare butt," Lillian cried as she leaned in close to Blair looking over her shoulder.

"You slapped her butt?" Blair said, eyes growing dangerous.

Tanner mistook the look as her playing. "To wake he..."

"No!" Blair put a finger up stopping him in his tracks. "You don't slap this butt. You never slap this butt. You don't slap any girl's butt." There was a real growl growing in her voice.

"I... But... I," Tanner stammered. He'd never seen Blair this aggressive.

"No! This is not the butt for you." Blair reached around to grab Lillian's butt cheek for emphasis exciting a little squeal from her friend. "This butt here is my butt. Not yours. Mine. This is mine to touch and slap. Not yours. That was wrong."

"I get it. I'm sorry, Lillian. It was a moment weakness. I came in and found two beautiful women entangled in a bed. My hormones pushed too hard."

"Doesn't matter. I don't care if you found us scissoring naked, it doesn't give you the right to get involved. Get your hands under control, reign in your beast, and get out."

"I'm sor..." Tanner tried to say.

"Get the fuck out, now," Blair's words were like ice as they hit Tanner. "Or dad will be the next person to walk into this room to find out what you've done."

Tanner turned and stepped out of the room. "I'll be waiting in the pickup."

"Scissoring?" Lillian was the first to recover.

Blair took in a few more steadying breaths and turned back to her friend. "All I could really think of. I can't say I know what two girls can really get up to."

"Oh," Lillian gave a sexy little look. "There are... plenty of things I could teach you that would blow your mind apart along with other things."

"Only if Mary's invited."

"Wouldn't have it any other way," Lillian said with a wicked little smile.

"You okay," Blair turned serious, kissing her friend's forehead.

Lillian nodded. "Shocked me is all. I was expecting to see you. Tanner is okay. He is still rather trustworthy... to a certain extent. Anyone else and I would have screamed a lot longer. Don't be too hard on him."

"He deserves what he gets," Blair replied. The smile said she was going to forgive him... this time. "We better get dressed and out the door."

"No scissoring," Lillian pouted sarcastically.

Blair looked around, arms out, palms up. "No Mary?" She countered mimicking the tone.

Taking out a cute shirt and skirt combo, Blair threw them on and looked at herself in the mirror. The skirt had a country flannel pattern of blues and yellows with the bottom finishing just above the knees. She felt... someone was going to need the easy access by end of day. The yellow top was light and spoke of the sun and great harvests. She would be surprised if anyone else thought of that though. They hugged her breasts a little too well.

Walking to the nightstand, Blair looked over and around it for her phone. "Lillian, you seen my phone anywhere."

"Umm, no." the lie was accepted too easily. "You wouldn't need it this weekend anyway. Can't even make a call."

"I told you, it feels like mum is with me when I have it."

"So, you're going on a trip with a really hot guy, and you want to bring mummy?"

"Well, no," Blair said sadly. "But I did want to say goodbye at least."

"She lives in here," Lillian reached over to touch her heart.

Eyes narrowing, Blair's mood instantly shifted. "You really are getting creative with ways to touch my boobs. Even got mum involved."

"I don't just sit idle, you know." Lillian breathed easier knowing Blair had moved on. She collected her things. "I'm ready when you are."

"Okay..." Blair looked her over. "Lil, you only put pants on under my shirt. My pants."

"I plan on going back to sleep when I get home. And I like stealing your things."

"Git," Blair said with a big smile, gesturing towards the door and shaking her head.

Outside and Tanner was waiting by the passenger door. He looked somehow official even though he only wore a white shirt and jeans. Opening the door and bowing deep, he waited. The sentiment was caught by both Blair and Lillian and after securing their bags in the back, Lillian ushered Blair in first to take the middle seat.

"My deepest apologies, Lillian," Tanner said renewing the bow. "I will endeavour to keep my hands to myself."

"You've always been nice to me, Tanner. Even when others were teasing me or putting me down, you gave me hope for humanities kindness."

Tanner rose.

"I will forgive you this once and pretend it was Blair's butt you were aiming for." Lillian smiled.

"Hey," Blair protested.

"Thank you. I will rewrite it in my mind to be the same," Tanner returned the smile.

"Hey!" Blair protested again and again was ignored.

As Tanner pulled himself up and into the driver's seat a hand caught him by the scruff of the neck and drew him close. "You do something like that again and I won't be as forgiving as our little saint back there. If you need a butt to smack in the future, you smack mine. Don't you dare miss." Before Tanner had a chance to reply Blair pulled him the extra millimetres for a strong, steamy kiss.

"Were you sure I wanted to be kissed," Tanner objected.

Blair kissed him again. "I don't believe you're in any position to protest having tried to slap my arse and fail miserably."

"Touché."

"Drive."

As the light came on and the engine roared, Lillian was giggling to herself profusely. "You two act like such a married couple."

"Our souls have known each other across the span of the universe." Tanner had not an idea where that line came from but it felt right. Wrapping an arm around Blair, she snuggled into him and soon fell asleep.

When it was time for Lillian to depart, she just nodded to Tanner while smiling at their softly snoring friend.

Violently, the world showed its bleary head. Like on a boat, Blair was tossed from side to side as she was forced to wake and discover the trouble they were in. And like on a boat after a storm, the turbulence settled to the sound of Tanner smashing the horn in frustration.

"Sorry, Blair, guy cut me off." Tanner gave an apologetic look. "How was the sleep? You've wasted away a few

138

hours."

"Sleep was good but you still need to practice your wake up techniques," she replied. Looking around, Blair saw the sun was just peeking up over a distant line of mountains. The sky had gained a some crimson and gold but was still a fair way off displaying the deep blue of the morning. A dark spot showing on Tanner's shirt drew her attention and Blair stared a moment before realising why it was damp.

"I'm sorry," she cried, hand moving to the edges of her mouth. Sure enough, a large trail of drool was evident and she wiped vigorously to remove it.

"Not the first time a girl has been wet while laying on me," Tanner pursed his lips thinking. "Wording could have been better."

"Not the first time I've been wet over you," Blair said, a cheeky grin spreading across her face. Then with feigned innocence, "wording could have been better."

Tanner could only shake his head and laugh. "Over the next rise we're going to see the town of Mackerel Springs. Best tidy your hair and get ready. It's going to be a big day."

"I hope so," Blair shot him a wink then shifted to the outer seat where a vanity mirror could be found behind the sunshade.

Over the next rise and the land dropped away into a deep valley. Sunlight had still yet to venture into the depths of this dark world. The town itself sat around the South Eastern end of a large lake fed by an underground spring. Blair could see near the lake a large field where stalls and rides where being set up. The Harvest festival was going to be bigger than she expected, looking more like a fair.

"We'll be working through to about 6. After that, no one's interested in the farming side of things and are here for the rides and side shows. We can wander the grounds a bit, then go to a restaurant for dinner. Bryan booked a couple rooms at a motel for us. Tomorrow's much the same, but we get to finish at 12," Tanner said.

"All sounds good to me but for the waste of money at Dad's expense," Blair replied.

"He is a dad after all. I know I wouldn't be putting our daughter up in a room with another guy. Even the comment about you being hot the other day, I thought he was going to deck me one. Pulled me aside once you were

139

out of site and gave me a good talking to. It was only that I told him about my feelings towards you and my intentions of leaving Astrid that he let me go."

Blair was smiling blissfully.

"What?" Tanner asked, unsure as to what tickled her fancy.

"You said *'our'* daughter... I like that," Blair leaned over and nibbled on his neck.

The car swerved a little as Tanner struggled to keep control. "Hey, hey, hey... I'm driving."

"How well can you drive... distracted," Blair didn't take her eyes from his pants.

"No! You'll send me into an embankment," Tanner said. "You stay in that seat with your seatbelt secure."

"You're no fun," Blair said with a little pout.

"Tell me that tonight."

"Won't be able to speak with my mouth full, now will I?"

"You're on the ball today," Tanner said with a smile.

"Do I need to say it?" Blair had her full lower lip in her mouth as if restraining it from saying the words on the tip of her tongue.

"Wha... No! you don't need to say it," Tanner said seeing the opening for Blair going balls deep. "Gotta work first. Stop distracting."

"I can't help what you're thinking, and I know every time you look at me today, you'll be picturing me *'on the ball'*." Blair loved the idea that giving him the prompt would make it happen more the more he struggled to stop his thoughts.

He glanced across... "Argh, stop! Stop. Work first, play later."

But she didn't stop. Blair was having way too much fun teasing Tanner that when they pulled up at the Festival, Tanner told Blair to go talk to the man at the gate and get there site number.

"You have a better idea what you asking for," she argued.

"I'm going to sit a while longer. I'm not getting out yet."

Tanner actually had a soft blush in the cheeks and Blair got the idea. "I can do that for you," she said leaning over to kiss his cheek. As she did a hand snuck down to grasp tonight's dessert and she felt it throb in excitement.

"Go!" Tanner said smacking her hand.

With a giggle, Blair jumped from the pickup and got the information from the official. "Head left to site 43," Blair said getting back in the vehicle. Upon reaching the site she looked down. "How's Tiny Tanner going?"

"I think you just fixed him with that ego boost." Tanner adjusted himself before jumping from the vehicle. "Come on, here on out, we will be serious about the job. Can you manage that?"

Ripping her eyes from his crotch. "Sorry, what?"

"Blair!" Tanner became stern.

"Okay, I'll behave."

She threw Tanner a cute little pout then got to work herself. Work she wasn't ready for. As much as Tanner and her dad had taught and practiced with her, Blair's mind went completely blank the moment the first customer walked up. Having asked Blair a question, Blair stood, mouth gaping, eyes wide as if the lady slapped her across the face. It was only that Tanner saw what was happening and stepped in that the woman didn't lose all faith in them.

"Sorry, Ma'am. Having just set up ourselves we are unable to direct you to where the nearest coffee stand is. You could try the information booth ten stalls back," Tanner replied politely.

As the woman walked off Blair turned with a stunned look on her face. "Was that what she asked?"

Tanner laughed. "Didn't you hear her?"

"I heard her talk; I just didn't comprehend the words. My mind shut down the moment our eyes met," Blair admitted.

"You're nervous. First job?"

"Well yeah. It wasn't going to be long before I was going to get one in the city, but for the time I had managed to scrape together a life with the minimal money I had."

Tanner nodded having seen her previous apartment. "The hand you've been dealt has seen you grow to be stronger than most your age. I know you can take whatever comes your way. If you want, pretend the people that come up to our stand are me. Talk to them the way you talk to me."

Blair just narrowed her eyes, tilting her head slightly to the side. "Good day sir, how can I service you today?"

141

Tanner smiled seeing his mistake. "Lillian then."

"Good day ma'am, how can I service you today?"

With a sigh, Tanner tried one last time. "And if Jacob was to come around asking about our products putting you in a position to be informative and show your superior knowledge?"

Cocking her head to the side, Blair thought a moment. "I can work with that."

"Good, cos here comes your first Jacob," Tanner said nodding towards a farmer checking out their stuff.

"Good day sir, how can I service you today?" Blair greeted the man. Tanner scoffed as the man eyeballed Blair up and down. Letting the comment slide the customer spoke of his farm and asked a number of questions of Blair in regard to their products and how it could help him. Blair, having broken the ice, fell into the role perfectly, giving the man the required information.

Tanner, listening nearby, excused himself into the conversation and touched on two features Blair either forgot or hadn't been informed of yet. All in all, the man seemed impressed but moved on regardless.

"Damn, I thought I had him," Blair said. Her brow was now burrowed deep in disappointment.

"If only for the servicing comment, he'll be back," Tanner said. "Most people will move on to begin with, especially this early in the day. The less time they have, the more rushed they feel to make a purchase or sign up for certain things. You did well. Said everything you needed to."

The praise just pumped up Blair's head to exploding having come from Tanner. With a Blush and a thank you she turned to the next customer. A customer that seemed to be more interested in Tanner. Blair smiled and decided to hang back until the ladies possible partner came wandering by.

And thus, the day wore on. Many people came and went and for everyone that Blair interacted with, she never missed a beat. Even picked up little bits of information Tanner threw her way, or just some mannerisms he used when talking to customers. She eventually found where the nearest coffee and food stalls were as by afternoon, she was getting hungry and drowsy. And as Tanner predicted the

142

serviceable man did return but was a little let down when Tanner had to be the one to service him as Blair was getting their third coffee.

"Shall we start locking down the stall for the night?" Tanner asked. The sun was drowning in the distant hills over the lake turning the water a burnt orange. And as the sun slowly died away, so too did the customers, being replaced with families and friends looking to enjoy the festivities of the event.

"Do we need to get it all packed away in the Pickup?" Blair asked. She wasn't looking forward to pulling everything down and remaking in the morning.

"Gods no," Tanner replied. "There's little here of actual value to many people. Plus, we have this." He pulled out a large canvas tarp. "We throw this over everything, peg it down and presto, we have a secure stand."

Blair didn't seem convinced.

"No one here cares. I've come back once or twice to find a peg or two out and the canvas sitting awkwardly but nothing's gone or even disturbed."

"I guess," Blair said, eyeing the product. There was nothing here she would waste her time in stealing.

"Well, let's get to it."

Unfolding the tarp, Blair noticed several other stalls doing the same. There was a feeling that nothing more could be done this afternoon shared amongst the hive mind of the stalls. Tanner threw the tarp over their belongings and Blair raced around pushing pegs in the ground at an angle to fight off any strong winds.

"Done," Blair called.

"Then shall we go have some fun?" Tanner asked motioning to the rides and attractions of the festival designed for the families.

A slight blush colouring her cheeks, Blair nodded sheepishly.

"I have just the thing," Tanner said reaching out his hand. As Blair took it, thinking to intertwine their fingers, Tanner pulled her in to wrap his arm around her. Blair, warm and fuzzy, nuzzled into his side as they set off.

Thinking of where Tanner could be taking them, some romantic ride or food, food was always welcome, Blair's spirits deflated instantly upon their arrival. But why should she have assumed any different.

Seeing her reaction, Tanner smiled. "One game. It's my favourite type of attraction and we had so much fun last time."

With a pout, Blair accepted one game of ball toss. "You're going to have to show me the throwing technique again."

"I was hoping you'd say that," Tanner said pulling the wiggly little butt of Blair's back against him. Leaning in by her ear, Tanner whispered. "Tell you what, you win you can ask anything of me. I win; I can ask anything of you, fair?"

"Fair," Blair said, knowing she'd be losing this one. She thought it a cute way to get to know one another though.

Tanner nodded to the game master raising two fingers. As he handed Blair her first ball Tanner leaned in close taking her hips and pulling her back to his chest. "That's good, cos I'll be asking that when we enter the hotel room tonight there'll be a no clothes policy."

A shudder of excitement ran through Blair as she melted into Tanner. This was far beyond what she was thinking and her body went crazy with desire. Without even trying or waiting for Tanner's instruction, Blair lobbed her balls carelessly into the stall. With desire in her eyes, Blair grabbed tanner by the collar and slowly pulled him into a kiss. Twin fires ignited in their hearts, building, merging, engulfing their very souls until the celestial world around them was stunned by its beauty and warmth.

Breaking the kiss, Blair pretended to yawn and stretch. "I think I'm about..." she yawned for real, the droning noise finishing on a little squeak, and looked sheepishly at Tanner. "I'm ready to call it a night."

Tanner laughed. "Come on then. Let's get you back to the hotel room."

Biting her lower lip, Blair nuzzled into Tanner's side as he placed the balls back. With a shrug and a tip for the game master, Tanner wrapped his arm around Blair and headed to the hotel. Like little butterflies tickling her stomach, Blair could feel herself getting excited. Two times now, she will have technically lost her virginity and both times were to the man she loved. This time though, Blair had him all night. She'd be able sleep in his arms, wake up by his side, see the first rays of sun dance across his

144

chiselled chest.

Subconsciously, Blair started to bob her head back and forwards, her cute little butt wiggling in opposite unison.

"You seem rather happy. Your little tails waggling uncontrollably." Tanner smiled at Blair. Never had he held someone so cute before. She was so breathtakingly pure, that anyone else was like nothing to him. Yet there was a perfect synergy between them, an enveloping aura that surrounded them as they drew near. Tanner new in this moment, looking down at that innocent puppy dog expression he'd found his person. He knew now what true love felt like and it was her. He knew with every fibre of his being this was true.

"Ruff," a little bark escaped Blair's lips and she waggled her butt into Tanners side.

Stopping a moment, eyes closed in silent prayer for strength, Tanner gathered himself. "Get on," Tanner said, crouching down before Blair.

"You want to give me a piggyback?" Blair eyes lightened, growing huge. "Then I best accommodate you. Jumping to his back, Blair nestled her head against his shoulder and felt his strength surge as he lifted her. Strong firm hands reached under her butt cheeks as she directed her legs around his hips. The long fingers curled over her rump to nestle a little deeper than intended. The angles working to have the tips of Tanner's fingers brush against her lips with each step. Closing her eyes, Blair allowed herself to drift along like in a dream.

A jolt caused Blair to open her eyes before she realised with sadness that Tanner was lowering her. It surprised her to be dismounting at the room as opposed to the reception where they needed to pick up a key.

"You fall asleep quick," Tanner noted. "I didn't realise you were serious at the fair about turning in."

"Oh my god." Wiping the spittle from the edge of her mouth Blair realised how deep she had just fallen. It hadn't even felt like she was sleeping, not able to get a clear grasp on where the piggyback ended and her own imagination kicked in. "I was so comfortable and warm against your back. I... I just don't know when I was out. I felt you the whole time." Blair was blushing terribly, eyes down. A kiss to her forehead, however, brought them back up to find that handsome smile of Tanners beaming down on her.

"Everything you do is so cute," he said before opening the door and walking in.

Like a moth to a flame, Blair flew in, all intentions to be burnt in hot, sticky, passionate sex.

Stopping in the centre of the room, Tanner paused not looking back. "I... I don't know what I'm doing. I want you, Blair, so badly. My mind has you running through it 24/7. You are sweet and innocent and I've brought you here, fuelled by my own desires. If you don't want to do this, I won't..." Turning as he spoke, Tanner's jaw dropped. He lost his voice midsentence, as if to make even the slightest noise would break reality. Too stunned was he to do anything.

Silently, Blair was able to remove all her clothing without Tanner hearing. Working under the sun this last week, Blair had bronzed over most of her curves. She understood for the best affect she needed to tan naked but the farm definitely didn't allow for that. Like a statue found in a Greek museum, this goddess was standing, one arm hiding the bare minimum of her rounded, pale, breasts. The other just slightly covering Tanner's entrée. Slowly, her eyes closed, she tilted her head down to her shoulder, the softest smile upon her face, her cheeks burning crimson. Opening her eyes, Blair looked at the man she loved, stunned to the spot, moved by her natural essence.

Blair's smile deepened, feeling the power she held, the same power he had over her. Dropping her hands and raising her head, Blair saw the current boy would not be approaching anytime soon. She would need to remind him that he was a man. With a sway of the hip, Blair moved across the short hotel room floor, her eyes locked to Tanner's. Blair was sure the twitch in the jaw showed he was trying to say something but couldn't get past the beauty before him.

Blair traced a finger down his still covered chest. "You speak of desire as if only men had it. You talk as if you dragged me back to this hotel room against my will. You act as though I didn't play a part in getting us to this point." Blair pushed Tanner back to the bed. "For that, your punishment will be to lay with hands behind your head while I have my way with you first."

For a moment, Tanner considered Blair as if he was finding new depths of her soul to love and enjoy. Too lost was he in her eyes to put up an argument that the tearing of his shirt caught him unawares. Eyes bulging, he made to rise but Blair just pushed him back down.

"Uh, uh, uuh. You're in trouble mister. You need to take your punishment," Blair said waggling a finger back and forth. She sat atop him, still swaying her hips causing Blair to grind into the large bulge between Tanner's legs. It was so hard to remain so patient. "You're not going to need that for what I'm about to do."

Relaxing, Tanner repositioned his hands behind his head. He was finally starting to look like a man again. Shifting back by way of some butt hops, Blair worked at the gates to the final stronghold holding her back from her prize. She knew what manner of beast lay within and this time, she was more than ready to tame it.

Buttons popped. Belt detached. Eyes connected to Tanner's, Blair pulled back his pants and boxers to throw them across the room. And still, she did not look at her prize, standing erect, like a massive stone obelisk of Egyptian craft. Creeping back across Tanner's chest, nibbling, and planting soft kisses in his erogenous zones, Blair's naked body lay along Tanner's, their beings absorbing one another's embrace. Shorter than Tanner, this allowed Blair to sit upon the top side of Tanner's obelisk, her opening teasing up and down the shaft with slow, rhythmic swaying.

Tanner was losing his mind in the explosions of ecstasy rippling up his body. With every sway of Blair's hips, Tiny Tanner grew stronger, gained more control, and started relaying information and imagery such as the timing for the perfect thrust. As much as Tanner fought this feeling, it became too much and in a moment of weakness, Tanner lost himself to the little TNT. Gaining control of the hips, Tiny Tanner launched himself with pinpoint precision to bury the whole of his length deep inside Blair's warm, firm, wet vagina.

"Eeeearrahhhahuuuuuuuuuooooooo," Blair squealed at the unexpected attack, eyes locked shut to the pleasure, and hips thrusting back all the way to Tanner's balls. They had both almost cum from that one movement and it was a long moment before either were ready to move again. With a few deep, calming breaths Blair found herself once more and locked eyes on Tanner. He was watching her reaction knowing he went out of turn. Blair's wicked smile at her recovery telling him it was still happening.

Raising herself to sit upright, breasts just out of the way as Blair continued to eye down Tanner, she reached down and slapped the side of Tanners Butt cheek. This caused him to jump a little sending a new shockwave through Blair. A shockwave she was expecting this time.

"And who told you, you could come inside?" Blair'd leaned back just enough that the base of the shaft was in view, their soft tufts of hair sitting apart. Blair traced her nails from the base of the shaft up to the stomach and back down again. Tanner getting the distinct impression she was talking directly to his cock. "You aren't ready to travel these halls. Too worked up and excited are you that you'll make a mess too quickly and leave without knowing the real pleasure this room could give you."

Slowly, lending herself to the wild electricity reaching inside her, Blair slid from Tanner's cock. It was all Tanner could do to hold back the flood, heeding the words of Blair. It was all Blair could do to stop herself from ramming straight back down. Tiny stood, strong and tall, watching as Blair shuffled back off the bed, her face close up to his one eye.

With great care and torturous patience, Blair circled Tiny's head with her tongue. The taste of her own sweet juices, a kink she hadn't been prepared to enjoy so much. Working her way down the shaft, Blair savoured every drop of herself as she cleaned Tanner before working her way to the tip once more.

"Warn me when you're ready," Blair told him seriously.

"Would you prefer any place that I would cum upon?" Tanner asked, a little disappointed she was one to spit.

"No!" Blair said. "When you're ready, I don't want to lose most of you halfway down my throat. I want to be able to bring myself back to where you can fill my mouth and I may savour everything that is you." A small pulse in Tiny told Blair she made the right choice. And she smiled back at him. "Oh, you like that don't you? Well then come on. Give me everything you've got."

148

Having practiced for this moment at home with a certain sizable cucumber, Blair got her mouth over Tanner's just as sizable cock. His moans only causing her to slide further and further until he was at her little dangly thing with plenty of length to come. Taking just a moment to get her last breath in and relax her reflexes, Blair went the distance.

When Tanner's soft, fuzzy pubic hair, tickled her noise Blair started to move back, humming a merry little tune. Blair almost loved being fucked here as much as she did down below. There was still the excitement, her pulse racing with each thrust, electricity sparking across her skin. But here there was more urgency to make her man cum. The depth of his cock had cut off her air supply which only seemed to heighten the fun.

Tanner's arms shot out to grasp the bed and he yelled a strong, guttural 'Now' at his imminent release. Blair pulled back until only Tiny's head was locked in the embrace of her lips. The moment Blair was in position the floodgates opened. Hot, sticky semen filled Blair to the point she needed to swallow three times before she could savour that sweet and salty delight. Enjoying every little bit, Blair would gently bite and suck on tiny, causing him to surge and give up those last few delicious drops to her waiting tongue.

Blair kept at it until Tanner could take no more and took control back. Lost in her own fun, Blair didn't see Tanner rising from the bed or leaning over. It was only when Tanner caught her under the waist did she notice. With a squeal and a giggle, Blair was picked up, legs first, into the air with ease to continue the rotation and land butt first above Tanner's chest.

"My turn," Tanner said latching onto Blair's defenceless butt cheeks and pulling her closer to his mouth. With thighs running either side of his head Tanner dove in. Forcing himself to slow down at the last, Tanner licked around the edges of Blair's labia while kissing gently on her thighs. Soft bites caused squeals from above and Tanner continued at a slow pace knowing Blair was enjoying every lashing and nibble. He would need a good 15 minutes to recover so no need to rush just yet.

The head board was fast becoming Blair's best friend,

taking her weight as she couldn't hold herself aloft without it. In seconds, she had gone from being in control to melting into a pool of wobbly jelly, unable to move properly. That tongue of Tanner's was a true master at its craft. It would build her up and let her settle. Smash her defences and let her recover. Bathe her in ecstasy before pulling back once more. Blair realised it was only toying with her, an even greater pleasure promised just over the horizon.

And then the first one came hard. Where Blair thought Tanner would slow, he didn't. His tongue flicking and curling around her clit, pushing her ever closer until he reached a hand up to cup her breast. That was all that was needed for the orgasm to come crashing through. Like waves in a sea worn blowhole, Blair exploded. Feeling Tanner tense and then ease again to gently pinch her nipples, Blair's waves continued for half a minute. It was amazing, his ability to make her squirt when she still couldn't get it herself.

Feeling the orgasm start to diminish, Tanner wasn't ready to just let her get away. Pushing her back towards the end of the bed, he was able to manoeuvre Blair around to be over her as she was laying. The breasts needed his attention most at the moment. His hands gently grazing over them as he gazed lovingly into her eyes. Eyes that couldn't hide the love, warmth, and enjoyment of this moment. Tanner was compelled to lean in and kiss Blair's soft lips. He'd been caught up in their act that he had forgotten to simply show her his feelings in the little things, the gentler moments, and this woke him up.

As two slender arms wrapped around his neck, the small, simple kiss grew. Stronger, deeper, did that kiss become that the fun ramped up once more. Fingers that were tracing areolas and pinching nipples became a hand that cupped and squeezed. The other busy fondling her curvaceous butt. Breaking the kiss, Tanner's Attention shifted to Blair's smooth neck. Kisses and biting, sucking actions trailed down to the shoulder. One causing a small hickey to appear but neither noticed.

From Blair's shoulder, Tanner jumped to the currently occupied breast. The nipple that was sitting between his fingers was now within his mouth. His tongue curling

150

around the tip, caressing the small bud, drawing it out to stand firmer, larger. And when it did, Tanner started waves of convulsing suction moving his head up and down slightly in the motion. As he sucked upon the nipple he wrapped it in his tongue pinching it upwards in velvet.

It started with an outburst of air but soon Blair's moans were rolling in waves. Tingles were racing right through her, passing every defence to attack her core as pure ecstatic energy. The hand that was playing off on its own, had heard the excitement and Blair felt him come around, trace up to caress the second breast heightening the moment. This allowed Tanner to jump between each breast heating and melting them evenly. The excitement was too much that it sent Blair over the top once more.

And then she felt it. The tip of Tanner's, again, rock hard penis was teasing back and forward ever so softly along her welcoming slit. Too lost was she in the ever building pleasure Blair hadn't notice Tanner bring his knees up under himself to gain leverage. Bringing her knees up to Tanner's hips, Blair wrapped her legs around his back giving him a sign she wasn't letting him get away. A sign he took vigorously, the entire length of his cock thrusting up inside her. The lance of pleasure charged up into her core, causing tremors of pleasure in its wake. As Tanner bottomed out the lance burst the large bubble of ecstasy. Blair felt this at first like an implosion. Energy and lust from every part of her body being drawn into that one pin point position. Muscles and limbs curling in towards the building bomb. When the body could take no more, the explosion occurred. Hands rushing down to grab the bed sheets, Blair's head smashed back in a silent scream of pleasure. Ecstasy, bliss, euphoria, an internal rapture, whatever this pure and exhilarating feeling could be referred to it was taking Blair over. Muscles trembled in uncontrollable fits. Eyes rolling to be lost in the back of her head. Air unable to be drawn. Blair had never known a moment such as this and couldn't even account for how long it held her. She just knew that if there was a heaven, this would be the state her body remained in.

When the waking world finally caught her, Blair looked around groggily trying to piece herself back together. Tremors continued to course through her veins feeding her muscles in fast recurring intervals. A blissful smile curling her lips as best it still could.

"Are you okay?"

Blair focused back on Tanner. Raising a trembling hand to gently touch his cheek the smile grew. "More than okay, Tanner. If you could do that a few more times tonight you will have won my soul. Even just that one moment was enough to win my heart, my entire life as it is is now yours," Blair said.

With a relieved smile, Tanner leaned in kissing Blair softly on the lips. A kiss Blair returned in all its love and gentle pleasure. As the kiss broke, Blair rolled her head to Tanner's ear.

"Seriously," she whispered. "You need to do that again right now."

A pulse rippled through Tiny as Tanner smiled, his eyes locked to Blair's. Without another word he started to move and Blair fell into the motion. Their souls as one.

A cool draft kissed Blair's skin causing goosebumps to rise. The wee hours of the morning had come too quick as she read 4:15 on the bedside table clock. A whole night of pleasure, sometimes even competing with the noise of the fair. The fair which consented defeat and went to bed closer to midnight. Blair felt sorry for the tenants in the rooms next door hoping they were able to sleep with so much going on but she could never be sorry for this night.

A warm arm embraced her only helping to heighten the tingling goosebumps against the cool of the night. Shifting back slightly, Blair's body found the curve of Tanner's and she fitted into it perfectly. It was amazing how so much could change in twenty four hours. How she could fall so deeply for someone, find so much pleasure in someone's arms. Blair smiled as her body responded to her thoughts.

"At least give me a little sleep tonight," she chided herself.

As if in response, her stomach let out a loud, long grumble reminding her that she hadn't eaten since lunch time, not counting Tiny.

Resigned to either remain awake all night from the now full blown hunger or to have at least something light and get a few precious hours sleep, Blair chose the latter. Being careful so as not to wake Tanner who had only moments before fallen asleep from exhaustion, Blair rolled from the bed. Remembering a vending machine was close to the room, Blair picked up her wallet and set off hoping to remain undetected with her minimal clothing.

Outside the air was crisp and clean. The cool breeze now embracing her gently as the draft could not. This feeling Blair enjoyed and she scanned for the vending machine previously seen outside the room hoping it wasn't just a dream. The target was finally located across the car park. It was amazing how her mind could notice something yet make up a completely different picture on where it was located. She blamed it on the warmth of Tanner's back.

As she approached Blair froze to the spot, fear entering her body with an icy embrace. Her eyes, catching something in her peripheral, had looked up to find the whole sky racing off into the west. The last time this happened, Blair lost a whole day and any progress she had made with Tanner. Now, she risked the same and felt herself starting to grow weak. Her knees began to buckle under her and her head swam. The last Blair saw as the world started to topple uncontrollably was Tanner running from the room to her side. Darkness engulfed her vision and Blair fell into the unknown.

Chapter 10 – A day, a year

A hand on her shoulder brought Blair back to consciousness. Her mind was still swimming and she felt there was a weight upon her side. Then a slap and a scream brought her to full awareness.

Taking only a moment to assess her surroundings, Blair knew with dread certainty the day had restarted. "Tanner, get out. We'll be down shortly. I'll be talking about what you've done in the car."

"But... I..." Tanner stammered.

"Now!"

Tanner left the room and Blair rolled over to assess her friend. "You all good?" Blair asked with a kiss to the forehead.

Lillian nodded. "Shocked me is all. I was expecting to see you. Tanner is..."

"...Okay. He's still rather trustworthy... to a certain extent. Anyone else and I would have screamed a lot longer. Don't be too hard on him." Blair finished.

Lillian's eyes narrowed. "What is this?"

"It happened again," Blair replied.

"What happened?"

"I slept with Tanner and the day reset," Blair said. There was a touch of sadness to her voice.

Lillian was a little confused, her mind cloudy at such an early hour. "Maybe you're cursed."

"Waaah... I just want Tanner to remember my body upon his, our souls as one."

"Aww Blair, at least you can try again tonight. Last time it was only a one-time thing." Lillian pulled her close stroking her hair.

Blair allowed Lillian to continue a while longer, the fingers feeling nice in her hair. The thought of this day over was also a nice thing. This time Blair could control the events to the same outcome. Take Tanner with the same vigour as yesterday... Today? "Yesterday," she said aloud.

"Mine or yours?" Lillian asked.

"No matter. You're far to calm with this information."

Lillian pursed her lips. "I don't know the truth of the matter. You seem convinced by it and I won't argue with that. I trust you."

154

"Thank you. It's all I ask," Blair said. "We better get ready. I reprimanded him a lot worse yesterday from that slap. Even organised a three way for you, me, and Mary."

Lillian's eyes bulged. "A what?"

"A three way. You know scissoring... other things."

"You have no idea what goes on do you?" Lillian asked with a laugh.

"Lots of things, I hear." Blair laughed. "It was a better flow of conversation yesterday. Seems forced and awkward today."

"It may be the same day but it's also a new day. Live in the moment."

A soft smile touched Blair's lips. "You're right." Standing, Blair started to get ready and while waiting for Lillian, had a search for her phone.

"What you after?" Lillian called as she wriggled into a top.

"Just mum. I couldn't find her yesterday and thought I'd look around..."

"You don't..."

"Yes, yes. I don't need to take mum on this trip. Still, I wanted to know she was safe."

"I'm sure she is and that you'll see her again. Ready?"

"I guess."

Blair and Lillian headed downstairs to find a pacing Tanner. Upon seeing the girls he ran over to the passenger door and opened it for them.

"Sorr..." Tanner started to apologise but Blair held up a finger in front of him then jumped into the Pickup. As Lillian came upon him, she lightly slapped his face a couple times. More of a pat really.

"Next time, concentrate on that cute, little rump crawling across the seat. It craves attention," Lillian said motioning to Blair.

As Tanner glanced across he was greeted with a little wiggle from Blair before she rested her butt in the middle seat. Tanner smiled knowing he'd messed up this morning but also that the situation had been diffused.

The rest of the morning followed a similar flow. Lillian made it home safely leaving Blair to snuggle up to her lover. The warmth and Blair's tired body giving way to her passing out with his arm around her. This time, however,

Blair's body woke in a more pleasant manner. No car cutting them off, likely because they had left at slightly different times throwing the timing of the trip out. Already the town was in view and Blair pouted. She'd planned to go ahead with the road head this morning but was going to be too late now.

Arriving at the fair, Blair fell into the setup much quicker and easier knowing what she was supposed to be doing. As a lady approached the stall, a smile crossed Blair's face.

"Good morning, ma'am, how can I service you today?" Blair asked. The shock upon Tanner's face was priceless.

The woman considered Blair a moment, looking her up and down before shaking her head. "Just... I was hoping you could tell me where the nearest coffee stall was."

"Of course, we've only just arrived ourselves and can't say for sure if they've set up yet but one row over towards that end of the row." Blair motioned towards the southern end of the fair.

As the woman started to leave, she paused. "Maybe later we could discuss other services...?"

Blair smiled and looked across at Tanner. "I have other service calls at that time sorry."

With a knowing smile the lady moved on.

"You need to be a little more careful with how you address customers," Tanner said. "The way you said that, some people may get the wrong idea."

"So if you came up to me in a store and I asked how I could service you, you wouldn't say with handcuffs and no key?" A look of innocence evident across her face which broke as she watched Tanner's expression change. A rich laughter filled the air as Tanner mumbled something about having a job that needed to be done.

And the job was done brilliantly. Blair felt like a primary school student having come across the answers to an upcoming test. Only this time a 100% mark wouldn't draw negative attention. Walking over to where the tarp for their stall lay, Blair looked to Tanner.

"I think we've done all we can for the day," Blair said.

"Better than that. You couldn't put a foot wrong, Blair. I knew you had this potential in you."

Even though the compliment was empty with what Blair

156

knew, she couldn't help but smile. Tanner didn't know she was reliving a day and therefore the words from him were so full of pride.

"So what's next? Dinner? Carnival games?" Blair asked as Tanner took up one side of the tarp and helped Blair cover their stall.

"Let's book into the hotel first, drop our stuff off and work it out from there," Tanner replied off script.

Blair considered him an instant before she remembered Lillian's advice to live in the moment. "A nice meal in a diner, a game of ball toss, and a ride or two back at the hotel room. Sound like a plan?"

"A ride or two then head back to the hotel room? I'm down for that." Tanner replied correcting Blair's wording.

"I prefer how I said it," Blair replied and footed it towards the hotel.

Tanner just shook his head and with a grin took off after Blair.

Key in hand Tanner opened the room and stepped inside, Blair following close behind. Walking to the bed Tanner placed his bag.

"Last time I was in town there was this nice, little Italian restaurant a couple blocks..." He jumped as the door to their room slammed shut. With a quick turn he found Blair shaking her head.

"No," she said simply. Her hormones had gotten the best of her watching Tanner's well-crafted butt walk into the room.

"Don't like Italian?" Tanner asked as Blair walked over placing a hand on his chest. A hand that trailed lower.

"I'm after something a little more... Meatier," Blair said and she pushed Tanner back towards the bed.

A strong jolt brought Blair to full consciousness. The warm breath from Tanner tingling over her ear. A strong arm holding her in a gentle embrace. Tilting her head, Blair read the time and a deep dread filled her soul. 4:15... again. It couldn't be happening again. It couldn't... Throwing Tanner from her, Blair raced from the room in nothing more than a small pair of royal blue, lace panties.

The stars were alive this night, racing across the sky as if time itself was running backwards.

157

"Nooo," Blair wailed. "No. no. no. no. Noooo!"

"Blair? What's wrong? Tanner asked racing from the room.

Blair didn't have a chance to reply however as the world rolled around her sending her into darkness once more.

And once again the hand shook her awake.

"If you slap her butt, Tanner, I will destroy you."

Tanner froze mid swing. "How did you..?"

"That butt is mine. I know the luring power it has and I'm warning you now. Touch my butt and I will destroy you. Get you to the car and I'll go down on you shortly."

Tanner made to leave then paused a moment considering her words. Shaking his head he continued on his way as Lillian stirred."

"What was that about?"

Blair leaned over and slapped Lillian's arse, including a quick squeeze. This excited a squeal from Lillian and she rolled back to the sound of Blair's laughter.

"Nothing my little flower petal. Just some friendly banter with Tanner while you slept," Blair winked.

"I hope that's all it was," Lillian's eyes narrowed as she considered Blair.

Blair didn't try to relieve Lillian's suspicions. What she did do though was spend a couple minutes on the hunt for her mum. Blair was so quickly running out of places to look she was starting to fall into despair. Right now she really needed her. She could talk to Lillian but with all the events of the day there wouldn't be enough time to get in everything she needed to. That and she didn't want to ruin the fair for her dad's farm just in case this was the day everything continued moving forward. It wasn't.

For the first week Blair tried doing or not doing things to force time to continue forward. One time, while watching the star's flight across the sky with Tanner, she had hoped he would also replay the day but it wasn't to be. After that Blair finally accepted her life was in the hands of the fates and she should just enjoy.

3 days later and Blair finally found the courage to get a little frisky on the trip to the fair. Tanner ended up stopping the car part way through with the feelings getting too strong for him.

158

20 days in and Blair had cracked the surface that was Tanner. She'd found a way to get him to talk about himself. Little things but over the span of the month, Blair was getting a well-informed picture.

Now, 30 days in, Blair had become comfortable with her situation. It wasn't a terrible day to repeat. She got to see her friend, be with the one she loved, any mistakes she made were soon erased, and it opened Blair up to be far more adventurous.

One adventurous move to celebrate her 100th straight day was to invite a certain coffee seeking customer to the hotel that night to join in the fun with her and Tanner. To Blair's surprise, this offer was even accepted. It was an experience to say the least. Tanner seemed a little uncertain to begin with but he settled in quickly. Blair and Merril put on a show for him, get Tanner's blood pumping, and Blair learned so much in that first hour. Firstly, that she really did only have eyes for the male population, as fun as it was, and second, some moves she could now converse with Lillian about beyond just the scissoring she knew... Blair paused in her thoughts of the night as something started to niggle at the edge of her memory. She ran through the events over and over again before a crimson blush crossed her face.

"That must've been some dream," Lillian said as they were preparing to meet Tanner downstairs.

"He didn't touch her," Blair exclaimed. "Tanner made it all about me." Blair couldn't believe that with two women in his bed Tanner still only pleasured her. That everything from Merril and Tanner was directed at her. Blair's love for the man instantly soared.

200 days falling in love and Blair won Tanner a large teddy in the ball toss game. Something Tanner himself had only done once for her in this time. She missed the soft fur of her oversized teddy... That was a really kinky night, she blushed. Something she might repeat with Tanner's prize. A shiver of delight ran up Blair's spine as they walked back to the hotel.

Day 319

"I'm going to get some coffee," Blair called to Tanner as she walked off into the crowd. There was a bounce in her step as she reached the coffee stall. Life, though predictable, was wonderful. Full of sound and colour, joy, laughter, love, passion. Blair wouldn't give these days up for all money in the world. And if Blair never broke the cycle and the world's destruction was the result, she would spend one more day in Tanner's arms, her death full of love.

"Two Vanilla Lattes, Miss," the shop keep said.

"Oh Gregory, but two visits and you've already memorised my order," Blair said.

The shop keep gave her an odd look. "And you my name it seems."

That's right; Blair hadn't learned it this time around. She simply smiled and watched as Gregory made the coffees.

"Blair..." A weak and disheartened voice sounded behind her.

Far distant memories tugged at her mind urging her to remember... remember... Jacob... Blair swung to find a pale and wobbly form standing close by. "Jacob! What are you doing here? Are you okay? What's wrong?" she raced over to stop him from falling to the ground.

"It won't stop," Jacob sobbed falling to his knees. "The days. They won't stop repeating."

"Gregory," Blair called catching the shop keeps attention. "Give the coffees to the next two orders." She turned back to Jacob and helped him up to his feet. "Come with me. There's a bench we can rest at under a tree nearby."

Leading Jacob through the maze of people, Blair shooed the current occupants of the bench to seat her little Brother. As she sat next to him the tears fell. Great racking sobs took over Jacob's body and he leapt into Blair's embrace crying unashamedly. Minutes passed and Blair's heart broke in two for the boy. He was clearly reliving the days as he had the last time and it seemed to be having terrible effects on mind and body.

Gaining enough control to slow the sobs into small tears welling at the edges of his eyes, Jacob fell silent. It had been too long since he felt a loving and wholly understanding embrace and he needed this. "I can't tell you how many times I've tried to stop the time loop. Am I

160

dead. Am I just a soul reliving its last day on earth?"

Taking Jacob's cheeks within her hands, Blair turned Jacob to face her. "You are not dead. You are Jacob. You are my brother and I love you." The words seemed to be reaching their mark.

"Then why can't I move on from this day? Why won't it stop?" Jacob seemed on the edge of breaking once more.

"I am right here with you. I have done nothing but repeat my days since the bonfire."

"And you're okay with it?" Jacob asked. "I can't get away from this horrible day."

"Aww Jacob. I'm so sorry this has happened. I've survived solely because I have Tanner with me. He saves me from the torment of the soul such a day could bring."

"Just like last time," Jacob said. He looked as though he wanted to smile but everything about him seemed so depressed.

"What do you mean like last time?"

"Tanner saved you at the waterfall."

Blair gasped realising that Tanner was the only common denominator. No, not Tanner. Sex with Tanner. She shook her head. That couldn't be it. Why was Jacob repeating then? He surely hadn't slept with Tanner or anyone else in the last 24 hours. But what else was there.

"Why isn't there anyone to save me," Jacob broke down once more.

Tapping his face a few times to get his attention Blair drew his eyes back to hers. "How did you get here?"

"What?" Jacob sobbed.

"How did you get here, Jacob? Dad surely didn't drive you."

Jacob shook his head.

"Then how?" Blair was relieved slightly seeing her decoy tactics worked.

"I did?" came the soft words.

"You did what? Walking is too far. Did you catch a bus?"

"I drove," Jacob replied.

This surprised Blair. "All that way? Where did you even learn to drive?"

"I taught myself."

"No. Jacob, that's amazing." Blair exclaimed. She really meant it too.

Jacob, for just a moment, forgot his eternal torment and blushed under the praise of his big sister. "I crashed so many times."

"I don't doubt it but look at you. You taught yourself how to drive." Then a thought struck Blair. "Why did you come, Jacob?"

Those sad soulless eyes looked up to meet Blair's cutting deep into her heart. "I needed to find you. I just want it to stop. I'm tired, Blair. So tired. Mentally. Physically. I feel my life draining from me." He paused a moment, hesitating with what he was about to say. "I tried to end it myself two days ago. The day was cut short and there I was again, the same roof above me as the last few hundred times."

That was more than Blair could take. Eyes spilling over with tears of her own, she pulled Jacob close once more, holding his whole being in her arms. "I may have a way to end this. I can't be sure but you will need to wake once more under that same roof."

"What do you mean?" Jacob couldn't allow himself hope.

"One more repeat. Tomorrow you need to stay at home. Act like it will be the final repeat Saturday you need to live out. That what you do tomorrow matters for your future. Can you do that for me?"

Jacob started rolling his head trying to find some confidence in her words but it was hard to muster. A hand grabbed his chin and pulled him eyes front.

"Jacob, will you do this for me?" her voice stern.

Finally, Jacob nodded.

"Good. Come with me. You need some food and some fun."

Without giving Jacob a chance to protest, Blair caught his arm and started almost dragging him through the crowd. It would've been dragging save that Jacob somehow managed to keep his feet moving. Pausing at three different stores, Blair bought some chips, a Dagwood, a large soft drink, 2 giant pretzels, and a bunch of fairy floss.

"This should get that energy of yours up. We can eat it at the stall." Blair said as they closed on Tanner.

To say Tanner was surprised was an understatement but when Blair explained how she found Jacob wandering the games and forced him to explain about how he'd stowed in the back of the ute, Tanner's expression quickly turned to shock.

"I could have lost my license if you were found in there," Tanner burst out, a fury boiling in his belly.

Blair stepped in front and kissed Tanner, stalling his momentum. "I'm angry too. He's acted recklessly and selfishly but there will be no one angrier than dad. Let's not be the bad guys in this. Let me take him around the show a bit. Build up my cool sister stance with him and tonight... Well let's just say he can have one of the two rooms to himself."

Tanner took a calm steadying breath. How could he be angry in front of Blair? How could he say no to her request? "Fine but not too long. I still need you here."

Blair looked around for pen and paper. Locating what she was after she started writing, filling two pages with lines stating either man or woman. "These are the customers that'll be coming along shortly. This column is their gender, then what they're after and finally, what will win us the deal."

"This isn't some game, Blair." Tanner started before a customer cut him off. Tanner looked to the man then the first line on the page. Man... "How can I help?" Tanner asked cautiously.

Blair watched the exchanged as she practically force fed Jacob with the food she bought. A smile crept across her face at its conclusion.

"One fluke guess doesn't mean anything," Tanner said

"Give me until Jacob finishes his meal. I get anything on that list wrong and I'll stay. Otherwise, I can show my brother around the fair and we meet back here at closing time... also written on the last page."

"You can be too confident and too stubborn at times, Blair."

She just tilted her head, eyebrows raised. The unspoken question of do we have a deal hanging heavy in the air.

"Okay," Tanner gave in. "But only until he finishes."

Three more customers approached the store in that time and three times Blair accurately 'guessed' their wants and needs.

"How?" Tanner asked simply. He now held to the pages

163

as if they were a sacred gospel and he, the last surviving protector.

Blair just winked. "I'll see you this afternoon. Maybe you could coax it out of me later with a tickle or two."

Tanner smiled. "It's on." And as Blair and Jacob walked away Tanner called out one last time. "Lead me down the garden path and I'll need to punish you later."

"Read the last line," Blair called back. It wasn't the first time she skipped work to play at the fair.

Tanner skimmed over the list to the final sentence. '*I would hope so,*' it read. He looked up with a grin on his face but the siblings had disappeared into the crowd.

Watching Jacob at the fair, knowing how he had been the last time, Blair's heart slowly broke. Where he was excited to try for a prize in the side show stalls, Jacob shot them a quick glance and kept trudging along. Where a ride could incite a scream of pleasure or fear, Jacob needed to almost be dragged onto them and then he sat with a blank expression. Blair could not begin to imagine the torment and psychological damage this boy had gone through. She needed to see him smile once more. She may not give up the time loop for all the money in the world but for this boys happiness... it wasn't even a question.

"We'll fix this," Blair said. "If tomorrow doesn't work than come find me each day. We can do whatever we please with no consequence. I'll see you smile again."

"Do I have to sleep in a different room tonight?" Jacob asked suddenly.

"Is that why you can't seem to enjoy yourself this afternoon?"

"I don't want to leave your side again," Jacob's face seemed to crumple in on itself.

"Jacob," Blair said waiting for him to calm. "I won't be far away. It will be as if we were living at home. You in your room, me in mine."

"But we aren't at home," Jacob started to protest.

Blair held up a hand. "Stop. This is something you need to be brave about. I know you're scared and don't want to be alone but there are things I need to do to end this for the both of us. I want to help you get to a timeline that will continue to move forward. For that to happen I need to

164

give up far more than you will ever know. Give me this night to prepare for my lose. Give me this night to say goodbye."

"I don't understand."

"Love. I will need to say goodbye to love. The day will reset once more before we are finally free. Will you just trust me? I know you don't understand but trust that I will save you."

Jacob was quiet a long time. When he finally spoke he sounded broken. "Okay."

"He still doesn't look too well," Tanner said glancing back at Jacob as the siblings returned to the store.

"He'll be okay after a day or so. Things will start to get back on track for him. For now, he is tired."

"There were two mistakes in your line up," Tanner said changing the subject.

"Oh?" Blair sounded innocently.

"The last customer was a no show."

"Reeeally?" Blair sounded as though she was mocking him. "And?

"You're 5 minutes late."

"Well, I needed to give you something to get a spanking out of," Blair said with a wink then turned to Jacob. "Come on, bro. Let's let Tanner close up while we get comfortable in the hotel. Race you there."

Blair took off at a run and Jacob followed close behind. It started as simply not wanting to be separated from Blair but soon the adrenaline and exhilaration of the race kicked in. It'd been too long since he could just play around like this, Jacob had almost forgotten how fun and silly it could be.

It was Jacob that arrived at the hotel first. He found the information for it in his dad's office and even made it here the night before just in time to fall into the abyss out on the street. He knew Blair would come up with something to stop the loop but Love? How do you say goodbye to love?

"I have a reservation for Anderson. I need the two rooms please," Blair said to the hotel receptionist.

"But there's three of us," Jacob said. The receptionist raised an eyebrow at Blair.

"Just the two rooms please."

165

Taking the key cards Blair passed one to Jacob and walked into the car park. She heard Jacob's footsteps behind come to a halt.

"It's Tanner isn't it. The love you need to say goodbye to. You need to say goodbye to Tanner. How will that help us? It'll only make you sad."

Blair didn't turn as she spoke. She couldn't face Jacob lest the tears would fall. "The first time we skipped a day, Tanner and I said we loved one another. In the replay I didn't get the chance as Astrid was allowed to stay. Now, when Tanner and I came here the initial time we said we loved one another again. We have done so every day since. I can't think of anything else it could be. The world is literally replaying the day as if it needs for Tanner and I to be apart. That the Fates wrote our lives apart."

"So why am I replaying days then?" Jacob asked unconvinced.

"It may be our shared blood or maybe how close we were that first time. I can't say for sure. If it works then we'll know, otherwise, I have only lost a day and know that this is not the reason. We would need to try other things after that."

"Maybe you need to sleep with Lillian," Jacob commented.

"You're just a little pervert," Blair said before giving Jacob a light slap and ushering him off to his room.

Jacob glanced back to see Blair wrap her arms around Tanner's neck and kiss him passionately before heading into their own room. He heard Blair say '*Love me like it's our last day on earth*.' Jacob understood the hidden meaning and was saddened by this. He had tried so hard to bring the two together and still it could never be. Blair could lose herself in a moment in time but never could she truly live a full and rich life with him. Jacob almost felt guilty to ask for it to end. Almost.

Chapter 11 – Siblings aren't allowed to get along

It was rare that Blair watched the movement of stars across the sky anymore but this night she woke an hour before her reset and coaxed Tanner into coming to watch the display. He was amazed at the odd movement of the stars. It almost seemed unnatural but the warmth of Blair in his arms and the blanket holding them together was enough for him not to question it.

It was a peaceful and endearing moment that Blair would never forget. The warmth of the man she loved, the cool breeze, the light display, all mixed together to make a perfect and beautiful memory Blair would take with her always.

One minute to go and it still hadn't hit her about what was to come. A small part of her believed the plan would fail and everything could continue as it had been with the exception of trying to give Jacob another smile each day. There was always hope for this.

The world started to spin as darkness began its decent. Leaning back, Blair allowed herself to fall, held protectively in the arms of her lover. The arms she was certain she could still feel as she awoke once more in her own bed. The arms that were not there at all but rather slapping Lillian's butt. This is where it needs to begin or I will never help Jacob, Blair thought to herself. A scream filled the room as Lillian saw the figure standing over her.

"Tanner! Get out!" Blair yelled at him. "You have no right."

"I'm... I'm sorry." His face had paled over regretting instantly what he had done. "I'll wait by the ute."

"Get the fuck out. You'll be lucky if we even come down to the Ute," Blair screamed. Any louder and the rest of the house would be waking up.

Bryan, however, was awake. He was just lying there feeling proud of how his daughter treated boys. He rolled over and allowed himself to doze when he heard Tanner's footsteps heading back down the stairs. Shotgun remaining where it was for now.

"Blair, are you okay? It was really just the shock of waking up to him. That's all. No harm done," Lillian said.

"For one, he had no right to touch you in any way

167

uncalled for. Don't ever let that shit slide. For two... this isn't the first time I've lived this scene."

"Another repeat day?"

"And another and another and another."

"Three times?" Lillian's mouth dropped open.

Blair just shook her head.

"How many? ...10?" Lillian asked, eyes growing wide.

"Try a number closer to a year. I crossed 300. I know I got that many at least."

Lillian was too stunned to talk.

"Jacob found me at the fair yesterday. He isn't doing too well. I need to end this and can only think of one thing that I haven't tried."

"Dare I ask?"

"I need to stop sleeping with Tanner," Blair said with a great sadness.

Lillian's mouth dropped even more. "You horny little thing you. You just said a year. Let's call it a year, and you haven't not slept with Tanner even one day in that time?"

"He's all kinds of snuggly."

"Sounds like more than all kinds of snuggly to me. I take it he doesn't know."

"Not a one, but the more I opened up to him the more he followed suit. Everything I did across the year he continued to do in a day, each day."

"So why is abstaining from Tanner the only way to move forward?"

"Because it is only the days I sleep with him that I repeat. He literally fucks me right back into yesterday."

"So why Jacob then?"

Blair threw her arms up. "I've asked these questions. You've asked these questions. Jacob's asked these questions. The one time I talk to Tanner about it he thinks I'm writing a book and the only question he kept coming back to was, you guessed it, why Jacob. There is no answer. He is stuck in the loop with me for better or worse. He has taken on the latter." Blair thought a moment. "There is a big favour I need from you."

"Anything," Lillian replied without hesitation.

"Jacob is extremely depressed. To the point he tried rather undesirable means to end his torment."

"You mean...?" Lillian dragged a thumb across her

168

throat.

With a nod and a pout, Blair looked down.

"We can't have that. Who else will give us spiced chocolates," Lillian said.

It took a moment for Blair to get the reference having been so long ago but when it clicked, her face went into a half smile, half disgusted look. "I'd take spiced chocolate over no Jacob any day."

"So what do you need?"

"He is close to your home at the Russell's. Can you drop in? Keep him entertained throughout the day. Tell him I'll be fixing things today and if I don't, invite him to the fair for me. He'll understand."

"I'll get it done, Blair," Lillian thought a moment before walking over to her bag. Reaching in she pulled out a small dark object that fit perfectly in her hand. "Please don't hate me."

Blair knew instantly what she had. "Why do you have mum?" Her face turned dark. "Do you know how long I've been looking for her? How much I needed her?"

Lillian bowed her head low and held the phone out before her. "I'm so sorry. For me it was only going to be a couple days at most. Mary wanted to do something nice for you."

Nostrils flaring, Blair could barely move her arm with how tense it was. Open palm, she hovered just over the phone, fighting her rage back. Finally, winning over her sanity, Blair felt it couldn't make any more difference now whether she had her phone or not. The day was going to be terrible either way. Curling Lillian's fingers back over, Blair encompassed the fist with her own hand. "Your bag was the only place I didn't look this whole time. I trust in you, Lillian. You can borrow mum a couple days."

"You sure? It sounds like you need the comfort and security."

"Yeah... but I do know I need to face this task myself."

"You're very strong, Blair," Lillian said.

"Let's hope so," Blair replied.

Taking their time the girls were almost 30 minutes later than any other time this last year. Tanner had been pacing out front, stressing, trying to work out some excuse he could give Bryan as to why Blair didn't come, why he slapped Lillian's arse. Upon seeing the girls, he felt as though it was the first intake of air he had had all morning.

With Tanner trying to apologise, Blair gave him the cold shoulder. Lillian did mumble a quick *it's okay* but Tanner remained looking at Blair. Dropping Lillian home, Tanner's fears only escalated as Blair moved to the outer seat and proceeded to fall asleep. He was sure he would make a more comfortable leaning post than the vibrating glass of the window.

Even when she woke, Blair barely looked his way. She remained quieter than when they'd first met and this concerned Tanner to no end.

"Are you ok?" Tanner asked.

"Mmm," was the reply.

Tanner decided this time and a number of times through the day to leave it at her one word answers or grunts. She was doing brilliantly with the business side of things getting very close to each of the customers that came to the counter. She was professional and could ignite an instant rapport with minimal words. She even corrected Tanner on a number of points with customers he was engaged with. It showed she wasn't unwell. Then what was it?

At the hotel after Tanner brought out one card key from the reception office Blair didn't say a word. Only walked into the office herself, leaving Tanner standing awkwardly outside. The receptionist was on the phone but Blair wasn't in the mood.

"I need the second Anderson room," Blair said rather loud.

The receptionist excused herself to the person on the phone before covering the microphone. "I'm sorry ma'am. The room was just given away to the next in line."

"I cannot spend the night in the same room with a man that enjoys fondling women in their sleep."

The receptionist bulked, her answer halting and jumbled. "Sorry, um, the rooms no longer. I haven't got more... Sorry, what?" The receptionist's attention went back to the phone. "You heard..? It is this room... You would do that..? That's very noble of you, Sir. I'll tell you what. Next time you book with us the room is on me. Thank you." Tears welled in the receptionists' eyes as she hung up the phone. "People... there is still beauty and warmth in the people of this world. Give me a moment Ma'am and I'll grab your key."

"Thank you," Blair replied with a grateful smile. Outside, she walked by Tanner. "I'm going to get an early night," she said before heading to her own room. Tanner continued to stand around a moment longer just staring at the closed door before he shook his head and walked to his room.

At one point in the night around 9:30 there was a knock at her door and then a scuffling of a second set of feet.

"Sir, move along. This isn't your room." It was the receptionist.

"My friend is in there," came Tanner's reply.

"Clearly there is a do not disturb sign on the door," the receptionist said. What Blair couldn't see in that moment was the receptionist leaning down to blatantly place a do not disturb sign on the handle all the while not breaking eye contact with Tanner. "Move along."

Tanner shifted from foot to foot trying to decide what to do before heading back to his own room. As quick as she could Blair raced to the window and tapped softly. The receptionist looked up to find Blair mouthing thank you to her. She simply nodded and returned to the office.

Then the moment Blair dreaded arrived. 5 minutes before reset and Blair tentatively crept outside. With a deep breath she looked to the heavens for the first time wishing the stars were racing across the sky. There was no movement to be seen. The stars remained, held in place by the procession of time, where they should always be.

Her heart dropped to the souls of her slippers. "Farewell, Tanner."

A knock at her door brought Blair awake. An ache ran through her face around her cheeks to her red rimmed eyes. Tears had kept her awake long into the early hours of morning and right now she didn't feel fit to do anything.

Another knock at the door. Blair rolled to the darker side of the bed pulling the blanket up over her head. It will go away. The knock will go away, she continued to tell herself.

Once more it sounded, more urgent this time and a

voice accompanied it. "Blair. We need to get to the stall," Tanner called.

Again she didn't reply, didn't show there was life within the room. How could she walk out there now? She was a mess and he owned the most perfect arms to save her. They had gotten passed yesterday but now she needed to be careful so that life continued onwards and upwards.

"Stop acting like a child and come do what you need to do," Tanner called. Blair could tell there was an edge to his voice now as his patience wore thin. Then, "Argh," when no response sounded.

It was better he was upset with her. Better that he stopped wanting her. It would be easier that way. She needed all the help she could get right now.

By the time 10am rolled around and it was time to leave her room, Blair had recovered at least physically. Her insides were still hurting terrib... No, best not think about that. The tears would come again and then there would be no way to hide her state of being. It was a terribly thin tight rope so high above the world.

Saying goodbye to the receptionist and thanking her for all her help, Blair walked to the fair. The main rides and sideshow stalls were already starting to pack up. The only customers now were farmers and other trades who came for the more important stalls at the festival. With less than two hours to procure their products before the official close of the fair, everything seemed more urgent.

Blair decided to wander a bit not wanting to face Tanner right now but as the stalls and customers started to thin further she decided to bite the bullet and go find her lift home. It was going to be hard to endure the small cabin of the pickup but she needed to get through it.

A hard look crossed Tanner's face when Blair finally turned up. Having called it at 11am most of the stall was already in the pickup. Just the table needed to be lifted up and everything tied down before they would be leaving. Blair made to take one side.

"If you're coming to help don't bother," Tanner grunted. "It's already well passed the time when that mattered."

Pausing mid bend, Blair slowly raised her head to look at Tanner, her eyes deadly. Eyes that could kill the unprepared or weak of heart. Without a word she spun towards her ride home and climbed into the passenger seat. She set her gaze out at the distant horizon running parallel to the Ute and there her eyes remained.

A number of angry words did Tanner bite his tongue over. Words that would stew and bubble as he continued to roll the events of the weekend through his mind. His mouth would open to speak out then clamp shut just as fast. It was when they finally rolled back into their home town that Tanner couldn't hold his tongue any longer. Pulling into a vacant park near a grocery store, Tanner rounded on her.

"What did I do?" He growled. "You've been ignoring me, your duties, everything around you, so tell me, what have I done to upset you so?"

"Nothing," Blair dismissed him with the first words she had spoken to him today. Her gaze remaining distant.

Grabbing Blair by the shoulder, Tanner reefed her around to face him. "Don't give me that shit. You've been in a horrible mood all weekend. What happened to you?"

Pain lanced through Blair's arm causing her anger to burst forth. "You think this is all about you, you arrogant swine. You arrogant, fucking swine. I have more things in my life than you that could upset me so. Yet, just because you believe the world revolves around you, that you're the only thing in my life, you forcefully and painfully push me to the edge when all I needed was some time to my fucking self. Fuck you, Tanner." Blair screamed in his face and, removing her seatbelt, made to leave.

Tanner's hand shot out taking her by the wrist and holding her in the car. Retaliation came swift and true as Blair's open palm connected with Tanner's face causing him to let go.

"You are just as bad as the men who accosted me in the alley the day we met. Go to hell."

This time there was nothing stopping Blair from leaving. As she stepped from the vehicle it suddenly lurched into life revving hard backwards into the street before screeching up the road, tyres spinning as he went.

It hit hard. She wanted to talk it over with him, make him see sense. She also needed to get him to this point and run him off. Even so, the dam finally burst spilling Blair's emotions all over town. Her feet started running not caring where they lead but always subconsciously guided to that one destination where she could freely break down.

Lillian heard her long before she saw Blair racing down the path way. She knew what had occurred and how devastating it would be for her. Jacob had been in the same state himself yesterday. His story tying so intricately into Blair's that there was no doubt some truth behind it.

Meeting her at the doorway, Lillian ushered Blair inside. There was nothing that could be said at this point to calm the girl. It needed to happen on its own before Lillian could help.

"MESH TAR WARASFERT HEOMWEE, TANNER," Blair cried incoherently, arms flailing to emphasise her point.

Mr Pertouski poked his head around a corner to see what was going on only to retreat immediately into a safe area of the house. Teenage girl tantrums were the worst.

"I know, I know. Come on, Blair. Come to my room and you can tell me all about it." She wrapped an arm around Blair's back and led her through the house.

"HUMIKLOPE GRONDRI FARRAPH." There were streams of tears and rivers of snot. It was not a pretty sight but Blair deserved forgiveness for that.

"I know." Lillian nodded, feigning understanding.

Upon the bed, Blair was wrapped up in the arms of Lillian. Lying on their side in a spooning position, Lillian was gently stroking her tangled hair. An hour... or was it hours? Time had passed without a sound, endlessly running in the background. Mr Pertouski had peeked in the door motioning to Lillian he'd contacted Blair's dad who would be over sometime before nightfall.

It wasn't much time to really talk and as Blair hadn't moved in a while she ventured to break the silence.

"My dear soul, not a word you have spoken this afternoon has been in any way comprehensible but deep to the depths of my heart I understood every utterance. I feel for you and with everything in life am here for you. You say the word and I'll jump."

"Break it off with Lamby," Blair whispered loud enough to get across.

Lillian tensed instantly, a dark look crossing her face.

174

Wriggling loose, Blair rolled to look her friend in the eyes. A soft, sad smile upon her face.

"If I was to ask that of you, I would no longer be a friend. I know that what you say still has unspoken limits. The moment I step over those, I would expect you to slap me across the face and walk away." Blair felt Lillian relax again. "I love you. I love your Lamby. I would feel far worse than now should the day come where I lived in a world that you two were not together. Still, you don't need to tip toe around me with pretty words. Speak your heart to mine."

Considering her words, Lillian realised she had been dancing around the events of the weekend just to save her friends feelings. They were already broken and scattered. It was her job to find them and bring them back together.

"Your plan worked then." It was not a question.

"I never had a plan to begin with. I went in just trying to keep my distance. Things got so out of control that Tanner became really angry with me. I told the receptionist at our hotel he abused people while they slept to get a second room. She had it out for him the whole stay. Then I, in not so many words, called him a rapist to his face when he only tried to work out what was going on and pulled me around. I screamed in his face and left on terrible terms. Yes, I stopped the time loop but who was to say that if I fixed the relationship today the loop wouldn't start again."

"It sounds like you're more upset because you needed to bring out the worst in yourself. That you needed to hurt Tanner and can't even apologise to him because it will bring pain and suffering upon Jacob. Do you hate Jacob?"

Blair considered the question. She had hated Jacob once for just existing. The rambunctious little boy was a bane to her very existence. This changed and the happy-go-lucky boy was now a true brother of hers. "How could I hate a child who is just as much a victim of the fates as I am? Jacob is family and I will do what I need to to protect him. He didn't ask that I do this. I chose to for him."

Lillian smiled and nodded her understanding. "I was hoping you'd answer thus. Are you going to be okay? Do you want me to come over tonight? Shall I send Lamby?"

"No, you go hold your girl. I'll be seeing you both in the morning. The suspension has been paid. I just need a little more time on my own to get my head straight. You've helped me more than you could possibly know this afternoon. How was Jacob fairing?"

"It really has affected him horribly. You were right that something needed to be done to help him. He is innocent in this and the torment of everything repeating over and over was getting to him. I think it really would have been selfish of you to have seen him in the state he was and continue to be with Tanner. Not that I enjoy seeing you two apart. Especially after that kiss."

"Kiss? When did we..?" Blair thought for a moment and as if lightning struck, memories of a distant bonfire and stolen kiss under the stars filtered in. Her eyes grew wide. "He will remember that. I think this may make it that much worse."

"Maybe he'll be too upset to bring it up," Lillian offered.

Blair didn't look convinced. "There was so much more to what we had then just the kiss. I'd be surprised if he doesn't bring it up once he's calmed."

"A problem for a future date. I guess your next issue will be explaining yourself to your dad."

With a pout Blair nodded. "I've been worried how this was going to go down. I really don't know what to say."

"That's because you haven't had a dad that long. If he's anything like mine just cry crimson and he'll be off playing a single player hide and seek. The men of this world seem to be too afraid to even acknowledge women issues."

"I couldn't. I don't think we've reached that familiarity yet," Blair said.

"The familiarity will only be reached if you open the door on this one. Think of it as an investment for when you're out of pads and need him to pick some up. He may grunt and groan but you'll be up a pack and no embarrassing stains that may be thrown around a store."

"I guess."

"Better do better than guess," Lillian said as her attention went out the window. "He just showed up."

"What?"

"You get knocked about every month, may as well get a little something back from them. It's all the advice I can give, now, come here," Lillian said holding her arms wide.

Blair embraced her friend and thanked her. Then, with a kiss on Lillian's forehead, Blair made her way outside.

"Are you okay, Blair? Tanner said you weren't feeling yourself and Cooper mentioned you were rather emotional on the phone."

Instinctually, Blair's hand moved to her lower belly. Before she was able to bring up the subject Bryan was already holding up a hand.

"Say no more. Your mother was a beautiful, kind, loving woman but hit that point of month and she was like a case of firecrackers exploding at even the slightest disturbance."

"I'm sorry dad." Blair's voice expressed a deep sorrow.

"Don't. You haven't let me down. I'm proud of you, Blair. I went over the numbers for the weekend and you were only just shy of Tanner's tally with half the amount of days. You really stepped up. Sunday will be put down as a sick day."

There were no words Blair could think of that could do justice to the feelings she felt right now towards her dad. He continued to prove himself time and again in the last few weeks. With overwhelming love for the man, Blair flung herself into Bryan's arms. Tears were rolling freely down her face and he seemed a little stunned from the contact. "Thank you, dad," Blair said softly.

Stuttering, and tripping over his own tongue, Bryan wasn't quite ready for the show of emotion. "I'll always have your back, Blair. You're my daughter and I love you."

"I love you too."

This made the trip home far more enjoyable. Blair didn't need to find a persona that may suit an imaginary mood. This was real and this was joyous. So much so that Lillian felt the love of the moment watching from her room and couldn't help but smile.

Now, Blair thought as they were bouncing up the drive way, there was one last loose end to come home to and that was Jacob. She needed him to be okay.

As if hearing her thoughts, Bryan spoke up. "Be gentle around Jacob at the moment. He's feeling a bit under the weather also. Caught something at a friend's house and is very low on energy. You may not even see him as he was sleeping when I left."

"I'll make sure he's comfortable. We need to get his spark up again. Can't not have his antics around the house. It would get too quiet."

Bryan raised a questioning eyebrow.

"Don't tell him I said that. Siblings aren't allowed to get along," Blair said with a wink.

Bryan simply smiled proudly. The family was finally feeling like it was growing closer.

As they made it to the house, Blair noticed Jacob sitting out on the porch, Shadow getting his quota of pats for the day. The car rumbled to a stop and Blair swung open the door ready to run to Jacob but paused. Shadow had decided her pats were that little bit better and made his way to the car to wait patiently.

"How can I say no?" Blair said before scratching the old boy behind the ears and giving him a nice belly rub. "I missed you too; now back to your bed. It's time for a sleep."

Like a great wave of exhaustion, Shadow listened to her words and wandered back to his soft bed. The bones were aching lately and this fluffy cushion the larger man placed here was a blessing.

"One more year, Shadow. Let me spend a little more time with you," Blair whispered before turning to her brother. "I hear you've gotten lazy around the house. Can't even be bothered to fart in a chocolate basket anymore. Losing your touch," Blair teased with a smile.

"Just gotta shake this thing I caught over the weekend. Life seems to be moving forward again so I'm sure things'll pickup."

"And what got you outside this afternoon?"

"Just waiting for the stars," Jacob said looking a little distant.

Blair caught his meaning and a lump came to her throat. "I have it on good authority they will be rather boring this evening. Come inside."

"Your sister's right. Get inside and relax a bit," Bryan said heading for the front door.

"You're sure there won't be a show?" Jacob asked.

"Not for a long while if ever again," Blair said with a weak smile.

"I'm sorry," Jacob's voice started to crack.

Reaching out Blair grabbed him and pulled him close. She held him for a long while before Bryan called out dinner was ready. "No Apologies. My life is what I make it. I am happy and have good friends and family around me.

How bout we come out here later when night falls and I'll show you just how boring the sky can be."

"I would love to," Jacob replied.

And true to her word Blair watched the stars with Jacob that night. They talked of their early lives. Things that neither could know of the other. With their relationship growing stronger, it helped to mend their broken souls.

The downside though was that, because the stars were boring this night there was still school to prepare for and the night needed to come to an end. Well for Blair anyway. Jacob had already talked his way out of tomorrow's school day.

"Get a good rest, brother. I want to see some of that colour return to your cheeks."

"I just needed time to move forward. I feel myself getting stronger every moment. Sweet dreams sis."

Chapter 12 – A life taken back

Walking in to school Monday morning, Blair felt like she was in a dream. People she had never met were saying hi as she walked by. It wasn't just a polite acknowledgment of a random person either. Many had used her name meaning they were going out of their way to speak to her. Some, even going so far as to call across the school yard while waving. On the main part Blair kept her head down, too shy and bashful was she to levitate her social status to that which was given to her.

Reaching her usual perch, Blair found that Lillian had yet to arrive. This was a rare occurrence as her dad was always arriving before the buses due to being on bus duty each morning. He liked this setup as it meant he wouldn't be elected for other tedious jobs. Scanning the yard, Blair spotted Mary at her regular table. A table where another student was waving at her. Blair tried to look away, acting as though their eyes never made contact but a niggling thought brought her back to the table. It wasn't a random student at all but rather Lillian who was trying to get Blair's attention.

Understanding why but not quite sure about the setup, Blair ambled over to the group. Before she had a chance to say anything, however, the group spoke in disjointed unison. "We're sorry."

Blair only shot back a questioning look. There could be a number of things the girls were referring to so hearing them out first seemed best.

"We've been mean, sometimes completely obnoxious, to you."

Blair recognised the speaker as Francesca. The girl was actually very articulate when she wanted to be having spoken on a number of assemblies. "I hadn't noticed," Blair said in reply.

"Well, not to your face. We've said every harsh and terrible thing under the sun about you and Lillian. We said it without giving you a chance, without finding out who you really were. Popular belief was that you were a blight on this school and so we accepted this as gospel. Can you forgive us?"

"I already knew where I stood. I was happy to be left out

of things, to drift just out of the edge of people's peripheral thought. I was happy to be alone as I've lived thus a very long time. I was happy until that one." Blair motioned to Lillian. "Barged her way into my world, started decorating without a please or thank you and told me this was how things were now. And so much did I find I needed a friend in my life. Someone who could flush away the greyscale and sepia tones to paint a, forgive the pun, rainbow of colours..."

"Hey!" Lillian tried to object.

"For me to find joy in. How could I not put myself in a position of ridicule to try and paint her world just as vibrant? I knew what I was getting in to. It was that very attitude I was looking to change. Don't fear that I have held a grudge."

Francesca nodded but her brows remained furrowed. "You've talked about changing the attitude of the school yet will still tease her sexuality?"

Blair pointed at another girl around the table. "Take Billy-Bob over there," Blair said.

"Sally," the girl corrected her unsure why she was singled out.

"Take, *Sally,* for instance. Maybe she loves to watch anime cartoons in her spare time."

Sally's eyes lit up at the mention of anime. "I do, I do."

Blair smiled. "Has anyone here teased her about it in jest?"

"Yeah but..."

"No buts." Blair held up a hand. "You tease her out of love. She knows that, you know that. Your words are designed not to hurt but to bring each other closer together. Even if it isn't your thing, you're still showing that you're involved and she is a part of your life. Any objections?"

The girls all shook their heads.

"This is the same. I would live and die for Lillian and know she will do the same for me. Lamby also. It was established early on that we tease each other freely without prejudice or harm. It is blatantly obvious when teasing is meant to hurt. She will never get that from me. I tease out of love even down to the butt slapping."

The girls all looked a little odd. "Isn't that a little

sexual?" Francesca asked breaking the silence.

"Again, no. From Lamby, sure. From me, it's just a 'good morning, how ya goin?' friend tap. You're all still thinking from a point of fear. Fear that Lillian will start hitting on you because she likes girls. Doesn't work like that." Blair looked around the group. "Though you may have some looks about you, I don't think anyone would get Lillian's attention. Not enough freckles."

Everyone turned on Mary. Instantly, her face grew crimson to a point the red cheeks almost hid the freckles all together. With a squeal Mary hide her face in her hands inciting a giggle from the group.

"I like this one," Sally said.

"I was thinking the same," Francesca seconded. "Blair, we've unknowingly held our little Lamby below water for too long. She's been drowning in our hate and malice hoping that someone would reach out a hand. You saved her. We've already asked Lillian to join our group. We hoped you would do the same."

Taken aback, Blair was lost for words. This sort of thing didn't happen to her. She was a loner...

"Blair, don't make up your mind straight away," Lillian said and motioned to an open chair. "Take that chair there while you make up your mind and we'll check in with you again, saaay... end of next year."

"HA!" Blair laughed knowing school ended for all of them end of next year. ...She wasn't a loner anymore. Taking the seat Blair sat and the girls started introducing themselves. When it was time for Mary to speak she became bashful and quiet. A jarring nudge in the ribs from Lillian brought her back to life and she reached out with a gift.

"Thank you," came the soft voice of Mary.

"It was my pleasure," Blair replied with a smile. She wondered what sort of upgrade Mary could have gotten for the ancient relic that was her mum. A new coloured case maybe. Opening the bag, Blair suddenly became quiet. A black, coiled, charge cable sat next to her untouched phone. A phone that could now be brought to life once more. Who knew what secrets were held within? Blair could get a deeper glimpse at the woman that was her mother. She couldn't determine exactly when the tears had

182

started flowing but this one gift was greater than anything she could ever think of getting. Standing, she ushered Mary to her feet before throwing her arms around her neck and kissing her on the cheek.

"You have given me the world," Blair said.

"As you gave me first," A rather emotional girl herself, Mary's tears mirrored Blair's.

Lillian reached out and slapped Mary's slowly descending hand. The hand that was creeping round back had returned to a safer elevation instantly.

With no context for the display, the table knew these three were already tight in such a short time. Anyone would be forgiven in thinking they had been friends since childhood. And as the hug was ending, Blair whispered some final words to Mary. Descriptive words on things she should try with Lillian. Things Blair learned from a coffee drinking woman far more experienced than these two school girls still learning their way. Things that had Mary's eyes going wide, the blush returning with a vengeance.

Everything settled, after that and Blair began to become better acquainted with her new friends. Sometimes through questioning and other times by just sitting back and listening. By first bell she knew this was her place in the school. These were her people.

It was late lunch when the first cracks in Blair's day began. Her new friends had helped to almost make her forget about Tanner. Or at least make things that much easier for her. But this lunch hour almost destroyed her. Blair sat watching as Astrid approached Tanner nearby. Listened as she spoke of her failures, her love for him, how sorry she was and jealous of how close he got to be with Blair. Astrid wove her sob story to weasel her way back into Tanner's arms. Tanner forgiving her and starting their relationship once more.

It was right at the moment that Tanner was deciding on accepting Astrid back that he looked at her. A dark expression crossing his face as his eyes locked with Blair's before he turned back to Astrid and said yes. Somehow that made everything worse and Blair turned away.

Instantly, Lillian had her arms around Blair. The other girls around the table, knowing all too well the pain of heartbreak, also gave their sympathies and love. It all became too much for a girl used to struggling through things alone and Blair broke free, running off. Lillian holding up a hand to ward off those wishing to give chase.

Having caused enough issues for herself of late, Blair somehow managed to think coherently enough not to truant as well. Ending her flight in the nurse's office, Blair was given a room for just such occasions and an invitation to speak to a councillor in the next room if so needed. It wasn't... maybe it was but to Blair, it wasn't. She was able to settle herself by sixth period bell more due to the fact that from now Tanner was only working the farm weekends. Days she could easily fill with sleep overs with her growing friend group.

Relieving herself from the quiet room, Blair made her way to class. A class that had Sally present and for the next hour, instead of doing art, Blair got to listen to the intricacies of some anime called Lost... Exile... Maybe.

Blair was still thankful.

The bus pulled away leaving Blair by her mailbox. The only chore her father had ever given her was collecting the mail. All others where done like clockwork as they had been before Blair called the farm home once more. Skimming through the letters, Blair found a bare envelope with only her name upon it. Blair knew it needed to be hand delivered not having a stamp and instantly the handwriting stood out as Tanner's. Whatever was held inside must be something he needed to get off his chest.

Placing the letter in the gift bag with her mum, Blair decided it was better she didn't turn up at home a horrid mess for what was said. The best place to read this was her room. She could read, breakdown, absorb, accept and move on. And for her sanity this had best be the last thing he did towards her.

The driveway seemed longer than it ever had now that she had something she wanted to get home for, wanted to get out of the way. And yet wasn't far enough as she didn't ever want to open it. Yet now she stood in her room looking in the gift bag at the letter. Reaching in, fear and nervousness swerved her arm to pick up the phone and charger.

"Here you go, Mum. Let's bring you back to life," Blair

said plugging the charger in at wall and phone. A moment of sheer terror took her heart missing a few beats as he phone remained unchanged. The long term without battery use had it needing a little longer to kick in and as the screen lit up, Blair could finally breathe again. The phone showed zero percent charged, 3 hours remaining. Blair knew it best for the battery to be fully charged before turning it on for the first time but 3 hours. That was going to be a long wait.

The gift bag could be seen reflected in the phone screen and Blair turned to look at it for real. The letter inside almost burning a hole to get out.

"I guess so. At least my inevitable wailing will waste a good chunk of time. Your right of course, mum," Blair said.

Retrieving the letter once more, Blair held it for almost five minutes gathering the nerve to break the... nope the seal wasn't used. Opening the flap at the top with tender care lest something reach out and steal her soul, Blair pulled the small piece of paper from the envelope.

Meet me in the barn at 8

~TA

That was it! Blair's mind screamed. She had to face him in the barn, in person, to get served. Fuck him. That was also still 3 hours off. Racing to her mum, Blair spilled everything that had happened since last she had seen her when Blair was able to hold the symbolic phone in her hands and express all her emotions. And there was a lot to say.

Intermission... Blair finished her meal as fast as she could and raced back upstairs, Bryan calling goodnight as he had a headache and was going to bed.

And as Blair divulged the last of her novel, no chance to wind down, the old clock in the hall downstairs chimed 8. It was time. Did she even decide she was going...? Yeah. She would have no closure otherwise if she didn't tell him to forget about her. Still in her school uniform Blair made her way to the back porch and slowly across the yard.

Quietly, timidly, Blair looked inside the barn where a soft light like dying embers glowed. And what her eyes saw she couldn't believe was real. A picnic rug lay on the hay strewn floor, candles upon this and a pie of some exotic nature could be seen in the middle.

185

Unexpectedly, a hand reached out to rest upon her shoulder, and like a haunting whisper, words filled her ear.

"Do you like it?" Tanner asked exciting a scream from Blair.

She'd been unprepared for Tanner's approach from such a quarter when he himself did nothing to hide his location. Too focused was she on the barn to see him. "What is this, Tanner?" Blair asked. She was wary and unenthused right now. The setup catching her off guard.

"I thought we could have some dessert and talk. We left things in a horrible state of affairs," Tanner said.

And an affair would be the state it is left in if dessert were to happen. He was back with Astrid now. "You can give me your words and leave. I know it wasn't a great place to leave things but I hold no grudge nor believe you would truly hate me. Just a fight nothing more."

"It wasn't just a fight. You said there were more things going on in your life than me, but I don't believe that something else had anything to do with last weekend. What are you afraid of?"

"Nothing," Blair replied, almost a little too quickly and Tanner caught it.

"We shared a kiss under the ever flowing stars. I could feel the joy and love you felt in that moment. Tell me you didn't feel anything."

Blair looked down and away. "I didn't feel anything," she said and a hand caught her under the chin. Gently it guided her back to look Tanner full in the eyes.

"This whole conversation you haven't once asked me to remove my hand from your shoulder. Look me in the eyes and tell me you feel nothing," Tanner said. He had a sad, almost empty image in his eyes burrowing deep down to his soul.

Blair chided herself having forgotten the hand lay on her shoulder, her body longing for the touch of those strong hands. She found across the year of love and other mischievous deeds that Tanner's hands, no matter where they lay upon her body fitted the area as if they were crafted only for her. The hand is still there, Blair, her subconscious called out to her but she was lost in those longing eyes somewhere, too far away to hear.

"It was noth..." Blair started.

186

In a desperate move Tanner sealed the last of the words away within a single kiss. A kiss that woke Blair's very soul from the slumber she placed on it. Electricity ignited sparks and a flame began within her body. The locks upon her heart started melting away into the abyss, and all Blair could see and feel in this one moment was the burning twin soul in front of her. Cosmic clouds drifted around them, worlds created and destroyed, stars folding into suns, expanding into giants, exploding into supernovas lit up the sky above. But all there was was Tanner.

There was nothing more she could do but melt into him. Lifting her into his arms, Tanner carried Blair into the barn. That one kiss destined to last the night. A night where the sky was lit with the ever streaking light of stars into the east.

"Jacob," Blair said aloud, her eyes shooting open. Throwing some bottoms on from her washing hamper Blair raced down to her brother's room. Without knocking she snuck inside and jumped on his bed.

"Argh, what is this? It's too early," Jacob growled.

"I need to warn you," Blair said. Hesitation caused the pause to grow.

"About the stars and another Monday to behold?"

"I'm so sorry. When did you find out?"

"When I saw you walk out to the barn," Jacob smiled. "It's okay. I knew this one was coming. I can't stop your love. But I can't live forever in a day either. I need to be the one to apologise and truly, I am so sorry, Blair."

Blair considered his words. "Can we make a pact?"

"What kind?" Jacob asked.

"We never need to apologise to each other. You will fail in life and so will I. If I hold strong you don't apologise. If I fail and we try again, I don't apologise."

"A pact indeed then. And really it isn't such a bad day to repeat. Dad gave me so much junk food thinking the sugar may raise my energy levels."

"How about trying a day at school this time? Ya know, spice things up a bit."

"I am actually feeling rather drowsy today. I don't think I slept right at all."

"Fair enough. It's what you took yesterday off for

anyway. May as well make it official." Blair laughed. "We good?'

"We're good," Jacob smiled a genuine beaming smile.

"Love you, Bro."

"Love you too, sis."

"Anyway, I'm going to go make some friends and give up some others," Blair said before racing out of the room and back to her own to prepare for the day ahead. With a good ten minutes before breakfast and a lot to share, Blair reached for her phone. She wanted to divulge everything from the previous day to her mum but... she wasn't there. Blair's brow furrowed.

"This definitely won't do. I won't repeat a day again until my phone has spent the whole 24 hours with me," she said aloud to no one in particular other than the fates.

Blair allowed the day to roughly flow along the same course. She teased Lillian and called out Sally for her love of anime. Even tried to sound knowledgeable by speaking of an anime called Lost Exile only for the Lost to be corrected to Last. Blair's emotions got her once more seeing the charge cable. It was just such a good present. And she accepted to sit and think about joining the friend group for the next year and a half. These friends were worth repeating every moment for.

It was recess that Blair changed things up. There was someone that she needed to speak to and this was the time it needed to be done. Before they reached their seat in the school yard where others would witness their talk Blair kept her eyes peeled for the long, blonde hair.

"So they let you back in school did they?" came a familiar voice from behind. At least she didn't have to look very far.

"Hi, Astrid," Blair said. The words tasted like bile upon her tongue sticking to the back of her throat. And she was alone. Even better.

"What, no little crude remarks? Not trying to feel me up today?"

"I was looking for you," Blair admitted.

"Here we go," Astrid rolled her eyes. "Look, I got in just as much trouble the other day as you did. My dad took away my car and grounded me for the next month. It's also put a black mark against my name. It's going to be that

188

much harder to get into college now."

"I want to apologise," Blair blurted out.

This was far from expected and Astrid narrowed her eyes.

"You were right to be wary of me when we met. I'd planned to steal Tanner from you and prove my superiority over you. And, this weekend when I had Tanner with me in a completely different town, I tried everything I could to win his attention."

Blair saw Astrid's knuckles whiten as she clenched her fist. She was clearly holding back.

"I'd want to hit me too. But I had already lost the moment I tried. He spoke of your splitting with him. He was sad over the weekend and even had a terrible outburst at me for what I was doing before driving off and leaving me in town. He didn't even take me home." None of this being untrue just worded in a rather misleading way.

"And you're telling me this, why? We won't be best, little bed buddies like you and Lillian." There was a softer glint in Astrid's eyes. The words had struck a chord in her but she wasn't going to outwardly express her thanks to Blair of all people for the insight into Tanner's heart.

"I just want you to know I'm backing down. I'll remain out of yours and Tanner's lives. And I am sorry for the trouble."

Astrid pursed her mouth as she considered the words. A simple nod was the nicest she was prepared to be before she started to wander off.

"He just wants to hear you were wrong, that you miss him, that you made a mistake and love him dearly," Blair called out. The pause in her walk signalled she heard but no words came in reply.

3rd Lesson and it was all over the school. Astrid and Tanner had made up. Being geography, Mary cast a worried look Blair's way but saw her friend smiling warmly. She even answered the next question in class so Mary accepted her friend was doing well with the news.

And yes, Sally still gave a class length, deconstruction of her beloved... umm... it was Lost Exile, right?

Sifting through the mail, Blair was actually angry this time to find a letter from Tanner. Upon opening it, nothing

189

had changed. Meet me in the barn at 8. Tearing the letter up Blair cast it into the softly flowing waterway beside the road. One night was a mistake, two nights and I accept that I am the other woman. The mistress to crush someone else's relationship, someone else's world. What made it worse was he knew what he was doing. He knew he would be tearing Astrid's heart and soul apart. She told herself to keep the rage going.

"Well, tonight you get to meet another Thompson. Let's see you put your arm on his shoulder."

Reaching the house Blair raced upstairs to plug in the charger before moseying into Jacob's room to see if there were any snacks left.

And 8pm came as it always had.

"Dad," Blair shook the sleeping man's shoulder. As his snores increased so too did Blair's ferocity.

Snorting, Bryan woke with a start looking around the room to get his bearings. "Blair? What's wrong?"

"There's someone in the barn," Blair said. The ability to imitate fear and worry was frightening.

Bryan settled noticeably. It was an odd reaction from a farmer with their farm being raided. "Did you get the mail today?"

Blair's eyes grew wide. "You knew? Are you pimping me out?"

"I'm stepping aside for love if this is something you are seeking."

"It isn't."

"Ok, I got this." A large grin took over Bryan's face and he reached over to retrieve a metal rod?

"That's a shotgun! Dad, you can't shoot him." Blair wailed.

"Salt rock shells but it is rare I ever get to use this. Only once has it been levelled on someone and never have I shot it."

"Why have it at all if you never use it," Blair asked.

Bryan was already making for the bedroom door but stopped a moment. "I bought this the day you were born. When your mother was resting with you in the hospital and there was nothing for me to do but wait I drove to the nearest ammunitions store. The moment I held your tiny form in my arms, looked into those adorable little eyes, I knew I would need this. It is only for you. It helped in the city. It will help now. With that he was clear of the bedroom and racing for the backdoor.

Jacob soon ran after him and Blair decided she might also watch the show from the deck. At least Tanner could see her position on the matter.

Reaching the rear of the house, Blair's face lit up. There was her dad, shotgun lowered on Tanner, telling the young man it was time to leave. Glancing over Tanner saw Blair and spread his arms. She just shrugged, done a cheeky little wave and walked off. Blair burst into laughter when she heard her dad finish the confrontation with a growling '*And I'll see you Friday."*

Guess he was still a good employee.

"Let's bring you back to life," Blair said to her mum as she pushed the power button. A splash screen filled the display and it went through a gut wrenchingly long start up process. When the main screen finally settled into place, Blair found it to be a rather bare and boring set up. Phone, messages, settings, camera, snake and gallery. Instantly, Blair tapped the screen to open the gallery and immediately became bashful. Using the correct button combination she navigated the ancient technology to open the gallery correctly.

Her heart dropped. Empty other than the pre-installed pics.

Messages... 1 message unopened. Again Blair was let down as it was a reminder on instructions for opening the voicemail inbox.

A couple calls to her dad were listed in the call log but nothing else of any interest.

"Mum, come on where is the excitement in your life?"

Settling on her bed, Blair quickly lost a number of games of snake before giving up in frustration. Clicking the top power button the screen went dark. Such an anti-climax to two days of waiting. Just some calls from Bryan and an automated message.

Blair's brow furrowed. Clicking the power button once more she read the message and followed the instructions.

"Welcome to your voicemail. You have 1 new message.

Message received from 2400 624 938 (Blair recognised this as Bryan's number. *This better not be a booty call*). *Message received at 12:58 p.m. 19-06-2004. To listen to this message press 1."*

This was the day after Blair's birth. Blair had a vision of Bryan polishing his new shotgun and telling her mother just how shiny it was.

1...

"My darling daughter."

Blair's breath caught in her throat hearing her mother's voice again. The tears were instant.

"Your father's run off talking about protecting you and left his phone behind. He's always been rather aloof at times. You're currently in my arms feeding and I can't stop looking at you. Such a little angel. So beautiful. You are my shining star, my darling. The moment you came screaming into this world I knew, I would love you right into the next life."

"I can't say for sure if you will ever hear this. Maybe I'll save it unopened until you reach maturity to listen to your mummy rambling." There was whimsical laughter before she started once more.

"I don't know what you may end up being when you're older, or if you are happy and healthy but I want you to know I love you dearly, always. If I was to give any advice it would be don't waste your life crying over toys, boys and the inevitable. Live your life with joy in every moment. Spread happiness wherever you go. Be like the stars in the heavens. Even though they may have disappeared from this universe billions of years ago, the light that they gave unto us is still just as bright and just as vibrant. You are my star."

"I love you, Blair..."

Blair held the phone close to her heart, her cheeks damp with tears. "I love you too, mum. I will live my life like the stars in the heavens. Thank you."

Epilogue – Sigrún and Airyck

At the time of her passing a rush of memory and feeling filled Blair's soul. Or perhaps, were unlocked for her to know her time before life. A golden soul of warmth and light, Blair's true name was revealed to her as Sigrún. The next, and more important, thing to come to mind was her twin soul Airyck, or Tanner as he lived on Earth. It would be only moments more for the eternal being living outside of time. Moments before Airyck also passed from the world.

Warmth washed through her as dazzling lights played before her eyes. The warmth she had missed for so long. It was everything to her beyond what the forming of words could do it justice and Sigrún knew her twin heart was here.

"Airyck," the telepathic words echoed into the void of space and in a swirling display, the second golden soul took form.

"My love, I have found you once again at the end of everything," Airyck said, the words traveling instantly to Sigrún's mind.

"And the start of more. Shall we retrieve what is ours?" Sigrún asked.

An icy chill pulsed through the two spirits as if frozen blood ran in their veins. Fear, like an uncontrollable urge, screamed for the beings to flee. Darkness took over the Earth growing in size and strength, threatening to engulf the two souls, their light to be devoured into non-existence.

But the souls remained, unchanging, seemingly unperturbed by this show of strength. And a show was all the dark soul was. To lesser beings whose life may have been hijacked this would have frightened them into running, all forms of confrontation forgotten. But not Airyck and Sigrún.

"Halt, foul being," Airyck pulsed the command and the darkness regressed.

Whisps of shadow, like snakes, sank back to form the dark being who corrupted the life that was to be Astrid. "You dare try to command me. I have fed of your souls for an age and grown strong in this time. You have not the strength to fight me. Even together, you are lacking. So

193

flee, wretched souls, lest I steal all that is you."

Laughter sounded around the scene causing Airyck and the dark soul to exchange odd looks. It was unheard of for a soul to laugh but the joyful terror that erupted from Sigrún made both souls cower. Airyck, simply due to never having experienced this side of his twin.

"Your petty words and antics may work on souls who have never kissed a dying sun or felt the pulsing heart of a supernovas birth, but they will not work on I. I who have swam the darkness beyond this ever growing, ever thinning universe. I have grown as this very earth has, forming in dust, building, expanding, holding life in my hands and finally being devoured into a black hole. I who it was that tenderly crafted and gifted that which you would call time upon this realm. Traces of my energy existed before the seed that was this universe burst from its shell in a violent and crude manner, to form all you see around you, your own being included. My essence can be traced to the universe before this one, before it collapsed upon itself, forming a cocoon. You, Renzel, will never know true power."

The dark soul listened as Sigrún gave her seemingly exaggerated speech. Many had before and many more will again. He had waited quietly to shoot her down once more until his true name was revealed. A name he had kept to himself since his life force formed a conscience. "How did you come by this name?" The thoughts seemed to come across in a stammering utterance.

Sigrún reached forward her hand. Bubbles of darkness seemed to try to rip themselves from Renzel. Pain and anguish ran through the soul as great goblets started to burst like pimples with golden light racing from them. On and on the stream of light fled from the dark being and into the glowing palm of Sigrún.

"You may have tried to steal my essence but it would be billions upon billions of years before it would start to take on your vibration. This essence *is* me. It knows all of your hidden thoughts. I know all of your hidden thoughts."

Renzel grew considerably weaker as the light exited his soul. Even more so than when he entered the life of Astrid. "What have you done?" He screamed.

"Only taken back what is mine. It seems more of your

energy had started to vibrate with mine and therefor returned to me also. All that would be left is Airyck's essence, and the scraps you awoke with." Sigrún turned to Airyck and extended a hand to begin.

As the dark soul screamed in terror and began to flee energy like lightning exploded from the darkness and raced to where Airyck floated, entering at the centre of the forehead. When he was done only miniscule drops of a sludgy substance remained.

"Must have been building that load for eons," Airyck commented.

"Renzel isn't even aware this form of his could only have originated from the universe before this one. Should he have taken a different path his light could have rivalled our own."

The two souls revolved close to one another emerging and playing in a display of love and greeting before coming apart once more.

"We were cheated of a life together but I would not give it up for anything. You found me when the fates, when the very strands of existence we wove through life, would hold us apart. That we found each other at all was a wonderful surprise," Sigrún said.

"I had enjoyed those five Sundays in Monaco beneath the silver moon," Airyck said remembering one of their special moments on Earth."

Sigrún laughed again, this time like a sunrise over the ocean. "Jacob was infuriated over that. He tried calling almost every hour, or sending messages to cease and desist."

Though he didn't have a mouth any who gazed upon the figure of Airyck could see that he was smiling. It beamed from his whole body. "Do you think we will ever come across Jacob outside of life?"

"He is here with us even as we speak."

Airyck looked around trying to feel out the third soul but nothing came back. Only emptiness and his confused expression was put forward to Sigrún.

"When I accepted the book written for me by Renzel, I crafted one extra line as I entered my life. This line it was that gave birth to Jacob. Having no book of his own, nor soul to fill his physical body it was a part of my soul that

195

became Jacob. It was why he was so affected by the time loop. The books were using my energy to reset each day. Energy they gathered from my sub form, Jacob. Jacob has returned to me now."

Feeling out with his essence, Airyck merged into Sigrún exploring her many facets. "Ah, I see now. There you are."

It was all Airyck had said before the twin souls, as one, moved off to their next adventure. An adventure that would see them become one being at its end. Two suns born in orbit of one another, synchronized to one another, revolving around and sharing in one another. It would be at the last breath of this universe that the two suns would come together, drawn in by their ever pulling love, and merge in an epic explosion that would echo out into eternity.

~ Fin

Thank you and I hope to see you again soon.

Books currently in the Aether

Veritas Rerum novels
Pyre of Souls
Veritas Rerum

Hail Atlantis

The Birth of Magic

The Elven King Trilogy

Mage Killer Trilogy

Sword of the Immortal Trilogy
Summoner Mage
Child of Darkness
The Immortal Knight

Novels of the Wandering Swordsman Kiyoshi
A Stolen Sword
Split Personality Swordsman

The Future Past

The Boatman – A book of short stories